WATCH YOUR BACK

Books by Terri Parlato

ALL THE DARK PLACES

WHAT WAITS IN THE WOODS

WATCH YOUR BACK

Published by Kensington Publishing Corp.

WATCH YOUR BACK

TERRI PARLATO

KENSINGTON
PUBLISHING CORP.

kensingtonbooks.com

KENSINGTON BOOKS are published by

Kensington Publishing Corp.
900 Third Avenue
New York, NY 10022

All Kensington titles, imprints, and distributed lines are available at special quantity discounts for bulk purchases for sales promotion, premiums, fundraising, educational, or institutional use.

Special book excerpts or customized printings can also be created to fit specific needs. For details, write or phone the office of the Kensington Special Sales Manager: Attn. Special Sales Department, Kensington Publishing Corp., 900 Third Avenue, New York, NY 10022. Phone: 1-800-221-2647.

Library of Congress Card Catalogue Number: 2024943020

ISBN: 978-1-4967-3862-2
First Kensington Hardcover Edition: January 2025

ISBN: 978-1-4967-3864-6 (ebook)

10 9 8 7 6 5 4 3 2 1

Printed in the United States of America

For my family

Acknowledgments

A heartfelt thank you to all the people who helped bring *Watch Your Back* to life. To everyone at Kensington Publishing, thank you for the time and talent you've dedicated to my book. I am so grateful. A special thank you to my wonderful editor, John Scognamiglio.

To my amazing agent, Marlene Stringer, thank you again and again. None of this happens without you.

To my writers group pals, Sandra Erni, Tacey Derenzy, and R.H. Buffington, I am so grateful to have such a supportive group of friends, who also happen to be very talented writers. And thank you to my dear friend, Karen Street, proofreader extraordinaire.

To my readers, I can't thank you enough for taking a chance on my books. I love hearing from you and talking with you at events. Without you, I can't do what I love.

To my husband and my children, thank you so much for your support. Everything in my world revolves around you. I am grateful beyond measure.

PROLOGUE
Nathan

Now

I'M FLOATING TO THE SURFACE IN A DARK PLACE, OR MAYBE THE DARKness is inside me. I have no idea where I am. Pain fills every corner of my body. My brain seems to quiver with disparate thoughts, and I can't seem to latch onto what's happened to me, and I'm scared shitless.

The sharp tang of Betadine fills the air, and the smell centers me. It nudges me to consciousness. I hear a clatter as a door opens. Then quiet when it closes. A light, cold hand touches my arm, and it feels like needles shooting through my body. But I can't see anything. And a mask over my mouth is pushing air into my lungs. I must be in the hospital.

I fight through the cobwebs of my mind, trying to remember how I got here. How this happened. It was dark. I was outside. She hit me in the back of the head. Something heavy, like a brick or a baseball bat. Then I tumbled down the deck steps. All twelve of those steep fuckers and landed on the concrete patio below. I lay there in the dark, shivering in the cold, warm blood oozing around my head. Then that's it. All I can recall.

Now I'm here. And *she's* here. In the room with me. Sitting close by my bed. I can't see her, but I smell my wife's lavender perfume, her signature scent. And I feel her presence. You always know when Eve enters a room. Tall, slim, shiny blond hair sweeping her delicate collar bones. She's not someone you'd forget or ignore. But our lives took a dramatic turn days ago. Weeks ago? I have no idea how much time has passed. It was a perfect storm, and she blames me. Granted, I am to blame.

But now I'm here and I don't know how bad it is. Will I die from my injuries? Maybe that's what I deserve. My heartbeat starts to ratchet up and a machine beeps, little electronic throbs that pick up in cadence.

She leans over me. Her breath flutters against my cheek, and I shiver. I can't move. I'm strapped to the bed, or maybe it's just that my broken body won't respond when I tell it to. I pray she goes away, or someone comes into the room. I hear her sit back and I relax. My broken ribs ripple as I breathe, bony fingers stabbing my right side, eliciting shocks of pain.

I wonder what she told the cops. Were the cops even there? I don't remember any of that, but I'm sure she had a good story at the ready. "Gee, Officer, I walked out on the deck this morning and there he was! At the bottom of the steps! Bleeding!" She would've gotten rid of the weapon before she called, of course. "He must've fallen. And you know what we've been through. He wasn't himself. Drinking too much. And we've been talking about having this staircase torn out and rebuilt for months. It's dangerous."

And they would've believed her. Everyone believes the illustrious Doctor Eve Thayer. When you're as beautiful as she is and a doctor to boot, people just stand in awe and want to be touched by the sunshine of your orbit. And I'm an ordinary guy. I manage a car collision shop and blend into the morass of everyday Joes. By some stroke of luck, I managed to marry a goddess. That's what I thought in the early days.

But now I'm here. Helpless as a bug on its back. Totally at her mercy. I hear the door open and footsteps.

"How is he this morning, Doctor Thayer? I just came on my shift," a young woman says.

"No change from last night." My wife's voice is silky and low. Everything about her is silky, but her words cut into my brain as if she held a scalpel.

"We were taught in school that you should talk to people who are unconscious because they might be able to hear you," the young nurse says.

I almost grimace. If I had the strength to move my facial muscles, I would. Someone telling my wife her own business. Eve hates that, like people are denigrating her, like she isn't the smartest person in any room.

"Yes. That's true," she responds softly. The nurse walks around my bed, maybe checking all the machines I hear beeping and purring nearby. Then she leaves.

I want to scream. *Come back! Don't leave me alone with her.*

But the door closes.

Eve leans over me again. "Get some rest, Nathan. I'll be back."

I hear the door open and close, and I'm alone and safe for now. But she'll be back. She said so, and there's nothing to stop her from surreptitiously finishing what she started. A pillow over my face or a syringe of something deadly injected into one of my IV bags. Is she really that vindictive? I try again to sort through what happened, but coherent thoughts start to fade behind the pain. Then there's nothing.

Part One

CHAPTER 1
Eve

Three Weeks earlier

SOMETIMES YOU NEED TO TALK TO A FRIEND. I KNOW MY HUSBAND IS waiting for me at home. He's probably already fed and bathed and put our sweet little girl to bed by now, so I've already missed that. My life is overwhelming me at the moment. Something I thought would never happen. But I never thought I'd be married with a baby either. It wasn't in my plan. The plan was medical school, work in a specialty, and pursue a professional life with a vengeance, which I've done. I didn't count on a weak moment and meeting Nathan Liddle.

When my workday ended, all I wanted to do was sit in a dark bar and have a drink with someone who's known me forever, so I called Rachel. She's my best friend from college, and the only friend I've managed to hold on to since I started medical school fifteen years ago. We were randomly paired as roommates freshman year and bonded quickly, learning the college ropes together. Occasionally another girl would try to join our circle, but Rachel and I were joined at the hip in those days, feeling no need to admit another person into our friendship, which sometimes had other people calling us stuck-up. But we weren't really. At least I didn't see it that way.

When I walked into our dorm room for the first time, Rachel had already decorated the walls with artsy prints and made up both beds with matching purple comforters and jewel-toned throw pillows. Most girls would've been irritated at her presumptuousness, but I was relieved and grateful. Rachel said we could change it if I wanted, but I was fine with her taking the initiative. The room was pretty and organized and I didn't have to worry about that. I only had to put away my clothes and the boxes of books I'd brought from home.

Rachel and I were so different but complemented one another perfectly. She was the outgoing, sociable one, while I tended to immerse myself in my books and schoolwork.

She sits across from me at a little table by the front window. We are a total mismatch still. She's an artist who works for a gallery on Graybridge Square. Rachel wears her dark hair nearly to her waist, dresses like some latter-day hippie. She never married, but instead has had a string of relationships, moving on as she became bored.

"So, what's going on?" she asks, twirling a dark tress around her finger.

I blow out a tired breath and take a sip of my pinot noir. "It's just been a day." I don't want to get into the issues that crop up in my professional life. Rachel isn't a lot of help there, so I stick to my personal problems instead. "And, well, Nathan and I are barely speaking to each other."

Rachel shakes her head, her dark eyes looking off over my shoulder. She warned me not to marry Nathan so soon. We'd only dated six months, but I figured it was Rachel's aversion to legal coupling that had her so concerned. I'd let my emotions rule me, which is out of character. But Nathan and I'd been happy in the beginning, even with a surprise pregnancy. We hadn't even talked about children.

She doesn't say, "I told you so." She's too good a friend for that, but I feel it.

"So, what are you going to do, Dr. *Psychiatrist?*"

Rachel has no qualms about throwing my profession in my face as if I should have the answer to every human problem. "I don't know. Work is crazy right now and I don't need this."

"It's always crazy, isn't it?" She smirks and nibbles an olive she fished out of her martini.

"Poor choice of words, and yes, it's always crazy." Over the sound system, Perry Como sings "I'll Be Home for Christmas" as people laugh and talk at the bar. It always seems strange to me to hear Christmas music in a place where people come to forget their troubles, and two days after the big day makes it feel even worse. The holidays are a sure-fire depression trigger. We see our numbers rise right before Thanksgiving and multiply until after the new year, then the numbers settle out, like a collective sigh of relief that the holiday season is over.

"But these last few months have been especially tough with the new hospital opening," I say. "I haven't been around much." I was tapped by our corporate owners to lead the medical staff at their newest private psychiatric treatment center here in the suburbs. Our main hospital is in downtown Boston. But since Nathan and I live out in Graybridge, the commute was attractive as well as the promotion. I see patients daily, some outpatient, some residing in our hospital wing. The increased pressure of leading a new facility has me working sixty hours and more most weeks, and Nathan and I have had very little time together, let alone family time with the baby. Why didn't I think about the extra hours, the workload, before I accepted the position? But in typical fashion, I jumped at the challenge.

"I'm not home enough, Rachel, and when I am, I don't have anything left for Nathan and the baby." It takes a lot for me to admit this. I've always prided myself on being able to handle everything that comes my way. I sip my wine, run a hand through my hair. *How do people do this? Marriage, career, children?* I sigh.

Rachel squeezes my arm. "Nathan knew that when he married you, Eve. He should be supporting you."

"Yes. I know. He does his best. He's taken on most of the parenting duties, and that makes me feel guilty."

"What are you going to do?"

"I don't know. I guess we need to talk. I don't want to throw in the towel this soon. And then there's Rosewyn. We owe it to her to sort things out, right?"

"So, talk to him."

"I will." That's what I need to do before I let things fester and get worse.

"You look exhausted."

"Yeah. At least the baby is sleeping through the night. That's helped. But I'm drained."

Rachel shakes her head. "Why do you work so hard, Eve? Really. You know Nathan would rather have you home more, and your mom doesn't give a shit. Who are you trying to impress?"

I sip my wine and sniff. "I know. It's just me. You know how I am." Growing up, I couldn't figure out what I'd done wrong. Why didn't my parents seem to realize I existed? I was their only child and had every material possession I could ask for. My dad was a highly respected cardiac surgeon. My mom kept a beautiful home and was involved in the community, but they were always busy, too busy to spend much time with me, so I worked like a dog, even as a little girl, to win every award, place first in every competition trying to get their attention. I think I went into psychiatry to try to understand their disinterest, and at long last, I figured it out. They were both narcissists. All that mattered to my mom was her social standing and her group of fawning friends. My dad was all about his work and the accolades he acquired. I realized once I got into my specialty training, that for people like them, no one else really mattered in the normal, human way. I could've won a Nobel Prize at ten and they wouldn't have cared, except to be able to brag to their friends as if they were responsible. It was a hard lesson to learn, but the epiphany changed my life, allowed me to realign my own thinking. I still work like a dog, but for myself. To prove to myself that I'm worth something, I guess. So, maybe I haven't figured everything out because, right now, my life is almost more than I can handle.

"Why don't you take some time off?" Rachel drains her martini and pushes the glass aside. "When was the last time you had a vacation?"

"What about the baby?"

"Take her with you. Load up Nathan's SUV and drive down to Disney World. Do something normal if that's what you want."

I smile at the thought of normal. "We should. We really should."

"Do it then. Forget about all this shit." Rachel waves her hand in the air as if the bar were a metaphor for my life.

Our server, a young woman with long blue hair, stops by. "Another round?" she asks, eyeing our empty glasses.

"What do you think, Eve? I'm game if you are," Rachel says.

Before Nathan, Rachel and I would often stay out late, talking, laughing. I feel guilty about that too. I haven't had much time for my friend, and we used to spend so much time together. But my mind flips back to my husband and our little girl.

"No. I'm good." I feel tears in my eyes, not like me, but I feel everything crashing into me at once. "I should get home."

"We're done," Rachel says. "We need our check." The server hurries away. "Really, Eve, get away for a while. Spend some 'quality time,' as they say, with Nathan and do some hard thinking about what's best for you. What do *you* really want?"

"Have Yourself a Merry Little Christmas" plays in the background. The red and green lights tacked around the window twinkle. I throw my credit card on the check. "Thanks for the advice," I say, and I mean it.

Rachel smiles. "Any time, Doc."

CHAPTER 2
Nathan

I HEAR EVE'S CAR PULL INTO THE GARAGE. IT'S A LITTLE AFTER 8:30 P.M., but I'm used to her late work nights. My gaze shifts back to *Monday Night Football*, which just started, still first quarter. She did text me a half hour ago to say she'd be home soon.

I'd left my dirty dishes in the sink. I'd warmed up leftover Chinese for dinner. Neither one of us cooks, so meals are pretty random. But Eve doesn't like a mess, and I consider jumping up and loading my dishes in the dishwasher before she gets into the house. I really don't feel like it. After putting the baby down, I planted my ass on the couch and don't feel like moving, but I do because I don't feel like having an argument tonight either.

I hear the hall closet door open and close. Then Eve breezes into the kitchen just as I shut the door of the dishwasher. She looks tired, more than usual.

"Sorry I'm so late." She pushes up the sleeves of her sweater and reaches for a glass, fills it at the fridge with cold water. "I, um, stopped off at Hartshorn's for a drink with Rachel," she blurts out like a confession. "She was having a bad day and called me."

"That's fine," I say, but I can't help but feel resentful.

"We just had one drink. How's Rosewyn? Did she take her bottle okay?"

"Yeah. She's asleep. No problem." I'd picked up the baby from the sitter, as usual. "You look tired." I clutch Eve's thin forearm. It's covered in new bruises. "What happened?"

She draws a deep breath. "Tough day. I had a patient kick me in the stomach and she must've left those bruises as well."

"Jesus, Eve. Are you all right?"

She nods. Leans against the counter, closes her eyes while she drains her water.

"You need combat pay for that job of yours." I've told her that a million times. Why, of all the specialties my wife could've chosen, did she decide to go into psychiatry? I've never gotten an answer to that that made sense, so I gave up trying to understand Eve's professional choices. But soon after our marriage, I discovered the steel that hides beneath that delicate exterior. If Eve Thayer wanted to go ten rounds with the champ, I'd put my money on her. It's not that she's so physically strong, although she's not a ninety-pound weakling either, it's just a strength of will like I've never seen in another person. Eve goes through life with that proverbial chip on her shoulder like she's daring you to try to knock it off.

When we found out we were pregnant two weeks after the wedding, I cried. I can't lie. We hadn't even talked about kids and neither of us felt ready. At first, Eve was devastated. Her work came first. She'd made that abundantly clear during our short courtship. But she rallied. We can do this, she said, and I believed her. And so far, we have. When Rosewyn was born, I was smitten, and Eve was thrilled too. We've been making it work, at least the parenting part.

"Did you have any dinner?" I ask her.

She shakes her head and moves toward the fridge.

"I left you half the Chinese."

"Thanks. I think I'll just have a yogurt."

We sit in the dark living room and watch football. Eve likes sports. That's one of the things we have in common. And we do have quite a bit in common actually. I feel guilty as I watch her spoon up her yogurt and delicately slip it into her mouth, her blond hair reflecting like a beacon in the light of the TV.

We met when she showed up at my collision shop two years ago. I saw her from the lobby through the plate glass window. It was near closing time when this white Lexus with front-end damage entered the lot. I watched as one of the guys met her as she pulled to a stop. She exited her vehicle like a Hollywood star arriving at the red carpet. She was tall, slender, with that dazzling hair and a sheepish smile on her red-painted lips. Like she was so sorry to be troubling us. I walked out and introduced myself and told my employee that I would handle this since it was closing time, and I knew he needed to pick up his kids from daycare. An excuse, but real enough.

She was so sweet and deceptively needy, and I reassured her that we would take care of everything, coordinate with her insurance company, get her into a nice loaner. Nothing to worry about. The process went as smoothly as I could make it, and in the encroaching darkness, in the empty office, she placed her hand, her long slim fingers on my sleeve and thanked me.

Then she asked if I wanted to go to the bar across the street for a drink. That was it. We were together after that whenever she was free. In the beginning, I didn't mind her work schedule. It left me plenty of time for the gym and my friends who were still single, although they were quickly dwindling in number. But Eve and I were happy.

But now, after nearly a year and a half of marriage, I think we made a mistake. We don't have much time together, and when we do, we don't seem to have much to say to one another. It's like during our whirlwind courtship we said everything we could think of. There's nothing left to tell.

And this new job of hers seems to have sapped all her energy. I don't think she's happy there, but she won't admit it, and she won't talk about it, like she's facing some big battle and she's in it alone.

So, life has become dull and lonely here in this old house that we were at one time so interested in renovating. The fixer-upper had so much potential. It's like it was a good idea, an exciting idea when we bought it, until reality settled in and we were just too damn tired to do anything about it. And taking care of an infant has taken center stage.

I feel my phone vibrate in my pocket. My eyes dart to Eve, but she's leaning back against the couch cushions, oblivious, empty yogurt container clutched in her hand resting on her lap. I check my screen, jump up, and head down the hall. She doesn't even notice as I leave the room.

CHAPTER 3
Rita

*T*ACKY CHRISTMAS DECORATIONS STILL TWINKLE IN THE SQUAD ROOM as I pass through with my morning coffee. Someone needs to take the initiative and take them down, but it's not going to be me. Seniority should buy you something.

It's a bit drafty, and the old building that houses the Graybridge Police Department is chilly. Chief Murphy told me he'd called a repairman to take a look at the HVAC system. But ironically, while the rest of the building is an icebox, it's hotter than hell in my cubbyhole office. I'm tucked away down the hall from the squad room where gray cubicles house most of the officers and our two young detectives. I force my window open a crack. We really need a new building but have made do with this 1970s retrofitted government structure since I've been out here in the burbs after years with the Boston PD.

I really can't complain. Things have been pretty slow the last few weeks and that suits me after the fall we had. I sip my coffee, heinous, but hot, and power up my laptop. I fish through my satchel, ready to call the lab about an open case. At the Graybridge PD, we're too small to have detectives assigned to specific areas like homicide, vice, or narcotics. Here, we do it all. Just as I find my phone, there's a knock at my door.

"What are you doing way out here so early?" I ask the attractive middle-aged man standing in my office.

He smiles; his eyes meet mine. "Thought I'd pay you a visit. I had a relatively free morning." Joe Thorne is an agent with the FBI. He works out of the Boston office. We're friends but have been seeing one another off and on for a few years, so I guess we're more than friends. It's complicated, at least for me.

"But I'm probably going to be busy out of town in a couple days," Joe says, "and I won't be around for a while. That's why I wanted to stop by."

I sit up straight and push my dark hair over my shoulder and hope my gray roots aren't too obvious. I was too tired this morning to put my hair up in its usual messy bun. And my appointment at the salon is still a week away. "New big case?"

"Yeah. I'll be in Maine for a couple of weeks, maybe more. Helping them out up there."

"Anything you can talk about?"

"Not now. You have time to grab a cup of coffee?"

I glance down at my sludgy, breakroom brew. "I can make time. Pretty slow this morning." Besides, I need to head out and talk to a woman who reported a break-in yesterday. I stand and reach for my satchel, throw a file folder inside.

We both drive since I have work to do afterwards. I pull my old van to a stop in the small lot next to the coffee shop. I'm wondering what's the big deal that Joe had to drive out here from Boston. Why not just give me a call and let me know that he'll be gone for a couple of weeks? Not like we're serious or anything.

The windows are steamy inside the shop, and we settle at a small table in the corner. The coffee is good and rich, a big improvement over the station coffee, and Joe and I both grabbed a donut, too, raspberry jelly for me, glazed for him. Junk food is my weakness. Oh well, I'll pedal ten more miles on my bike tonight.

"So, how's work?" he asks.

"Slow for a change, which is nice."

"Especially this time of year. How was your Christmas?"

"Pretty good. Saw Danny and Charlotte." My brother and his daughter are my closest relatives. "And Collin, of course. He and

André had me up for dinner." My upstairs neighbors own a café and catering business, so a meal at their apartment is always amazing."

"How's Danny these days?" Joe asks.

"He's good. Semester's over and he's working on an article about literature in Colonial America. I think that's what he said." My brother is the most well-educated of my siblings, a professor at a small private college. He and I are the youngest of the nine McMahon kids. And while Danny is a successful and accomplished professor, he's also a functioning alcoholic, something that few people realize. Joe and I meet him for dinner occasionally, and Joe has taken a concerned interest in him as he knows how close Danny and I are.

We finish our donuts; my fingers are dusted with powdered sugar. Joe wipes his hand over his mouth, lingering on a scar from a long-ago knife fight, which he still hasn't told me about. The day is so overcast, the coffee shop is dim. And in the low light, I can't help but appreciate Joe's dark eyes, feel a tingle when he looks at me.

He reaches for my hand. "I've got tickets for Eric Clapton," he says.

Joe and I share an affinity for classic rock. "Really? I've never seen him."

"Me neither. I thought you might like to go next month."

"Sounds great. When exactly?"

"Let me find the tickets." He pulls reading glasses from his shirt pocket and scrolls through his phone. Virtual tickets. Nothing is like it used to be when you held on to concert ticket stubs like some treasured trophy and pasted them into a scrapbook. Joe finds what he's looking for and passes his phone to me.

"Oh, right," I say, assessing the concert details. The venue is in upstate New York. Far enough away to have to be an overnight trip. The implication dawns on me. Despite our dates, Joe and I, for some reason, haven't slept together yet. Well, except for the one time when we first got together a few years ago. Then we lost touch and only recently reconnected. I don't know why I've avoided taking the next step. Me, I guess, always pulling back.

"You don't have to go, Rita," he says. "My son said he and his wife would take the tickets if I changed my mind."

I swallow. "Yeah. Funny how our music has stood the test of time. Lots of younger people appreciate it."

"They do." He waits for my answer.

Get a grip, Rita. Spending the night with Joe doesn't mean we're getting married or anything. I've just gotten so comfortable being on my own after divorcing my husband, Ed, years ago. I sip my coffee and Joe chuckles, squeezes my hand, and lets it go.

"Think about it while I'm gone."

I pull into the driveway of a large, two-story. It's located in one of Graybridge's strangest neighborhoods. That is, one that's difficult to figure out. The houses are older, though not historic. It was a beautiful neighborhood thirty years ago but has been in decline the last five or ten years. Some houses are still nicely maintained, but others have seen better days, peeling paint, rotted clapboards.

This house, like some of the others, is being renovated. No one lives here yet, but the angry homeowner greets me at my van door before I can get out of my vehicle.

"You the detective?" a husky, flannel-shirted woman asks.

"Yes. Detective Rita Myers," I say, slinging my satchel over my shoulder and standing on the cracked driveway.

"Wilma Parnell." She shakes my hand with a firm, painful grip. "Come on in."

She turns and strides quickly up the sidewalk, which is bordered by weeds, limp with melting snow. The porch creaks as we make our way to the front door, which stands open.

Inside, the place is chilly. Music echoes down the hall, some country melody full of angst and longing. In the kitchen, Wilma shuts down a paint-spattered boombox. Tools are spread out on a Formica countertop and the cabinet doors have been removed and stacked on the floor against a wall. The smell of sawdust hangs in the air.

From my satchel, I pull a copy of the report our officer filed yesterday. They'd taken a statement, checked the place out, and dusted for prints. Wilma waits as my eyes sweep over the paper. "You noticed the missing items yesterday morning?"

"Yeah. I got here about eight-thirty, and the front door was open. Someone had jimmied the lock. I thought maybe some homeless person, you know? Looking for a place to warm up. But when I looked around, I noticed a small toolbox was missing. And I could tell that someone had been rummaging around in here. That box and the stuff in it were brand new. Over a hundred bucks worth of stuff, Detective."

"I'm sorry about that, Ms. Parnell. What was in it?"

Wilma counts on her fingers. "A set of Allen wrenches, a couple of screwdrivers." Her gaze meets mine. "A *drill*."

"Anything else gone?"

She swipes her graying, curly hair over her shoulder. "Oh, yeah. A crowbar too. It was sitting next to the front door when I locked up. It wasn't worth much, but still. I can't afford to lose equipment. I went into my 401K just to buy this place."

"You going to flip it?"

"Maybe. Haven't decided." She rocks back on her heels. "But I can't freaking lose money on it."

I walk through the first floor, making notes. Hard to tell what might've been disturbed in all the junk sitting around. "You seen anyone hanging around the property?"

"Not that I noticed. There's some teenagers down the block that hang out in the street occasionally. Don't know what they're up to. But not by my place. At least not while I'm here." She seems to consider. "But they might have something to do with it."

We tour the second floor, which is empty, cold bedrooms, and nothing looks disturbed.

"Let's take a look outside," I say coming down the stairs. You never know. The perp might've dropped something in the yard that might point to his or her identity. I worked a robbery at a convenience store once where the suspect left his wallet at the scene, right on the counter, with his driver's license inside. Some criminals make my job too easy, but that, of course, is not usually the case.

I stop to examine the jimmied lock on the front door. It's a simple design. You wouldn't need professional knowledge to break it, so the perp could've been an amateur. Maybe it *was* a homeless person looking for a place to warm up and decided to take the toolbox on his way out, to sell maybe. Graybridge doesn't have a huge homeless problem, but like every place else in the country, that population is growing.

Outside, we trudge through the slush and the long, weedy grass. Don't see anything interesting as we round the house and enter the backyard. Nothing of note here. Backdoor is secure. An old rusty swing set sits in the corner near a back fence, whose boards have fallen away in spots. A tall house rises up on the other side. Looks neat and lived in. Maybe the neighbors saw something.

We head back inside and Wilma leans against the countertop. I go back over the report and my notes. "So, Ms. Parnell. Before the break-in, you were last here when?"

"Friday."

I clear my throat. "All right. You worked most of the day and locked up around four-thirty?"

"Yeah. It was getting dark."

"Then when you got here yesterday, you noticed the front door?"

She nods. "They must've been in here over the weekend."

"Okay. When you looked through the house, you saw that the toolbox and crowbar were gone. That all?"

"I guess."

"Okay." Doesn't look like much of a crime, but I know if you're the person whose property's gone missing, it's a big deal. "You don't have any surveillance video?"

"No. Didn't want to spend the money." She puts her hands on her hips, surveys the kitchen. "But maybe I should. Shit."

"Not a bad idea." I take one last look around, note the fingerprint dust around the sink and countertop area where the toolbox had allegedly been sitting.

"You think they'll be able to ID the SOB?"

"Maybe. We'll run the prints through the system."

Wilma nods. "Well, they better not come back." She picks up a claw hammer.

"Just keep your phone handy, Ms. Parnell. And think about installing cameras."

"So, what's next?"

I stash my notebook and the file folder in my satchel. "I'll check with the neighbors and see if they saw anything. And we'll let you know if we get a hit on the prints."

She nods. "Thanks, Detective. I thought this was a safe neighborhood when I bought the place. Don't need any trouble."

CHAPTER 4
Eve

I WENT HOME LAST NIGHT DETERMINED TO HAVE A FRANK AND REASON-able conversation with my husband, but, in the end, I was too damn tired. So, we sat and watched football until I fell asleep on the sofa. I woke up during the third quarter and wandered into the nursery, checked on Rosewyn, who was sleeping like a little angel in the glow of her Winnie-the-Pooh nightlight. Then I headed into the bedroom. Nathan was already softly snoring curled up at the edge of the bed.

We had no time for more than a quick hello in the morning as I was running late. No time for the type of discussion I know we need to have. I cuddled and kissed my little girl. Then I quickly fed Oscar, the fat tabby I adopted long before I met Nathan, and jumped into my car.

I turn into the winding driveway of the Graybridge West Psychiatric Center. The company I work for bought the property years ago. It had been built in the 1940s and functioned as a psychiatric hospital until it was closed in the early 2000s after years of complaints of patient neglect and mistreatment. The plan was to demolish the old structure and rebuild from scratch. But the building lingered, vacant, a drain on the company's books until last year when they decided to refurbish the existing building and another smaller building next to it. The smaller building is now a rehabilitation center where they do occupational therapy and help people with various injuries get back to their old lives as much as possible. Years ago it was part of the psychiatric hospital. It was where the most seriously, and sometimes criminally, mentally ill patients were kept, along with facilities for shock therapy and other treatments that have fallen out of favor.

I walk through the whooshing front doors of my building. I smell a tinge of old-building smell that defies the cheery lobby paint. I think the remodel was more cosmetic than anything. Our elderly receptionist is on the phone and waves as I walk by.

I see my colleague, Doctor Brian Tanaka, in the hall on my way to my office. He's about my age, handsome, with a wife, four-year-old son, and two-year-old daughter. He seems to be able to handle home life and professional life with an ease that's foreign to me.

"Good morning." Brian smiles. "Rough day yesterday. I heard about Frances. How are you feeling?"

I instinctively rub my stomach, although the pain from the kick was minor. "I'm okay. It wasn't too bad. Just a glancing blow, thank goodness. How is she this morning? Have you heard?" She's my patient, but our tussle was the talk of the facility yesterday, and I'm sure the morning staff has heard the whole story.

"Slept like a baby all night, Glenda said."

Thanks, probably, to some medication, but that's good news. Glenda is our night nursing supervisor, an older woman who has been in psychiatric nursing for more than thirty years. "Great. I'll check on her shortly."

"Oh," he says. "Meeting with the administration at noon. They just sent out an email."

"Great. No lunch again today then."

"Nope." He raises his eyebrows.

I sigh, close my office door, and get settled at my desk. I power up my laptop and run through my appointments for the day. Then I skim quickly through my inpatient charts to see if there is anything I need to address from overnight.

My first outpatient arrives in thirty minutes, so I hurry to the inpatient hall to do my rounds.

* * *

I finish just in time to greet Donald Barry as he signs in at the desk. He is forty-three. I've been seeing him for a couple months and things haven't gone well. In fact, I'm going to suggest we transfer him to another doctor.

He leans back in his chair, squeezes his eyes with his fingers. "Doc, I think we *are* making progress."

"Don, I think you'd get more out of seeing Dr. Tanaka. It's been nearly three months, and your anxiety is still about where it was when we started."

He slumps forward, his blue eyes red, dark bags beneath them. "Well, I haven't been totally honest with you, Eve, Doctor Thayer." He clears his throat quickly. "I haven't been taking the medicine."

"Why is that?"

"It made me feel woozy and tired."

"Why didn't you say anything?"

He shrugs. "A man's supposed to be able to handle things, not have to rely on something like medicine. My ex-wife took a pill for every fucking thing."

His ex-wife is a sore spot. They divorced six months ago, and he's been trying to find a new relationship, online mostly, and so far, he hasn't been successful. I've diagnosed him with borderline personality disorder and anxiety, and the fact that he's not taking his medicine is concerning.

"Don, I only prescribe medication when I think it's crucial to your well-being. If you don't take it, we can't make any progress."

He runs his hand through his unkempt, graying hair. He's fastidiously neat, pleated trousers, immaculate white shirt. It's only his hair that's a mess, out of place. "All I need is a new girlfriend. Someone who'll listen to me, be with me." His eyes meet mine.

Yup. He's going to have to start seeing Doctor Tanaka or find another treatment center. This isn't working.

I stand and circle around to my desk.

"What are you doing?" he asks, leaning forward in his chair.

"Don, I really think you'll benefit from seeing another doctor."

He gets to his feet. "But I want to see you. I'll take the fucking medicine."

"Yeah. I know. But Doctor Tanaka is really good, and I think he can help you better than I can." I start to amend his chart.

"Give me another shot. Write me a new prescription."

He's balling his fists and I glance at the door. I really don't need this today. "Let's walk out to the lobby. We'll get you set up with Doctor Tanaka for next week. At least give him a chance."

"Will you still be here?"

"At the facility, yes." I stride for the door, and he follows. When I reach for the doorknob, my sleeve slides up my arm exposing ugly purple bruises.

"What happened?" Don asks.

"Nothing. No big deal."

"Are you all right?" He takes a deep breath, lets it out slowly. "Who did that to you?"

"No one. I bumped into my desk," I say, and know he doesn't believe me. I walk quickly into the reception area and stop in front of the counter. He moves next to me, too close, as I make the new appointment.

He huffs out a breath. "Fine! I'll see the other doctor, but I'll see you here, too," he says, and storms out the front door.

I walk back to my office. The outpatient wing is quiet this morning, and chilly. The fluorescent bulbs buzz slightly overhead. I don't think they did much more than paint on this side of the building during the remodel, saving the bulk of their budget for the inpatient wing which needed updated security measures and modern equipment. I turn a corner and nearly run into Glenda, who waits by my office door.

"Sorry, Doctor Thayer. Didn't mean to scare you." Glenda is short and stocky, built like a rugby player. Her gray hair is cut very short and her glasses gleam in the overhead light, hiding her eyes.

"I just didn't expect to see you. You're usually gone by the time I get here in the morning."

"On my way out in a minute. That new girl, Megan. She's still not up to speed, so I had some things to straighten out this morning. Some people aren't cut out for this type of nursing."

"Is there a problem I need to know about?"

"We'll see. I'll let you know. Let's give her another week or two to learn the ropes. Oh, and I wanted to tell you that Frances was quiet overnight."

"Thank you."

"And you're all right?" Her gaze shifts to my bruised arm.

"Of course." I glance at my office door. I need to get back to work.

She nods. "Comes with the territory. Had my share of tussles with patients over the years. All righty then, I'll head on home." She turns on her heel. Then calls back to me, "Have a good day."

CHAPTER 5
Nathan

*T*HE MORNING HAS BEEN SUPER BUSY. THERE'S NEVER A LACK OF BUSI-ness in this line of work in a big metro area. First thing, I was greeted with a car that was barely recognizable. We needed to total it, no question, and one of the estimators was already completing the paperwork when I got to the office.

"Don't think anyone walked away from that," he said as I stopped by, sipping lukewarm coffee.

"Yeah. I saw." I grimaced. Just paperwork, then off to the junk-yard with that vehicle.

The rest of the morning passed pretty smoothly, and I was able to relax a bit in my office. I tried to fix it up when I went from assistant manager to the top job. My old boss retired right before I met Eve, and I was promoted to his corner office. He'd had pictures of his family all over the walls and framed awards for professional accomplishments. Potted plants on the floor by the window and all kinds of knick-knacks on the desk.

I haven't bothered with much. A picture of Rosewyn in a pink sweater set, slobber on her little fist, sits on the corner of my desk. I hung my college diploma on the wall, BS in business management. That and my interest in cars got me this job, but you don't need a college degree to do it. My old boss had a high school education and worked his way up. But times were a little lean when I graduated, and jobs weren't exactly falling into my lap. I had experience in the car business. My dad owned a body shop for years and I worked for him as a teenager, so here I am, but I like my job well enough.

It's lunchtime and I check my phone. There's a knock on my open door.

"Hey, Nathan. We're headed over to the barbeque place. You want to come?" Greg is one of our techs, tall, skinny, and a whiz with automobile electronics.

I clear my throat. "Not today. I need to run some errands."

"Okay. See you later." He moves off down the hall. I grab my jacket and head out.

She's waiting for me at our usual place, and I feel guilty, yet excited, and I weigh one against the other. It's just I've been so alone these past few months, and I don't know that Eve really cares what I do anymore. She's so wrapped up in her work, does it really matter? I still care about her, but what am I supposed to do?

End it and go to couples therapy or something. That's what I should do.

Nicole is stretched out on the bed at our usual hotel. I turn and shut the door, throw the deadbolt. She smiles as I approach, loosening my tie and kicking off my shoes.

When I met Nicole a few weeks ago, Eve and I hadn't had sex more than a couple of times since the baby was born. Every time I got close to her, I felt her pull away, shut down. And she didn't even know she was doing it. I don't think. It was as if she was closed off in her own world. She'd remember herself and kiss me, nuzzle my neck, but then start a conversation about work or something she'd seen on the news. It was like she'd be with me just so far then pull away. I had no clue what was going on with her. I kept waiting for her to talk to me. I'm not great about initiating intimate conversations, and neither is she, so where does that leave us?

I was at my wit's end. It was six o'clock on a Friday and I decided to do something to try to get us back on track, so I made reservations at Eve's favorite restaurant. I called the sitter and got the okay for her to keep Rosewyn until later. I figured I'd surprise Eve, but when I called her at work, she was in a rush. She was about to fire one of her nurses and it wasn't going to be pretty, so she hurried me off the phone and said she'd be late. So, my plan fizzled before it had even gotten started.

Then Greg popped into my office and said he and a couple of the guys were going over to Lucia's, a Mexican restaurant/bar across the street, the one where Eve and I had that first drink together. Did I want to go? Already had the sitter lined up, so absolutely.

She was sitting at the bar with a friend when I ordered a craft brew. She said her name was Nicole and she worked in Woburn for some big computer company. We chatted. She was blond, like Eve, with big blue eyes and a petite slender build. She was wearing a sweater that slid off one shoulder exposing creamy skin, something Eve would never wear, totally arousing. Her friend had to run, so I invited her to join me and the guys, and she readily accepted.

It felt good and natural to be out with friends, drinking, laughing, just relaxing. After a couple of hours, the guys left one by one until it was just Nicole and me. I learned that she was divorced. Had a college degree although I can't remember what she said her major was, maybe she didn't say. She was a local, friendly as hell, and the attention felt good. Then she suggested we go to a hotel nearby. She was temporarily staying with her grandmother, and I couldn't bring her to my place, obviously. So, that's how it started.

"Hey, there," she says, sliding the sheet down her naked body. "I couldn't wait to see you. Once a week just isn't enough." She smiles as I climb in next to her.

"We'll see what we can do." I smooth back her long hair that shimmers as it slips through my fingers. Take her mouth with mine.

It's been nearly a month that we've been meeting at lunchtime. After that night at Lucia's, she called me at the office and asked me out to dinner. And I leveled with her. I'm married. I expected a shit storm, but she actually didn't seem surprised or too concerned. I didn't intend for it to go any further, but she was game for meeting once a week for lunch and/or lunchtime sex. And I gave in.

Now I'm a little worried. I don't want to get mixed up with a fatal attraction, but so far, I haven't seen any red flags.

"It's fine," she whispers in my ear, her warm breath tickling my cheek. "This works."

She'd told me she wasn't looking for anything serious. She was still getting over her divorce. That's why she was living with her grandmother. Her ex had wanted the house, and she was content for him to buy her out. She was trying to figure out her life right now and seeing me was a nice distraction in this transition period.

So, I enjoy the sex and the attention. She texts me a few times a week just to say something nice, keep my spirits up since she obviously knows that my wife and I are having problems. I'd told her a little bit about Eve, that she was totally absorbed in her career and that we'd drifted apart. Nicole was understanding and said that we could be there for each other, like a little crutch to get us through a mutual rough patch.

CHAPTER 6
Eve

WHEN I DID MY MORNING ROUNDS, FRANCES HAD STILL BEEN ASLEEP. I was anxious to check on her since our run-in yesterday and see how her medication is working today. My first afternoon patient is set to arrive in ten minutes, so I stop to see Frances first.

She's sitting in an armchair next to the window. She's fifty-eight and homeless. Our corporate owners make a big deal about devoting ten percent of our beds to the indigent. Which is great, but it also makes the company look good and gives them some tax breaks. No one has been to see Frances in the three weeks she's been with us. She's about thirty pounds overweight, weight that seems to hang in loose folds from her otherwise bony frame. Her long hair is a tangled nest of gray with streaks of chestnut brown, a shade so pretty that you wonder what it was like when she was young, before the streets and mental illness claimed her. We've diagnosed her as being on the schizophrenia spectrum. When she attacked me, we'd just tried a new medication with her. Obviously, it didn't work the way we wanted it to and she's back on her old medicine, which zones her out too much. Medication is tricky and doesn't work the same for everyone. It's more of a guessing game than you'd think.

"Good afternoon, Frances."

She turns her head slowly in my direction, her face puffy from meds and other medical conditions.

"Hi." Her voice is a whispered grumble. I wonder if she even remembers the scuffle we had.

"How are you feeling?" I scroll through her chart on my laptop.

She doesn't reply, just stares out the window at the bare winter woods beyond the grounds. Old psych facilities tended to be built out in the country, away from society as if trying to hide the patients away. Most new facilities attempt to keep people as part of the world and are situated in more populated areas. This place has that pre-modern feel from when it was built in the forties. We're out on a country road, down a winding driveway, isolated.

"Frances?"

"I'm okay."

It's been tough getting much out of her, and our therapy sessions have been challenging. Frances doesn't like to talk about her life, and I can only imagine how fraught with difficulties it has been. Sometimes she mentions a husband, but she says that he died, or he left her. The details are always sketchy as if she's thinking back to a time so long ago that she's not sure that it even happened. She also says that she had a child once, one day it's a boy, the next day a little girl. Despite our best efforts, we haven't been able to track down any family for her.

"Would you like the TV on?" The room is so quiet, so devoid of human life. I sigh.

"Sure," she responds at last. I click on the flat screen mounted high on the wall. A talk show with laughter and brightly attired women appears.

"Not that shit," Frances says.

I flip through channels until she stops me at a nature program where the camera follows a tiger slinking through the jungle. "I like that better," she says laconically.

"Can I get you anything?"

Her dull eyes meet mine. "Yeah, you can get me the fuck outta here."

"Soon, Frances. You're not strong enough yet." She's not stable enough. I know that the staff is looking at places to send her when she *is* stable. Back in an office down the hall, people are working on her case, trying to figure out what to do with her. She coughs, an old smoker's hack, and reaches for a plastic water cup, her hand shaking.

"Okay," she says, lips wet. Her eyes travel back to the TV.

"I'll stop in later," I say.

"Okay," she says again, and I leave the room, pulling her door closed.

My last outpatient appointment of the day is Marie Williams, a thirty-five-year-old who has been dealing with depression since her parents were killed in a car accident four months ago.

She sits demurely in the armchair and heaves a big sigh, tucks a pale tress behind her ear, smooths her silk blouse.

"I had a pretty good week," she says. "Until yesterday."

"What happened yesterday?"

"A guy nearly hit me at the intersection of Main and Westberry."

"Were you hurt?"

"No. He hit his brakes in time and swerved back into his lane, but it brought back my parents' accident, so I freaked out a little. Then I started thinking about them all afternoon, how my life completely changed in an instant. I didn't sleep well last night." Her eyes tear up as she glances out the window.

"That must have been frightening." I get that more than she realizes. Someone ran me off the road a couple of years ago. That's how I met Nathan, at his shop. The cops were never able to find the culprit. It was late, dark, and I couldn't give them any helpful details. But I wasn't hurt, so it wasn't a big deal.

"Sometimes that scenario keeps spinning in my head. If only I'd driven them to their appointment that day like I planned." She wipes her eyes with her fingers, her nails polished a deep red. "Dad shouldn't have been driving. I should've taken his keys away."

"You know that wasn't your fault?"

"Yes. Of course. But I can't help thinking about it sometimes. I told them I'd reschedule the appointment and take them at a later date. It was a routine appointment. It could've waited, and I had an emergency meeting that I couldn't get out of."

"So, what did you do yesterday after the near miss?"

She blows out a breath. "I went home. Tried to do some work. I called a friend and we talked."

"Good. How do you feel today?"

"Better. I got some exercise at lunchtime and that seemed to help, too."

"How is your medication working?"

"Great. Since I started on it, I'm pretty good most days. So much better."

"That's terrific. Anything else you want to talk about?" We still have ten minutes left.

She fidgets with her scarf. "My parents' estate. That's still not settled."

"That can be difficult. Do you have someone handling it?"

"Yes. I've got a great attorney. I'm thinking of taking a trip when it's wrapped up. Maybe Paris."

"That sounds lovely." Marie is a human resources consultant and appears to be pretty successful. She self-pays for treatment. Says it makes more sense since she is a private contractor and carries only minimal insurance. And money doesn't seem to be a problem for her.

She talks about her mother, sorting through her things, and that brings another tear to her eye. She reaches for a tissue from the box on the end table. But sorting through a loved one's possessions can be therapeutic, and despite the tears, it seems so for her.

We're finished, and Marie and I stand. She slips into a three-quarter length, camel-colored wool coat and pulls dark leather gloves out of her pockets.

"See you next week, Doctor Thayer. And thank you."

Marie's progress gives me some sense of professional satisfaction. And I need that right now, when my life seems to be getting the best of me.

CHAPTER 7
Nathan

*B*ARBARA SINGLETON IS THE PERFECT BABYSITTER. EVE AND I WERE going to hire a nanny to come to the house, but after interviewing half a dozen college-age girls with limited experience caring for infants, we found Barbara.

At fifty-six, Barbara has raised a son who is off at college. She's married to a pilot who is often away, and she needs something to occupy her time. She wasn't interested in taking in a slew of kids, just one at a time. She lost a little boy she'd had since he was six weeks old to kindergarten and an after-school program and was ready for a new infant to dote on.

She lives a few blocks from us, so that was perfect, too. Last week, I noticed a FOR SALE sign in her front yard, and Eve and I panicked, but Barbara reassured us that she and her husband were only looking to downsize and would stay in the area.

She meets me at the door with Rosewyn cradled in her arms. My baby girl smiles when she sees me, and I melt, every damn time.

"We had a great day!" Barbara says, pushing back her dark hair with her free hand. "I think she's trying to talk, Nathan."

"Yeah. She's been pretty vocal lately. Eve thinks *mama* is coming any day." Barbara turns and I follow her into a beautiful, but babyproof, living room.

"Most babies say *dada* first," she says. "But our Rosie is definitely her own girl." No one calls her Rosie except Barbara.

When we were first trying to figure out daycare, I suggested Eve's mom, but that elicited a quick huff of breath from Eve. "I wouldn't trust my mother with Oscar," she'd replied. And my mother-in-law hasn't turned out to be the most attentive grandmother. She's surrounded Rosewyn with plush toys and more little pink outfits than she could ever wear, but mostly she's concerned with what Rosewyn will call her when she starts talking. Grandma is definitely out.

Barbara places Rosewyn in my arms and gathers her diaper bag. I already know there's a note in the front pocket outlining every bottle, diaper change, and nap that transpired during the day.

"Oh, Elephant is in the kitchen. I'll be right back," she says.

I wander around the living room, baby on my hip, and jounce her around, the way people do, trying to make her giggle, which she does. I notice an end table loaded with pictures in assorted frames. I'd seen it before, but never really looked at the faces. There are several of a boy, her son, I assume, pictures of the same kid at various stages of growth. But there's also a tiny picture in the back of a newborn swaddled in that same blanket every hospital uses for their babies. There's a tiny pink bow pasted on her bald head. I pick it up for a closer look.

"Who's this?" I turn and Barbara is standing at my elbow, stuffed animal under her arm. Her face reddens and she takes the picture from me.

"My daughter." She places the picture back on the table and turns away. "I'll put Elephant in the diaper bag." She strokes Rosewyn's cheek.

We walk to the big front door. "Thanks, Barbara."

"Bye-bye, Rosie," Barbara says. "See you tomorrow!"

When Rosewyn and I get home, it's dark already. Winter in New England. I set her in her playpen and turn on the Christmas tree lights. We need to take it down, but we haven't had time, and Rosewyn enjoys the lights and shiny ornaments.

I go through her bag and put stuff away, restock it. By the time Eve walks through the door, the baby has been fed, bathed, and dressed in her pajamas. I'm sitting in the living room watching TV, baby on my lap.

"How was your day?" Eve calls from the kitchen. "I've got tacos," she says before I can answer.

"Great."

"How did Rosewyn do today? Any issues?"

"Nope."

Eve sets a plate of Mexican on the coffee table for me and picks up the baby. She coos and nuzzles her and that makes my heart momentarily happy. Eve returns to the kitchen with Rosewyn on her hip then comes back balancing her own dinner and a glass of wine.

"How was work?" I ask around a fish taco.

"Fine." Eve manages to set her dinner and glass on the end table without spilling anything then sits with the baby on her lap.

My mind flips back to Nicole. They're so different. Nicole is chatty, warm, bubbly, and Eve is, well, Eve. Quiet, introspective. You never know what she's thinking. It's like she wants to be alone. A Greta Garbo wannabe. It didn't bother me in the beginning.

"Did you know that Barbara has a daughter?" I ask.

"What?" Eve sips her wine.

"Today when I picked up Rosewyn, I saw a picture of a baby girl with other pictures of her son."

Eve's forehead furrows. "When we interviewed her, she didn't mention a daughter, only the son. You sure the baby was her daughter?"

"She said she was."

"Huh."

Eve settles back in the chair, Rosewyn bouncing on her lap. My baby girl slobbers, her tiny fingers in her mouth, and kicks her legs as Eve tries to eat her tacos.

"Maybe she just forgot to mention the daughter," I say.

"Could be," Eve responds, leaning her head back on the chair cushion, her dinner sitting on the end table. She's already tired of the conversation, or maybe she's just tired.

CHAPTER 8
Rita

BEFORE I LEFT WILMA'S, I CHECKED WITH HER NEIGHBORS, THOSE who were home anyway, and they hadn't noticed anyone suspicious hanging around, so I don't have much to go on. Back at the station, I work at my desk until my shoulders start to ache.

It's getting late. I walk through the squad room on my way back from the vending machine and notice that Chase is still here. He sits at his desk in his cubicle, working on his laptop. Pictures of his wife and their little boy are pinned to the gray fabric walls. Detective Chase Fuller and I have been partners for a couple years now and, despite the age difference, have become a pretty good team. He leans back in his chair. His short dark hair and his baby face make him look even younger than his thirty-something years.

"What're you still doing here?" I ask.

"Sara and Charlie are at her parents' house tonight, so I figured I'd catch up." He scratches the back of his neck. "But I'm heading home in a couple minutes."

"Yeah. Me too. You hear anything about the prints from the Parnell case?"

"Nothing in the system."

"Probably an amateur then. Ms. Parnell thought maybe a homeless person. Or could be teenagers making mischief."

"What's next, Rita?"

"Well, we don't have a whole lot going on around here, thank God. Let's have a cruiser make a point of passing through the neighborhood the next few days. See if they see anyone hanging around that might be up to no good. And I'll keep in touch with Ms. Parnell, make sure nothing else has disappeared."

"You want me to call Roy's?" Roy owns the closest pawn shop to Graybridge.

"Yeah. Do that. There's a description of the stolen items in the report."

My office is ice cold. It was hotter than hell this morning. Seems the ancient HVAC system has revolted. *Too hot, hey? I'll show you!* I'm sitting, tidying my desk, getting things ready for the morning when my cell phone rings. My brother's name pops up on the screen.

"Hey," I say while searching my desk drawer for a candy bar that I'm sure I stashed in there recently. The vending machine choices had been subpar.

"Hi Rita. What are you up to?"

"Working. I don't get a gazillion days off like you academic snobs."

He chuckles. "Yeah. Right. Listen, what are you doing New Year's Eve?"

"Isn't that a line from a song?"

"Maybe. I'm having a little get-together at my place and wondered if you wanted to join us."

I was looking forward to relaxing at home, watching old movies, and eating junk food.

"You could bring Joe," he adds.

"He's out of town on assignment."

"Well, come anyway."

"Who's going to be there?"

He sighs. "Charlotte and her boyfriend." His daughter, who I'm close to. "And some people from work."

The sound of his voice more than anything has me relenting. Danny and I are close, the closest of all the McMahon siblings. And I can tell he's going through a rough patch. He is currently between girlfriends and that always leaves him adrift with too much time on his hands, which has him spending too much time in the past. A past where all nine of us were alive and relatively happy. We didn't have much growing up in Boston, but neither did anyone else in our predominately working-class Irish neighborhood. But we were happy enough.

"All right. What time?"

He gives me the details and tells me not to worry about bringing anything. His mood, I can tell by his voice again, has improved, and that is enough for me.

It's dark and cold, typical New England December weather, when I pull up my van at the curb in front of my building. My first-floor apartment is cold, too, and I turn up the thermostat even before I turn the lights on. It's a small one bedroom but it's enough for me. I rub my hands together trying to thaw them out as I walk over to my ancient stereo. I flip through my vinyl collection, select an old Elton John album, one of my favorites. I sigh as I place it on the turntable and drop the needle. I drink in the heavenly music that emanates from the speakers as I pour myself a glass of red. Wonder what's in the fridge that will suffice for dinner?

Right on cue, there's a knock on my door. Collin, my upstairs neighbor.

"Hey, Rita. You're home late. I thought things were slow at work."

"Come on in," I say, and step aside. "Yeah. They are. Just slow getting myself together tonight."

He's carrying a covered casserole dish. God bless him.

"I brought you beef stroganoff from the café. I made too much. It didn't go over as well as I'd hoped." He arches a dark eyebrow, purses his lips.

"I'm sure it's delicious."

"It really did turn out terrific. Just a quiet day at the shop all around, I guess. The cold weather must be keeping everyone at home."

"Wine?"

"Sure."

Collin and I sit in my small living room. We've become good friends in the years he and his partner, André, have lived in the apartment above mine. Their café and catering business keeps them hopping. Between that and my schedule, we don't see each other that often, but Collin always looks in on me, brings me food. His family is all in Florida, and I've become something of an honorary aunt for him, which suits me. He's a good neighbor and a good friend.

We catch up. Gossip about the other people in our building, have a few laughs at their expense, nothing mean-spirited. Collin is too nice for that. He finishes his wine and heads back upstairs.

I flip the album over, then microwave the stroganoff and eat it standing at the counter. It's so good. I refill my glass and collapse back on the couch. I pull my satchel over and dig out my notebook. Flip through the pages. It's a little bigger than your typical detective notebook. I need room for my sketches. All my life I've drawn pictures. They help me think, organize my thoughts. While talking to Wilma, I'd sketched the first-floor layout of her house, and I think about that now. Would a homeless person have taken the toolbox and the crowbar? Seems like there might've been something smaller, more valuable to lift. But who knows? I set my notebook aside, sip my wine, close my eyes, and listen to the music.

CHAPTER 9
Nathan

*T*HE WEEKEND IS FINALLY HERE AND I'M GLAD TO BE AT HOME, EVEN if it is New Year's Eve. Before Rosewyn, it was a night to party big time, but I think I like this better, even if Eve and I are in this strange, polite world we've fallen into. Maybe we'll figure it out in the new year. I've been thinking the last few days that we should try. I should try. When it comes down to it, I love Eve, and when I look at our daughter, I know I want us to be a family—stay a family. Maybe Eve will forgive me for Nicole. I'll end it. Start fresh, and when I tell Eve what I've done, as a professional maybe she'll understand, and we can put it behind us.

I could keep the affair to myself. I don't think Eve has any idea. But that's just not me. When I was a kid, I took a ten-dollar bill from my mom's purse one day. There was a video game I wanted badly, and I didn't have enough money to cover it. Mom didn't suspect that I was the thief, and I was filled with guilt. I tossed and turned in bed that night and couldn't sleep until I tiptoed back downstairs and confessed. Mom was hurt more than angry, but she was glad I told her. I was grounded for a week and the video game was confiscated until I earned the ten bucks and gave it to Mom. It was a life lesson that stuck with me. A little thing maybe, but it taught me that I don't do well keeping secrets of wrongdoing from the people I care about.

If I'm going to work things out with Eve, I can't have that be-tween us, but the thought of telling her fills me with dread. What if she won't forgive me? That thought has my stomach in knots.

I sip a beer and try to relax on the couch as dark settles in. Eve has Rosewyn on her hip as she walks through the house closing cur-tains.

We just finished dinner, takeout from our favorite Italian restau-rant, a little more festive for the holiday. The dishes are still in the sink. Eve got up to tend to the baby, who'd needed a diaper change, right after we'd finished our meal. I grabbed a beer and settled in the living room without thinking too much about it.

Eve has finished her tour of the house. She looks exhausted, hol-low eyed, and sets Rosewyn in her playpen.

"We should take the tree down," she says, and runs her hand through her hair, sending blond tresses askew.

"I'll get the bins from the attic."

"Not now, Nathan. Tomorrow. I'm too tired to do it tonight."

"Right. Okay."

She sinks down in a chair and picks up the TV remote, starts flip-ping through channels.

I drain my beer and sit with the empty bottle in my hands. I really don't know how to tackle what's wrong between Eve and me. My parents' marriage, what I remember—my mother died when I was in middle school—didn't seem a whole lot different from my own. They didn't talk much. Dad worked at his car shop. Mom had a part-time job at the supermarket. My older brother was always at school or after-school sports. I thought we were happy enough, typ-ical. Maybe we were. But I don't remember my parents actually be-having much like a couple. They were pleasant enough to each other, but that's about it. We functioned. It never occurred to me that maybe we *were* dysfunctional. Who the hell knows? Then Mom got sick. Six months later she was gone. And I felt lost; the house felt empty.

I jump up from the couch. "I'll take care of the dishes," I say.

"I almost forgot."

"You want a refill?"

She lifts her glass. "Thanks."

After I've refilled Eve's wine, I head back out to the kitchen and start cleaning up. With my hands plunged into hot soapy water, my phone vibrates with a text. It's sitting on the counter where I can see it. Nicole.

Eve walks into the room, passes by on her way to the refrigerator. I grab a dish towel, hastily wipe my hands, pick up my phone and shove it in my back pocket. Eve tops off her glass and sets the empty bottle on the counter.

"Should we take Rosewyn to the park tomorrow? If the weather's nice," she says.

"Yeah. Sounds like a plan."

Her gaze drops to the counter where my phone had been resting. "Then maybe Monday we can call that contractor about the deck."

That was one of the projects we'd talked about when we bought the house, creating a new outdoor space with all the bells and whistles.

I nod. "Let's do that. I can call." Maybe the new year *will* mark a new beginning.

Something like a smile appears on Eve's face, lifting her full lips, showing a glint of white, even teeth. Her hand briefly touches my shoulder, squeezes lightly. She sips her wine. "Thanks for doing the dishes."

Kitchen tidy, I slip off to the bathroom and look at Nicole's text. **Happy New Year's Eve!**

I wonder if I should respond. Say something neutral. I'm definitely going to break it off, but people are vulnerable on this night. I'll wait until next week. I type: Same to you! And leave it at that.

Back in the kitchen I stand in front of the sliding glass door that opens onto the deck. There's a light in a window in the house behind us. That's strange. No one lives there. It's been empty since we moved into our house. But it looks like someone is over there with a flashlight. Then it winks out and everything is dark again.

CHAPTER 10

Rita

*M*Y WHOLE BUILDING SMELLS LIKE HEAVEN. COLLIN AND ANDRÉ ARE catering a big New Year's Eve party in Boston. They left an hour or so ago after cooking all day. I heard them running up and down the stairs carrying trays of food. And I felt the cold air from the open front door in the building's shared foyer seeping under my door.

My brother's party starts in thirty minutes, so I reluctantly get off the couch and head into my bedroom. I slip into a pair of slim black pants and notice the waist is a little snug. Too many holiday treats. I'll have to do better and put in more miles on my bike. Middle-age spread is no joke. I try to keep myself fit because I don't want to fall behind my younger colleagues. Mostly I've been successful, and I want to keep it that way. I pull the blue cashmere sweater Danny gave me for Christmas over my head and settle the soft fabric down over my hips.

I brush my shoulder-length hair and apply a bit of make-up. I think of Joe as I stand before my bathroom mirror and wonder what's holding me back. New year, new me? I smirk at myself. We'll see.

There are half a dozen cars parked outside Danny's impressive two-story house. He was always one of the more sociable McMahons. Lights blaze in every window, giving the place a warm glow on a cold, dark night. We'd had a bit of snow for Christmas, which made everyone happy. When we were kids, nothing was more depressing than a green Christmas. Even as adults, I think we all become kids when Santa is on his way. But the snow has pretty much melted, and we're left with the cold air and an iciness in the wind.

Charlotte greets me at the door with a hug.

"So glad you're here," she says. "Dad said you were coming." I glance through the foyer at the crowded living room. Well-dressed men and women chat and sip wine from Danny's best crystal. A young man comes up behind Charlotte.

"Detective Myers." He extends his hand. He's tall, athletic, looks like he could be in a commercial for aftershave.

"Rita, please, Stephen." I hope like hell that's his name. Only met my niece's boyfriend once.

He nods. "Can I get you a drink?" We walk together into the dining room where other partygoers stand in knots and laugh in that light phony way people do when trying to be polite.

I spot Danny by the sideboard talking to an elderly gentleman. Danny is perfectly turned out, as usual. Dark suit, snow-white dress shirt. No tie though, to be more casual. His dark hair is neatly coiffed, and the bits of gray that were present before the holidays have disappeared thanks to a trip to the barber probably. The elderly man walks off just as we approach.

"Hey," Danny says and grabs me in a hug. I smell whiskey on his breath mingling with his cologne.

"Nice get-together," I say as Stephen hands me a glass of red wine. I'm impressed he remembered what I like from the one time I met him. I take a big sip. I'll need it to spend an evening with Danny's college colleagues.

"Yes. I had a nice turnout," he says. "You'll remember some of them from last year's party."

I doubt that, but I don't say so. "You're turning this into something of a tradition."

"Yes. I guess I am."

"Charlotte!" A tall woman with big teeth, who seems way too excited, calls from across the room. Charlotte gives me a sheepish smile as the lady corrals her and Stephen and leads them into the living room.

"So, how are things?" I ask Danny as we stand alone by the big dining room window.

"Fine. New semester starts in a couple of weeks. So that's good."

But the look in his eyes tells another story. *Jesus.* I worry about him and wonder how many drinks he's had. He seems pretty sober, but then, he holds it well.

"Joe should be back in a week or two," I say, although I'm not sure about that. "You want to do dinner?" Danny likes Joe and Joe seems to have a good effect on him.

"That sounds great." He clears his throat, his gaze on the Persian carpet. "Have you spoken to Maureen lately?"

Maureen is our eldest sister. She lives in our house in Boston, the one where we all grew up. It's like since Ma died, Maureen has taken over the old place like some medieval guardian, deciding who can touch what, like Ma's possessions are ancient relics.

"Not recently. Why?"

"I haven't spoken to her in a couple of weeks. But I was wondering if you wanted to take a ride down there." He glances toward the window to the black night beyond. "I want to look through some things in the attic."

"Good luck with that," I say, before I think better of it.

His jaw tightens. "It's not all her stuff, Rita. There are boxes of our things there, too."

"Yeah. I guess." Maureen has given Danny a few boxes from the cluttered attic already, but she's been pretty stingy about it.

"Would you go with me?"

I'd really rather not. I'd rather let the past rest in the dusty attic where it belongs. But I'd do anything for my brother. I sigh. "Okay. Sure. Let me know."

The evening passes in typical fashion and I try to be the polite guest, do my best to make small talk with people I have nothing in common with. At five minutes to midnight, someone turns off the classical music that has been playing all evening and turns on the TV to one of the countdown shows. Danny and Charlotte have run through the crowd, handing out delicate flutes of champagne. We all join in with the TV people, counting backward from ten. The TV people scream "Happy New Year!" And we join in with that, too. There's a flurry of clinked glasses and chaste pecks. Danny is at my side and swallows his champagne in one gulp. He slips an arm around my waist and sighs.

CHAPTER 11
Nathan

*T*HE WORK WEEK STARTS COLD AND BLUSTERY. I'M TRYING TO LOOK at the new year as a new start, a clean slate, like everyone else, I guess. The time I had with Rosewyn and Eve over the holidays has given me the strength to try again, try harder. I feel guilty as hell over Nicole and texted her to meet me for lunch.

We've met a couple of times at this out-of-the-way diner, so I feel pretty secure that no one I know will spot us here. Even if they do, we just look like two businesspeople grabbing a quick lunch. I'm sitting in a red vinyl-covered booth in the back, sipping the ice water a middle-aged waitress plunked in front of me. I look out the window and see Nicole walk around the corner, scarf over her mouth against the chilly breeze. Her blond hair, not too far off Eve's color, flutters in the wind.

She slips out of her coat, pulls off her gloves, and sets them on the seat before sliding in across from me.

"How was your New Year's?" she asks, cheeks red with the cold.

"Fine. Quiet. You?"

She smiles. "Fun, actually. I went out with some friends from work."

"That's good."

The tired waitress stops by. "What can I get you?" She pulls a small notepad from her apron pocket.

Nicole glances quickly at the colorful plastic menu. "I'll have the chicken salad and a Diet Pepsi."

I order a grilled cheese and tomato soup for some reason. It was what my mom used to make for me when I was sick and home from school, but I haven't had it in years. The waitress glowers at me like I should've ordered a steak and I'm a poor excuse for a man. Then stuffs her notebook back in her apron and walks away.

"So, what's up?" Nicole asks.

"Um, well," I don't know if I want to get into this before we eat. Will she storm out? Make a scene?

Nicole places a hand on my arm. "Nathan. I can see it all over your face." She grins. "You'd make a terrible actor, you know that?"

I sip my water.

"You've had time to think over the holidays . . . about us, am I right?" she says.

"Well, yeah." I'm such a fucking coward. I can't even break up with my mistress. She has to do it for me.

"Me too." Her dark lashes flutter down over her eyes for a moment. "I think it's time we both moved on." She manages a slight smile and sighs. "Life is a little crazy right now. I've got my hands full with a big project, and I'm trying to get my grandmother into an assisted-living apartment, and that has been a nightmare with paperwork and doctor's visits." She rolls her eyes. "You're a great guy, Nathan. You came along at just the right time." She glances out the plate glass window at the busy street.

I go from shaking in my boots to exhilarated. I squeeze her hand. "It was great, meeting you."

"Yes. You're a terrific person, Nathan, but we both deserve better than sneaking around, meeting in hotel rooms. It's time."

I blow out a relieved breath as our food arrives. Nicole chats along about her grandmother and her best friend at work and a million other things that have me zoning out and thinking about Eve.

When we finish, we walk out to the parking lot together. She reaches up and gives me a kiss on the cheek. I watch her as she walks down the block and turns the corner, the ends of her red scarf flapping in the wind.

* * *

The afternoon drags, but we're really busy. New Year's Eve is kind of the Super Bowl of car accidents and by the end of the day our lot is full to bursting, wrecked vehicles parked everywhere. I'm antsy to get home, ready to turn over that new leaf with Eve. I'll even suggest we go to counseling together. My gaze shifts out my window where a tow truck beeps as it backs up, a shattered red convertible chained to its bed. My mood slips. What if Eve throws me out? Demands a divorce? I wouldn't blame her. Sweat sprouts on my upper lip and I cover my mouth with my hand. I'm a piece of shit for what I've done. And I'd take it back if I could. Hopefully I haven't ruined everything.

Finally, it's closing time and I head out to Barbara's to collect Rosewyn. Barbara meets me at the door with an uncharacteristic pucker in her brow.

"Anything wrong?" I ask.

"I was just about to call you when I heard your car." She turns and leads me into the living room. Rosewyn is asleep in the playpen, but I notice her cheeks are flushed and her wispy dark hair is damp. "She's running a low-grade fever," Barbara says. "She was fine all day, then when she woke up from her nap, she was fussy. I think she has an ear infection, Nathan." Barbara scowls at me as if this is my fault.

Rosewyn has had them before, not too many, like some kids, but a time or two. "Poor baby," I say. "I'll call Eve and see what she wants me to do."

Barbara nods. "I'll get her things."

I pick up my daughter and her eyes slit open, then shut again. She cries that I-don't-feel-good cry and I feel guilty. I'll stay home with her tomorrow and for as long as she needs. I can feel the heat coming off her little body and wonder if her fever is more than low grade.

Barbara returns with Rosewyn's diaper bag. "Be sure you call the doctor first thing, Nathan," she admonishes like I'm some irresponsible teenager, and like I'm not actually married to a doctor who'll know what to do. "And keep her covered up outside." Barbara follows us to the front door. She places a hand on the baby's forehead. "She feels warmer than she did. Be sure to give her something for the fever and get her to the pediatrician. If they're closed, go to urgent care. There's one about a block from your house. Don't wait until tomorrow. These things can escalate quickly in a baby."

"Eve will check her and make sure she's okay."

At the mention of Eve, Barbara's brow furrows. She nods and fusses with Rosewyn's blanket almost as if she doesn't want to let her go.

"We'll take care of her, Barbara, don't worry."

"Call me and let me know."

"Yeah. I will." I duck out into the chilly evening, holding my daughter close to my shoulder. After I get her settled in her car seat, I glance back at the house. Barbara is at the window, watching.

CHAPTER 12
Eve

*R*OSEWYN HAS AN EAR INFECTION. NATHAN CALLED ME LAST NIGHT as I was leaving work. He'd picked her up from Barbara's and she was feverish. I checked her ears with the otoscope I keep in my medical bag at home. I don't need it much where I work, but it's come in handy with the baby. I called her pediatrician, who's a friend of mine, and she called in an antibiotic at the 24-hour pharmacy. I could've done it myself, but I always like to check in with Doctor Marsh so I'm sure any issues are noted on Rosewyn's records.

Nathan is home with her today and I'm grateful. What would we have done if his job was more like mine? Then I feel guilty. I could've stayed home with her. My appointments could've been rescheduled. My dad was a pretty renowned cardiac surgeon, and I don't ever remember him staying home on a workday for any reason. And I never wanted to be like him. That's why I didn't plan on having kids. That way I couldn't be a bad parent. I sigh. Nathan's a great father. He would never dither about taking time off to take care of Rosewyn, so I don't have to make that choice.

I have a pretty full docket today and finished up my morning rounds quickly. Frances seems to be doing better. We've eased back on her dosage and things have gone well so far. She even played a game of checkers in the common room with a young woman whose room is next to hers. Frances is usually reluctant to interact with the other patients, so that was a good sign. I make a note to myself to check in with the office to see how their plans are coming along for when she's released. They are also still trying to locate a relative for her, so I'll check on that, too. Hopefully, there's someone out there who's a next-of-kin.

After lunch, I have four outpatient appointments. Dr. Tanaka told me that Don had skipped his appointment last week but had rescheduled for today. I cross my fingers, hoping that that works out.

Marie settles into the armchair in my office, her expensive coat and gloves draped over the back.

"How was your week?" I ask, notepad on my lap.

She tips her head. "Up and down."

"Why was that?"

"New Year's." She bites her lip and picks at a piece of lint on her black slacks. "When I was a kid, my parents used to make a big deal out of it. They never went out with friends and stayed home with me instead. They said it was too dangerous to be out on New Year's Eve. Everyone would be crowding the bars and drinking too much. So, we had our own little traditions. Dick Clark. Bubbly juice instead of champagne. They didn't drink, so we'd watch the ball drop on TV, the three of us, and toast with our juice." She sighs. Marie looks up at me, brushes away a tear. I lean over and hand her the tissue box.

"A nice memory?"

"Yes. I had such a happy childhood when I was little." She clears her throat. "But other than that, things are going well."

We talk about her job, which seems exciting, full of travel and upscale hotels and dining. I almost envy her. She can do as she pleases. No ties. No one to let down. Her life is her own.

She's divorced and taking her time about getting into another relationship, which is prudent. She spends a lot of time with friends and, except for her parents' deaths, seems to be happy. I don't think she'll need many more appointments, but that's up to her.

I walk out to the reception desk with Marie, and we laugh over Mr. Whitson's dog. Mr. Whitson is an inpatient, who insisted on bringing his rat terrier with him. It's normally not allowed, but his wife has money and influence in the community and somehow got it approved by the board. Edgar, the terrier, who is named after Poe, is currently doing his business right outside the facility doors, much to the chagrin of the aide whose duty it is to walk him three times a day.

Marie looks down at her shiny Jimmy Choo pumps. "I'll be careful where I step." She smiles. "See you next week, Doctor Thayer."

I feel a presence over my shoulder. Don stands beside me. He leans against the counter.

"Nice to see you, Doctor," he says.

"You too, Don. How's it going?" I step back, hold my breath.

"Okay. How are you?" His eyes shift to my sleeve where faded bruises lie beneath the cuff of my button-up blouse.

"I'm fine, Don. Did you see Dr. Tanaka today?"

"Yeah. It was all right."

I breathe a sigh of relief. "Well, that's wonderful." I turn to head back to my office.

"Doctor Thayer?" he calls.

I turn reluctantly.

"You sure I couldn't see you again?"

"Why don't you give it some time? See how things go with Doctor Tanaka."

He nods, his gaze on the floor. "Oh, I've been talking to a woman online." His eyes meet mine. "This one might actually work out."

"That's great."

"Or not." He smiles. "Have a nice day, Doctor Thayer." He turns and exits through the sliding doors, gingerly skirting the mess that the aide is trying to clean up while holding the dog's leash at the same time.

Back in my office, I scroll through charts, tidy up for the day. I need only to do evening rounds, then I'm headed home. I check my phone. Nothing from Nathan since just after lunch when he reported that Rosewyn seemed better. Temperature dropping. I text him that I'll pick up dinner on the way home.

It's quiet in my office. This side of the building, the outpatient side, is pretty well deserted after hours. The heat rumbles, rattling the vents and reminding me just how old this structure is. Out my window, it's full dark, and I hear the wind blowing through the bare trees and sleet starting to ping against the window. I shudder and slip into the cardigan I draped over the back of my chair. I'll do my evening rounds then get home.

My heels click against the old tile floor. I walk quickly toward the lobby, past the shadows in the nooks and crannies. I stop for a minute and listen. Is there someone here? Brian? But I turn and glance back up the empty hall. Must just be the wind.

The lobby area is brighter, and a nurse stands there talking to the receptionist. I swing around to the inpatient wing, buzz myself through. One of the aides is settling patients back in their rooms after dinner.

The last patient I need to check on is Frances. She's sitting in a chair near the window. The room is dark, lit only by the bedside lamp.

"Frances?"

"Yeah."

"How are you feeling?"

She shrugs. There are shadows under her saggy eyes and nose. Someone combed out her long hair and braided it, giving her a hollow, ancient look, like a painting of a crone from a medieval fairy tale. She looks years older than she is, a testament to a hard life.

I glance over her chart. Nothing new there. Vitals all the same. Medication on track. "Can I get you anything before I leave?" I ask, my eyes on my laptop screen.

"Yeah," she croaks. "You can get rid of that little girl."

I glance up at her. "What little girl?"

"The one that keeps bothering me, laughing. I heard her in the hall by my door. I wish they wouldn't bring her up here."

"Who?"

"She won't stop laughing." Frances boxes her own ears. "I can't sleep with her out there."

I blow out a breath. Schizophrenia sufferers often have auditory hallucinations. I was hoping her medication would quell those. She hasn't complained of them in a while. One step forward, two steps back with her.

"I'll see what I can do, Frances." I consider her medication again. What will give her the relief she so badly needs?

"I'd appreciate it," she says.

I stop on my way back down the hall and talk to Glenda, who's just come on duty.

"I'll go check on her," she says. Glenda rolls her eyes and marches off down the hall.

In the lobby, Frances's day nurse is walking toward the front door, her shift over. I call to her and ask her about Frances, but she says that Frances didn't mention hearing a little girl to her. Then I ask the receptionist if, possibly, someone had a visitor today who had a child with them, but, of course, no one did. I sigh and head back to my office to do a little research on medications. Maybe I've overlooked something that might suit Frances better.

An hour later, I head for home.

Nathan opens the door for me when I arrive carrying a bagful of food from his favorite Chinese restaurant. "How's it going?" I ask, setting the bag on the table.

"Not bad. Rosewyn is sleeping. Her fever's down."

"Great. The antibiotic must be kicking in." I'm glad we were able to start it last night. "But she'll probably not want to go to bed at her normal time," I say, glancing at the time on the microwave. It's nearly eight o'clock and she usually goes down for the night at eight-thirty.

"Well, she missed her afternoon nap," Nathan says, as he unloads the cartons from the takeout bag. "She was still a little fussy, but then she perked up, took her bottle about a half hour ago and fell asleep on my lap, so I put her down."

"Maybe she'll sleep through."

Nathan shrugs. "If she wakes up in the night, I can get up with her. I already called out for tomorrow."

His dark hair is mussed. There's spit-up on the shoulder of his flannel shirt. But when Nathan smiles at me and his dimple deepens, I sigh. I walk over and throw my arms around him and it's all I can do to keep from crying.

CHAPTER 13

Eve

*I*T'S FRIDAY AND IT'S BEEN A BUSY WEEK, BUT ROSEWYN IS FINALLY BACK at the sitter's, ear infection nearly resolved. Rachel called me and invited me to lunch, and it feels good to be out of the hospital for a while.

We're sitting in a little Thai restaurant near Rachel's gallery. There are heavy red curtains with gold accents at the windows. Outside, people walk by with their coat collars pulled up against the winter chill.

"So, how's Rosewyn?" Rachel asks. "She's back at the sitter's then?"

"Yes." Rachel and I had talked on the phone yesterday, and I told her about the baby. "And Nathan's back at work."

"That's good." Rachel spoons up her Tom Kha Gai, tips her head. "How are things with you and Nathan?"

I take a deep breath. "Better, I think. He really is a good guy, Rachel, a good father."

"Uh huh. But what about the two of you?"

I almost don't want to talk to her about this. It feels too personal right now even for a best friend. And I don't really know what to think about Nathan and me. "Maybe we should go away, like you said. Get away from everything here and just be ourselves." She nods, and I change the subject. "What about you? What's been going on?"

She clears her throat, pushes her long dark hair back over her shoulder. "Work's been a beast. Aaron's been an asshole since after the holidays."

Aaron is her boss, an elderly man and an over-the-top perfectionist. "That's his usual persona, isn't it?"

"Yeah, but it's been worse lately. Sales are down and there's that new gallery in Boston that he's sure is cutting into our revenue. And one of our best-selling artists has left us for them, and that's got Aaron batshit."

"So, what are you going to do?"

"I don't know. There aren't a lot of choices in my business." Rachel blows her bangs off her forehead. "If I have to, I can always go back to graphic design, corporate work. It would pay the bills, but I'd rather cut off my left arm. I hate office work."

"What about Peter? How are things with him?"

"We broke up. He was getting too clingy. 'What are you doing, Rachel?'" she mimics. "'Can I stop over after work? Let's go see my sister in Worcester tonight.' I'd had enough of him. So, I'm solo now, and I think I'll stay that way for a while." Rachel smacks her hand on the table and turns around in her seat. "Where did our server go? I could use another drink."

While I'm drinking tea, Rachel often likes a couple glasses of wine with lunch. Working at an art gallery, that's not a big deal. But I can't go back to the hospital with alcohol on my breath. "So, what are you doing this weekend?" I ask. "You want to come over to the house? I wanted to ask you about paint colors for the living room." When I was pregnant, Rachel painted the nursery a soft pink and hand painted roses in strategic places on the walls. It turned out beautifully.

Rachel sips the wine our server hands her. "So domestic, Eve. Sometimes I can't believe you're the same person I met all those years ago."

I laugh. "We all change."

"Yeah. I guess. I really miss our girls' trips. Remember St. Barts the spring before you met Nathan?"

I chuckle. "That was one for the record books."

"God, I miss those days. Oh, I almost forgot. Remember that guy I dated in college?"

"Which one? There were so many." I smile.

"Yeah, well, Andrew, the geeky one down the hall, sophomore year." Rachel taps the table with her manicured fingernails. "You remember," she continues. "He lived across the hall from that weird girl with the frizzy dark hair and glasses."

I search my memory and the people start to fall into place. I remember Andrew, tall, sandy blond hair, and the girl who lived across from him, vaguely. She was younger than we were, a freshman. She was a little strange, and I got the feeling that she wanted to be friends, but while I always said hello when we passed in the hall, Rachel and I weren't looking to add an underclassman to our circle. And then I remember something else about her. "The girl who had the thing with the professor?"

Rachel arches her brows. "Yeah, the professor who had a thing for *you*."

I shiver. Professor Daniels. He never did anything to me that I felt I could go to the administration about. It was just an awkward smile in my direction, a hand on my shoulder, excessive praise in front of the class for my work in his Drama I seminar, a class Rachel and I took as an easy elective.

"He was so creepy. I definitely remember him, but I barely recall her or Andrew either." Our undergrad years are pretty hazy for me. Rachel's memory of our college life is much better than mine. "What about Andrew?"

"I just read online that he's running for mayor. I could've been the first lady of Boston if I'd stayed with him."

I smile, sip my tea. "That I can't picture."

"Me neither." She sighs. "You and I used to have so much fun."

She means before I got married and that puts my back up. So maybe my life did veer from the course I'd set out as a twenty-something. "So, do you want to come over tomorrow?"

A shadow slips over her face and I wonder what's on her mind. Rachel can be blunt, outspoken, but sometimes it's hard to tell what she's thinking. She's moody, my mother would've said. People are complex, that I know as a professional. They have different facets to them, and it isn't always easy to get to the core of who they are or what they're thinking. Outside of my office, I can't poke at people and unpeel the layers. And we're all entitled to our inner selves.

"What about you and Nathan? I don't want to get in the middle of that," Rachel says.

"I told you we were doing a little better."

"Well, that's good, but I think I'll just stay home this weekend."

"You sure? Everything okay?"

She sips her wine. "Yes. I'm good. Maybe next weekend we can plan something."

I sit at my desk, glance out the window. The afternoon has grown dark and dreary. Wintry wind rustles the bare trees, which scratch the glass like boney fingers. I'm catching up on paperwork when I hear my phone buzz. I'm about to ignore the call until I finish the chart I'm working on, but when I check the screen, my heart stops. Nathan.

Meet me at Barbara's NOW

What could've happened? I pull out of the parking lot and onto the road. Did Rosewyn have more than an ear infection? Did some latent illness hide behind the ear infection and bloom into something serious?

Something bad has happened to my baby.

That thought rolls through my brain over and over as I speed through town and near Barbara's house.

I struggle for breath as I pull up in her driveway. Cop cars are parked in the street. I search for an ambulance but don't see one. I throw the gearshift into park and run. An older cop grabs my arm and stops me. I try to break free, twisting and turning in his grasp.

"Hold on there," he yells, pinning me against him.

"My baby. What's happened?"

"Are you the mom?"

"*Yes!* Where's my baby?" He slowly lets me go as Nathan, escorted by a younger cop, walks over. "What happened!"

Nathan's face is red, tear stained. "She's gone, Eve," he stammers.

"What do you mean she's gone?"

"Let's sit in the patrol car," the older officer says, motioning with his chin.

"No! I've got to get inside."

The younger cop stands in front of me, hands on his hips. "It's a crime scene, ma'am. You've got to stay out here."

A *crime* scene? "Where's Barbara?" I scream at Nathan.

"Mrs. Singleton is inside," the older officer says. "We're waiting for detectives."

My knees start to buckle, and Nathan grabs me and pulls me to him.

The next thing I know, Nathan and I are sitting in the back of a police car, heat running, windows steamed. The older officer sits in the front seat and turns around to talk to us.

"Please tell me what's going on," I say through tears.

"We got a call from Mrs. Singleton about thirty minutes ago."

My gaze wanders to the tall white house as if he's telling me a story.

"She reported that the baby was missing." He takes a breath. "She said she went into the bedroom to check on her and the baby was gone from her crib."

"How is that possible!" I scream. "Where is my baby? Did you search the whole house? It's not like she could just walk away!"

"Yes. We've searched the house. We've got detectives and K9s on the way."

"I've got to get in there. I've got to see Barbara. This has to be a mistake." I'm screaming, tears falling down my cheeks. Nathan's arm is around my shoulders and he's crying quietly.

I collapse back against the seat. Neighbors have gathered in the street, their eyes quietly searching. Did one of them take her? Did someone take my daughter, or did something else happen? Something Barbara won't tell. My mind flips back to when we met her and discussed placing Rosewyn in her care. We were impressed by Barbara's perfect home, her perfect life, her warmth. Was it all a ruse just to get her hands on my baby? I'm shaking, gasping for breath. Nathan squeezes me so tightly it hurts.

The back door of the car opens and a middle-aged woman in a white blouse, dark pants, and blazer stands there. "Mr. and Mrs. Liddle?"

"Yes," Nathan says.

"I'm Detective Rita Myers. Let's go inside."

CHAPTER 14
Rita

I HAVEN'T WORKED A MISSING CHILD CASE SINCE MY DAYS WITH THE Boston PD, and those were usually settled fairly quickly. A noncustodial parent running off with the kids or a child who wandered away at the park. In all the cases I dealt with, except one, there was a happy ending. But that one, a baby dead in a dumpster, still haunts me. And I hope to God we're not dealing with a similar outcome here.

This is a really strange case. Upscale neighborhood in the middle of the afternoon. No signs of trauma. It's like the baby just disappeared into thin air, as the saying goes, and it gives me a pain in the gut. The uniformed cops have already gone over the house inch by inch and found nothing. The crime scene team is here and setting up. K9s are on the way as well. When there's a child involved, the wheels of law enforcement move quickly.

Mrs. Singleton is on her way to the station where Chase will question her more closely. This is a big step for Chase. But I trust him. He's coming along well and has good instincts. He's also the father of a little boy.

We've been cleared to sit at the kitchen table and Mr. Liddle and his wife, Doctor Thayer, take seats. She coughs, her hand at her throat. I look through the cabinets, find glasses, and bring them each a glass of water.

I sit opposite the Liddles, pull out my notebook, and turn to a fresh page. "Okay, Mr. Liddle, I understand you dropped the baby off this morning?"

"Yes," he manages through trembling lips.

"How long has Mrs. Singleton been caring for your daughter?"

"Since she was six weeks old."

I glance down at the notes I'd gotten from Officer Connors. "And she's nine months old? Eighteen pounds, dark hair. Wearing denim pants and a long-sleeved, ruffled, pink top?"

"Yes." He's a quivering mess. Eyes dripping, nose running. His wife is sitting like a statue, eyes unfocused.

"Anything unusual this morning?"

"Nothing out of the ordinary," he responds.

"No problems with Mrs. Singleton before this?"

"No. Nothing,"

I sketch their faces in my notebook. Let them think a minute. There's noise outside and we all look toward the window. The dogs have arrived, and cops are leading them through the backyard. This elicits a sharp cry from the missus.

"What happened to our baby?" Mr. Liddle asks. "Where could she be?"

"We're doing everything we can to find her. Does she have any medical conditions?"

"No. She's a healthy baby." He starts to cry again. "Why?"

The wife pinches his arm. She's shaking, lips trembling. "She has an ear infection, but she's better. No fever. She was fine to go back to the sitter."

"Doctor Thayer, where were you when you were notified about the baby's disappearance?"

She clears her throat, sits upright. "At my desk, at work. Can we speak to Barbara?" Her voice is an even staccato, like she's on autopilot. No tears now. But a redness in her face, like anger. Not unusual. People react in different ways to trauma.

"Not now."

"Where is she? She must know where Rosewyn is."

"She's with another detective. They're taking her down to the police station." The parents are distraught, of course, but there are questions that need answering and I proceed to ask them about everything in their lives, including the relationship between them.

I see a flicker of consternation when the questions get personal, but it's my job to ferret out the subtleties that lie beneath their answers. I add to my sketch of Doctor Thayer. A tightening of the lips when talking about her marriage. All was not well there, I suspect, long before the baby disappeared.

"What do you think happened, Detective?" she asks.

"We don't know at this point." I lean back in my chair. "I can tell you this much. Mrs. Singleton says that she put the baby down for a nap upstairs. Then she worked in the kitchen repotting houseplants." I glance at my notebook. "She says that she needed potting soil and went into the shed in the backyard to get some. Then she went back to work in the kitchen."

"She left the house!" Doctor Thayer explodes. "With my baby upstairs!"

"Just to the shed in the backyard. She came back inside and finished with her plants. Cleaned up. Then she went upstairs to check on the baby and found the crib empty."

"And you believe her? Rosewyn just *vanished!*"

"That's what Mrs. Singleton told us. When she saw that the baby was gone, she called 911."

"Have you found anything at all that will help us find Rosewyn?" Mr. Liddle asks, shaking himself out of his stupor.

"So far, we found nothing disturbed or unusual in the house or the yard." I glance out the window at the team swarming the shed and garden and hope like hell they don't find the baby buried there. I turn back to the parents. "But the front door may have been left unlocked."

"You're fucking kidding me!" Doctor Thayer screams and jumps to her feet. "What about security video? This is a nice neighborhood. Someone must have cameras around here."

"Our officers are conducting a house-to-house search and they'll be checking for that."

Doctor Thayer paces like she's thinking through a puzzle. "What about the real estate agent? The house is on the market. Could she have brought someone through who saw the crib and then came back when they figured the baby would be here?"

We noted the FOR SALE sign in the yard when we arrived and the lockbox on the front door. "We're looking into that. Detectives are contacting the agent." Maybe there's something there, but we'll see. I tap my pencil against my notebook. "Do you have a lot of money?" I ask.

"Not too much. We're okay, not rich though," Mr. Liddle answers.

"My mother is quite well off," Doctor Thayer says. "Do you think this is a kidnapping?" Her lips start to tremble again, and she leans against the kitchen counter, her hands at her throat.

"We don't know. But we'll look at everything." I need to get down to the station and check on Chase. He has orders to keep Mrs. Singleton there until I arrive and go over the interview. "One last thing before I leave you in Officer Connors's capable hands. Who do you know who might have an interest in your daughter or want to hurt the two of you?"

They look at one another, mouths open. Mr. Liddle says, "No one that I can think of. Who would do this?"

"What about you, Doctor Thayer?"

She shakes her head. "I don't know. Couldn't it have been just some random person? Someone walking by. They try the door and it's unlocked, and . . ." Her voice trends up toward hysterical.

"Could be. We're looking into that as well," I say calmly.

I'm about to stuff my notebook into my satchel when Doctor Thayer stops pacing. Her eyes meet mine. "Wait. A patient of mine. Donald Barry."

"What about him?"

"He's angry because I transferred him to another doctor."

"Okay. Why did that make him angry?" I write his name in my notebook.

"He formed an unhealthy attachment to me, so I transferred him to a male colleague. But I don't know that he would take my daughter. It doesn't make sense." Tears start to wet her cheeks again.

"But he was angry with you?"

"Yes."

"Anyone else?"

Mr. Liddle looks at me. "You really think it's someone we know?"

"We want to cover all our bases."

Doctor Thayer walks back to the table and reaches for her water glass.

"Where'd you get those bruises?" I ask.

"Oh." She pulls her sleeve down over her wrist. "Another patient. Frances Martin. But she's inpatient. She couldn't have gotten out of the facility. She couldn't have taken Rosewyn."

Still. I want to run by Doctor Thayer's hospital. See what we might find over there. "Okay. If you think of anyone else we need to look at, please let us know ASAP." I close my notebook and stand. "Officer Connors will take you home and stay with you." I motion Anna over. She's one of the best, and I don't have to explain every little thing to her. "She'll help you guys out. Keep you informed." And she can monitor their movements and all communication with friends and family.

I leave them there, mouths open. But I don't have time to sit with them and hold their hands. I have a baby to find, and time is the enemy.

CHAPTER 15
Rita

BACK AT THE STATION, WHAT HAD BEEN A SLEEPY, ROUTINE DAY HAS been turned on its head. The chief has already talked to the press. In a missing child case, the media is your best friend. An Amber Alert went out first thing. You want everyone in the community acting as your eyes and ears. Chief Bob Murphy meets me in the squad room.

"Anything, Rita?" His gray hair is disheveled as if he'd been repeatedly running his massive hands through it. Bob and I have worked together for decades, starting our careers as rookie cops with the Boston PD. We've been through a lot together, but nothing prepares you for a missing child case.

"Nothing new. Nothing helpful from the parents yet. I sent them home, with Connors to keep an eye on them."

He nods. "Nothing new here either. Chase questioned Mrs. Singleton, but I want you to have another go at her. This is your investigation, Rita, and the department is at your disposal, everything we've got." His cell phone rings, and he pulls it out of his jacket pocket and turns away.

I text Chase to meet me in the conference room and leave Mrs. Singleton with a uniformed officer in the meantime.

It's all-hands-on-deck and the chief has already got everyone on task. Detectives Lauren Broderick and Doug Schmitt are writing notes on the white board, tacking maps next to them. They've swung into action quickly and I'm pleased. Lauren is our youngest, newest detective, and without a doubt the smartest person in the building.

Her youthful face is red with emotion as she turns toward me. "Anything new, Rita?"

"No. I just talked to the parents and sent them home. But I didn't really learn too much from them." I turn to Chase. "Anything out of Mrs. Singleton?"

He shakes his head. "She's a basket case. I didn't get anything that our officers hadn't already found out. She says she has no clue what happened to the baby. Her story stayed consistent no matter how many times I asked her."

I nod, shift my gaze back to Lauren. "Do a background check on Mrs. Singleton. That's your focus. Oh, and a Donald Barry, a patient of Doctor Thayer's. See what you can find out about him, too. Doug?" He turns. He's older than Lauren and Chase, yet still more than a generation younger than I am. Doug and I butt heads occasionally, but it looks like he's focused on the task at hand today. He's even loosened his expensive tie and neatly draped his suit jacket over a chair. "You coordinate with the uniformed officers. Gather everything they've learned from the scene and the door-to-door interviews. I'll talk to Mrs. Singleton in a few."

I have Chase follow me with his laptop to my office. "Let's take a look at the tape," I say over my shoulder. I want to see what transpired during his interview before I talk to Mrs. Singleton.

I shut my door and Chase sets his computer on my desk and queues up the tape.

Mrs. Singleton sits at a little gray metal table, hunched over, her arms wrapped over her stomach.

Chase starts with a few innocuous questions, sets the day, time when the incident occurred. Then he has her detail what happened from putting the baby down for her nap until Barbara went to check on her an hour later. He has her run through this several times, and like he said, her story never changes. Chase's voice is steady, calm. But then he ramps up his questions, stands, and leans across the table.

"Where is the baby, Barbara?"

She blubbers and shakes her head.

"You were the only one there. You know what happened to her. Where is she?"

Barbara cries. "I don't know." Her hands fly to her mouth.

"Come on, Barbara. You know where she is. We'll find her eventually, so why don't you just make this easier on everyone and tell us what happened to her?" He draws back, paces the little room, but Chase doesn't let up. He peppers her with questions, insinuates that Barbara has done something awful to the baby. When she collapses forward, her head in her hands, all the while denying she knows anything about what happened to the baby, Chase sits, his voice calm and even again.

"Okay, Barbara. Maybe when you checked on Rosie, you found her unresponsive, maybe she wasn't breathing. Maybe she passed from natural causes. I had a friend whose baby died from SIDS. It was awful. A tragedy. Babies die sometimes, and it's nobody's fault. Is that what happened, Barbara? You found Rosie deceased and you panicked? Could've happened to anyone. No one would blame you. Why don't you tell us so we can put everyone's mind at ease?" I nod along as I watch the tape. Barbara pulls herself together and sits back, tears staining her face.

"No, Detective. That didn't happen. She was just gone."

Chase stops the tape.

"Good work," I say. "You did exactly what I would've done. You went at her hard, got her emotional enough that she might've spilled. When that didn't work, you eased back and gave her an out."

Chase rubs his hand over his mouth. "But I didn't get anything out of her, Rita."

"Maybe there wasn't anything to get."

"You think she's innocent?"

"Possible. You want to come in with me for a minute?"

"Sure."

I head toward the interview room, Chase on my heels. Mrs. Singleton is crying quietly, dark, shoulder-length hair mussed, nose red. Someone brought her a box of cheap, value-brand tissues and she pulls a clump from the box as we enter the room.

Her red-rimmed eyes go straight to Chase. "Has my husband called?"

"The airline said they'll contact him. He's halfway to Reno."
Chase hands her a paper cup of coffee he picked up from the
breakroom on our way. A peace offering of sorts.

She nods and snuffles. Chase introduces me and he and the uniformed officer leave.

While Chase has questioned Mrs. Singleton about her involvement, I want to know what she has to say about anyone else who
might be an interested party.

"Okay, Mrs. Singleton. I've read over the report. I'd like to ask
you about the people in the baby's life." Her eyes meet mine and I
think I see a little relief that we might be interested in someone besides her.

"Anyone else ever pick up or drop off the baby other than the
parents?" I start a sketch of her in my notebook.

She clears her throat. "No. Just Mr. Liddle. I've rarely seen her.
She works long hours."

"What's your impression of them, the parents?" You can't rule
out one of them actually being involved. It was obvious that all
wasn't well between them.

"He seems like a good father, attentive. He's a nice man. But
she's a bit cold. I don't think she spends much time with Rosie
from what I can gather." Mrs. Singleton blows her nose. "I don't
think she's a very good mother, Detective. Maybe I shouldn't say
that."

"So why *are* you saying that?"

She shrugs. "Just an impression."

"You sure there's nothing else about Doctor Thayer?"

Mrs. Singleton shakes her head. "Like I said, I've rarely seen her."

"You ever witness anything strange between them when you did
see her?"

She blows her nose again. "I haven't seen them together since
they talked to me about watching the baby months ago." She draws
a deep breath. "I'm worried sick. Rosie's such a sweet little thing."
Mrs. Singleton dissolves into tears.

I flip through my notebook. "Where are you planning to move?"
I ask.

"What? Oh, my husband and I are going to downsize. Why?"

"Just wondering," I say, and scribble in my notebook. "Have you bought a new house yet?"

She shakes her head. "Not yet."

"Were you planning to watch the baby after the move?"

She blows out a breath. "I don't know. My husband thinks I ought to stop, that it's getting too much for me, but I don't think so. We haven't decided what we're going to do yet."

"Why would it be too much?"

She shrugs. "It's not really. My husband's getting ready to retire. I think he wants it to be just the two of us."

"You've watched other kids before the Liddle baby?"

"Yes. I had been taking care of a little boy. I had him from the time he was an infant until he started school."

"What are his parents' names?" I raise my pencil.

"Um. Robin and Mike Parker."

"They live here in Graybridge?"

"Yes. Over on Maple Street."

"Okay." I turn the page in my notebook. "Did your real estate agent bring any buyers through the house lately?"

"Yes. A few. But I can't recall their names or anything. You'd have to ask her."

"We will. Just wondered if you'd been around, seen anything strange while they were there."

"No. I wasn't home. Do you think one of them could've taken Rosie?"

"Possible." I shut my notebook. "Okay. Well, we've still got cops at your house, so you need to find somewhere else to stay for a while. Somewhere here in town."

"I can go to my sister-in-law's. She lives here in Graybridge. Is that okay?"

"That's fine. Leave us her address and keep your phone handy." I stand and grab my notebook. I need to see what Lauren's found. I stop by the conference room and motion for her to follow me to my office.

Lauren, computer on her lap, sits in the chair opposite my desk. I close my office door. I need a quiet space to think through what we've got so far.

"You hear anything from the guys on scene?" I ask.

"Nothing. Doug said the neighbors didn't see anything either. And so far, no video."

"What about this Donald Barry?"

She glances at her computer. "He's forty-three. Works for an IT company. Divorced. Lives at the Grand Valley Apartments. I took a quick glance at his social media, what was public. There weren't too many pictures. It doesn't seem like he's got much of a social life, but I'll need to dig deeper."

"Let me have his address, phone number." I write it all down in my notebook. I'll take a ride over there and see if I can catch him. "Can you find me a phone number for Mike and Robin Parker?" Lauren can do this in a fraction of the time I can. By the time I've glanced through my notes on the interview with Mrs. Singleton, she's got them and dutifully rattles off three numbers, two cells and a landline. "Thanks. What did you find out about Mrs. Singleton?"

Lauren leans back, brushes brown curls from her forehead. "Nothing so far. She's clean as a whistle. Not even a traffic ticket. I did find out that her maiden name was Torrence."

"One of *the* Torrences?"

"Yes."

"Huh." They're an ultra-rich family who've had a couple of unsavory minor incidents that have gone public. But with their money and their charitable endeavors, they've managed to smooth things over and have retained an overall respectable status.

"Keep digging, Lauren."

Something about Mrs. Singleton has me unsettled. There's something odd about her, like she's sitting on the edge of a cliff, and it wouldn't take much for her to jump off. But is it guilt because she did something to the baby, or guilt that the baby disappeared on her watch?

CHAPTER 16
Nathan

W<small>E'RE HOME, SITTING AT THE KITCHEN TABLE. OFFICER CONNORS</small> has been nice, but reserved, a notebook in her hand. The small radio on her shoulder crackles quietly in the background. I can't sit still, so I jump up, wipe tears from my cheeks and put on a pot of coffee, hoping this simple task helps to steady me. Eve follows me to the counter.

"So, who is this angry patient?" I ask.

She explains about Donald Barry, but how would stealing our baby make Eve want to take him back as a patient? But then maybe he just wanted to punish her. Get even. Then my conscience pricks me when I think of Nicole. She's probably heard about Rosewyn by now. It must be all over the news. Could she be involved? My insides turn to ice. But she seemed perfectly fine when we broke up. And what would she gain from taking Rosewyn? I sneak a look at my phone. Nothing from her. I think about the guys at work. Rack my brain. Anyone there who could possibly be involved? But I can't see that as a possibility. If it wasn't Barbara, it *must've* been some random stranger.

The doorbell rings and Officer Connors jumps up. "I'll get it."

Eve and I exchange glances. There are news vans parked in front of our house. Maybe Officer Connors is talking to the media. But she returns to the kitchen with my mother-in-law on her heels.

Althea Thayer is nearing sixty, her blond hair is short and neatly styled, her clothes and jewelry, expensive and perfect. Heavy perfume precedes her like her own atmosphere.

"Eve!" she shouts, and wraps my wife in a hug. "What is going on? Have they found my granddaughter yet?" Her anger and indignation have my back up. Althea has spent so little time with Rosewyn, she wouldn't be able to pick her out of a baby lineup if her life depended on it. Eve makes no excuses for her. She knows her better than anyone, and I'm sure her mother's presence will only add to Eve's pain.

Althea turns on Officer Connors. "Why haven't they found her yet?"

"Mrs. Thayer, everyone at the Graybridge PD is working Rosewyn's case."

"What about the FBI? Have they been called? I've got money, you know. Has there been a ransom demand?" She turns on Eve.

"No." My wife winces and moves away from her mother.

"Why don't we all sit down?" Officer Connors says. "Let me get everyone some coffee and we'll talk through this." Before heading to the counter where the coffee pot sits, she rips paper off her notepad and hands it around. "Write down anything that comes to mind, no matter how insignificant."

She's smart. She's giving us an assignment, something to ground us. But I stare at the paper and can't think of anything. My mind has gone completely blank. Althea is writing like a mad woman, figuring anything she has to say is of utmost importance, probably. My phone vibrates in my pocket. "I've got to go to the restroom," I say, and leave the kitchen.

I shut and lock the door behind me. I have a text from Nicole.

I saw it on TV! I'm so sorry, Nathan. Do they have any clues? Let me know. I'm here if you need me!

I respond.

Nothing yet. Thanks.

Officer Connors's gaze meets mine as I walk back into the kitchen, but she doesn't say anything. Is my guilt written all over my face? *Jesus*. But all I can think about is Rosewyn. Is she all right? Is she hungry? Scared? Tears start again and I wipe furiously at my eyes. I feel so helpless.

CHAPTER 17

Rita

I NEED TO GET MOVING. I CHECK IN AT THE CONFERENCE ROOM, CON-
fer with Detective Schmitt. Nothing to report. Next stop is the
chief. He's in his office on the phone when I pop my head in at the
door. He covers the receiver when he sees me.

"I'm headed out to see Donald Barry," I say. "The man Doctor
Thayer told us to look at."

"Good, Rita. Keep us in the loop. Take Chase with you."

I almost forgot about my partner. I was so laser focused on the
task at hand, but it would be prudent to have backup. A perp with
a kidnapped baby is dangerous. "Will do."

I make a beeline for my old van, Chase nearly running to catch
up. "I'll drive, Rita," he calls, and heads to an unmarked department vehicle.

"Right. Okay," I say, and change directions. My van isn't as reli-
able as she used to be.

While Chase drives, I call the Parkers. Mrs. Parker picks up. She
has a sunny, friendly voice until I identify myself.

"We heard about the baby on the news!" she cries. "And I recognized Barbara's house. I can't believe it. Barbara is amazing. How
could this have happened? Have they found the baby? Barbara
must be a wreck!"

When she finally lets me get a word in edgewise, I say, "Mrs.

Parker, I just have a few questions for you. I've heard from Mrs. Singleton that she cared for your son for a number of years."

"Yes. And she's wonderful. Just the perfect babysitter. I can't imagine what could've happened to that poor baby."

"In all those years, there was no problem with Barbara?"

"Nothing. No. She was so good with Jayden."

"Have you seen her lately?"

"About a month ago, Jayden and I met her at the library for story hour. He misses her. Then we went for hot chocolate afterwards."

"She seemed fine, happy?"

"Of course. She always is."

"She say anything about the Liddle baby?"

"Just that she was a sweet little thing. I got the impression that Barbara was thrilled to have a girl to take care of. She bought a small pink teddy bear for her and a brown one for Jayden while we were out."

"Anything seem amiss at all with her?"

"No. She's awesome. God, I can't believe this. I hope you find the baby and that she's okay. Barbara must be devastated. Should I call her?"

"That would be fine. Thank you for your time, Mrs. Parker, and please call if you think of anything that might be helpful."

"Will do."

The Grand Valley Apartments are only about a ten-minute drive from the station. It's nearly full dark when we pull into the parking lot. Mr. Barry is on the first floor in the back of the building. I hear the TV blaring—sounds like news—as I knock on the door. It takes him a few minutes, but finally he opens up.

We show him our identification, and the look on his face is confusion. But he leads us into a neat living room where a huge flat screen displays the local news. A reporter is standing in front of the police station talking about the missing baby.

We sit opposite Mr. Barry. He's a tall man and hunches over, his elbows on his knees, thick graying hair nearly shielding his eyes.

"Doctor Thayer gave you *my* name?" He looks up. His eyes meet mine. There's anger there.

"We're looking at everyone who knows Doctor Thayer."

He grunts. "I would never be involved in something like this. You'd have to be sick to take someone's baby. Poor Eve. Is she all right?"

"No. She's not, Mr. Barry." I've got my notebook on my lap. Chase is clicking away on his phone.

"Jesus." He stands, paces the room. "Who would do something like this?"

"That's what we're trying to find out. What do you think of Doctor Thayer, Mr. Barry?"

"What do you mean?"

"Do you like her?"

"Of course. She's . . ." He thinks a minute, looks at the ceiling. "She's a special lady." His lips tighten.

"You're angry with her, though? I heard she's decided not to see you anymore."

He swings around in my direction. "That's just temporary. We'll get back together soon enough."

Okay. This guy is super creepy, and I'd like to poke at him some more, but we need to move quickly. "Where were you this afternoon?"

"Here. I work from home a couple days a week." He opens and closes his fists.

"Anybody see you here?"

"No." It dawns on him what we're really asking. "I was on a couple of conference calls."

"When? What time?"

He scratches his head. His gaze shifts to a big clock on the wall.

"Were they just calls, or video?" I ask.

"Both. I mean a couple were calls and one was a Zoom."

"Okay. What time?"

"The Zoom was this morning. But the calls were off and on all day."

"All right. You mind if I look around?"

"Be my guest," he says sarcastically.

"Give Detective Fuller the details on those calls. Times, who you talked to."

"Fine."

Chase raises his head from his phone. "Shoot, Mr. Barry."

He smirks as he cuts his gaze to Chase.

While Chase takes down his information, I move through the small apartment. It is neat, Spartan, tidy to the extreme. No signs of an infant anywhere, not that he couldn't have hidden her someplace else or dumped her body. Still. There's nothing here.

Chase and I head out to the psychiatric hospital where Doctor Thayer works. There's a flurry of excited voices in the lobby, a receptionist, nurses in blue scrubs, someone in a white coat. They've all heard about Doctor Thayer's missing baby. But no one has a clue. I isolate one of the nurses and ask about Frances Martin, but she can't tell me much. The facility administrator, Mr. Jacobson, a tall man in an expensive suit, strides over to where I'm standing. I tell him we know that Ms. Martin attacked Doctor Thayer a few days ago. That goes nowhere, as I suspected, but I needed to cross her off our list. There's no way, he tells us, that Frances could've gotten out of the facility. He shows us the locked doors and cameras.

We also check on Doctor Thayer, go over her schedule with the receptionist. She's been at the facility all day, except for an hour at lunch. It would be pretty tough to take the baby away someplace in that amount of time, but I'll check on her lunchtime activity. It's not out of the question that one of the parents had decided to take the baby. One of them could've enlisted a friend or family member to take Rosewyn someplace until they could join her. Not terribly likely, but everything is on the table at this point.

We swing by Mr. Liddle's place of employment, Graybridge Collision. It's a nest of activity. Pneumatic wrenches whir and car engines thrum as we pass the work bays. Inside, the lobby is neat and has that clean, yet motor oil smell that all car places seem to have. I talk to the assistant manager, who tells me that Mr. Liddle was at work all day except for lunch, when he was with him and a couple of the other guys. So, Mr. Liddle is in the clear unless he had someone grab the baby for him, but, again, that doesn't seem likely.

It's getting late by the time we return to the station. No one has gone home and, with the addition of the night staff, the place is bursting with noise and light and empty pizza boxes. It's organized chaos and the chief is in the middle of it all. He looks like he's aged a decade since we left a few hours earlier.

We meet in the conference room, the chief and us four detectives. We go over everything we've got. Nothing is of any help and I'm feeling the heat. We decide on a game plan. Lauren and Chase volunteer to stay through the night. The chief sends Doug home. He wants at least one of us to get a good night's sleep, if that's possible. I volunteer to go stay with Doctor Thayer and Mr. Liddle. I'll send Officer Connors home to get some rest, too.

CHAPTER 18

Nathan

*I*T'S DARK OUT. I STAND ALONE BY THE KITCHEN WINDOW THAT LOOKS out on the backyard. The house hums with light and voices, tension so thick I think we'll all crack at the slightest movement. Rosewyn should be having her bath. I should be getting ready to give her the last bottle of the night. My eyes feel like sandpaper. My tears have dried up; my throat is full of phlegm, and I feel like I might choke.

I look across the room at the kitchen table. Rachel is here now, having muscled her way through the reporters and cops out front. She's sitting next to Eve, her arm draped around my wife's shoulders. She gives me a critical look now and then. We aren't close. We're too different, and I've always gotten the impression that she thinks I'm not good enough for Eve, that somehow I trapped her into this marriage and got her pregnant on purpose and against her will. Still, she's Eve's friend and if it helps Eve to have her here, then I can deal with Rachel.

Althea's still here too. Demanding to talk to someone "higher up," throwing around her contacts with bigwigs at the state level. I try to block out their chatter. Everyone has something to say except me and Eve, seems like. My wife sits at the table, hunched over an untouched cup of coffee. I want to put my arms around her and cry with her, but Rachel is planted on one side and Althea on the other.

Oscar winds around my legs. Eve probably forgot to feed him. I wasn't a cat guy when I met Eve, but we've grown on each other. I fill his bowl, give him a pet, and my gaze shifts to the cupboard over the stove. I take down a bottle of whiskey from the top shelf and pour myself a glass. We rarely drink it, but it's all I can think to do. But then my mind wanders to my closet upstairs. To my old jacket hanging there in the back, the one with a half-full pack of cigarettes in the pocket. I'd quit a month before I met Eve. I'd taken up the habit in college and kept telling myself I'd give it up eventually. And I finally did. But I kept that last pack as if it was a test. I was stronger than the cigarettes. But I think of them now. Crave just one. My fingers twitch and I take a big sip of Jack Daniels, let the burn slide down my throat.

"What are you doing?" Rachel stands at the end of the counter, hand on her hip.

"Nothing, why?"

"You might want to join us. Eve could use everyone right now."

"Yeah, I know. I'm coming." I drain my glass and place it in the sink, and like a dutiful puppy, I rejoin the crowd at the table. Officer Connors gives me a sidelong glance, then goes back to her notebook. Althea scowls in my direction, but Eve seems oblivious, in another place.

I can only sit still so long before I need to get up, get moving. I feel like I'll turn into a statue sitting there.

"I'm going to the restroom," I say as if I need permission, and head upstairs. I stop at Rosewyn's door, push it open. It smells of my baby girl, powder and something soft and sweet. I walk to her crib and run my hand over her pink blanket while tears sting my eyes. I pick up Elephant and tuck him under my arm. *Where are you, Rosewyn?*

I start to leave the room but decide to put the stuffed animal back where he belongs on the dresser next to her crib, waiting for her return. I walk into the master bedroom, to my closet. It's cold inside as I stretch my arm past my dress shirts and work pants, back to my old jacket. My fingers reach into the pocket. Nothing, and my heart sinks. Then I try the other pocket and there they are, like an old friend, waiting for when I need them. I slip the pack into my hoodie pocket. Good thing I pulled that on when we got home. The house was cold at first, but now with so many people here, it's heated up. But I kept the old sweatshirt on. I was wearing it yesterday. Yesterday when my baby was here in my arms.

Downstairs, there's new chatter. Something has shifted and my heart momentarily leaps in my chest. Good news? Then I realize it's just a changing of the guards. Detective Myers is here now. She and Officer Connors are conferring in the living room.

I sneak out the sliding door to the deck. The cold biting wind nearly takes my breath away. I reach into my pocket, fumble with the pack, and pull out a cigarette. Tucked under the cellophane is a book of matches. I stick the cigarette in the corner of my mouth, strike the match, and sigh as I suck the comforting smoke into my lungs. Tears from the cold gather at the corners of my eyes and the tobacco does its work. It fills a suppressed longing like nothing else, and I feel the tenseness in my shoulders start to give way.

"What the fuck are you doing?" Rachel stands in the open doorway.

I cough. Crush the cigarette on the deck railing like a guilty teenager. "What?"

"Are you *smoking*, Nathan?"

"What does it matter, Rachel? For God's sake."

She shakes her head and walks back into the house.

CHAPTER 19

Rita

W HEN I GOT TO THE LIDDLES' PLACE, THERE WERE STILL A COUPLE of reporters stalking the front yard, but I called a quick "no comment" as I walked by. Inside, I conferred with Officer Connors, then cut her loose.

The Liddle house is full of chatter, people huddled around the kitchen table. A dark-haired woman introduces herself as Doctor Thayer's friend and an older woman as her mother. The baby's parents, who seem to be the only quiet people here, hang their heads, faces red with emotion.

"Mr. Liddle, Doctor Thayer, can I have a word?" They both rise and their faces blanch. "We don't have any real developments," I add quickly, and they start breathing again.

I have them sit on the couch and I perch on the edge of a chair facing them. They look terrible, as is to be expected. I run through my visit with Donald Barry, my trip to the psychiatric hospital, and Graybridge Collision. They nod along.

"What about Barbara?" Doctor Thayer asks in a croaking voice.

"We've questioned her closely. But she hasn't given us any reason to believe that she's involved." But we'll see.

"I just thought of something," Mr. Liddle says, his mouth hanging open. "There's a picture of a baby girl, one of those newborn pictures, on a table at Barbara's. I saw it the other day." He glances at his wife, eyes wide. "I asked her who it was. She looked really uncomfortable and said it was her daughter."

"Okay."

His eyes lock on mine. "She told us when we interviewed her that she only had a son. And there were no other pictures of a girl grown up or anything. So, what happened to the daughter?" His voice starts to rise.

Doctor Thayer jumps to her feet and covers her eyes with her hands. "What if something bad happened to *her* baby girl?" She swings in my direction. "What if she killed her?" Doctor Thayer's voice is filled with hysteria. Anguish over her own child fueling her words. "What if she killed Rosewyn?" She collapses back on the couch.

Mr. Liddle says, "Or maybe she took Rosewyn to replace her daughter, and she's hidden her someplace."

"She could've done that, right?" Doctor Thayer pulls her own hair, clutching thick handfuls of blond tresses.

"What if she's got Rosewyn someplace and we can't find her? What are we going to do?" Mr. Liddle cries.

Things are quickly spiraling out of control, one parent spurring on the other in their desperation. "Okay, guys. Let's take a breath. There's probably a perfectly good explanation for the picture. We are questioning Barbara carefully, and like I said, we have no reason to think that she did anything to Rosewyn. Let's take this one step at a time." And I hope that I'm right.

They are crying quietly in each other's arms now but nodding like they get what I'm saying, winding down from their outburst.

"Why don't you both get something to drink while I check in with the station?" I don't know if they actually heard me, but I want to talk to Chase and see if there's anything new. "Excuse me a minute." I wander out to the kitchen, past the table, out to the deck, where cold air nearly slaps me breathless.

Chase answers right away and tells me that nothing has changed since I left.

"Okay. I want you and Lauren to look into the Singletons' family, specifically their kids." I tell him what Mr. Liddle told me about the picture of the baby girl.

"That's strange."

"I thought so, too. Might be nothing, but you never know." I end the call, look up across the yard and catch my breath. If I'm not mistaken, that's Wilma Parnell's house backing up to the Liddle residence. This is the tall house I saw from her place. When I drove out here it hadn't clicked that this was the same neighborhood. Coincidence? Maybe. Maybe not. My heartbeat ratchets up.

I switch my phone to flashlight and make my way down the steep deck staircase to the concrete patio below. It's dark as midnight back here and a little creepy. There doesn't appear to be anything in the Liddles' yard that I can see. But there's the wooden fence with the missing boards dead ahead. It's definitely Wilma's house on the other side. It sits in darkness. Too late for Wilma to be working there, but what if her break-ins have something to do with the missing baby?

I walk slowly through the wintry grass and patchy snow. I wish I had my real flashlight, the one I keep in my van. The phone light isn't great, but I don't want to take the time to go back. I push on the loose boards that make up the old fence. Then walk along until I find a place where they've fallen down enough that I can step through.

I stumble a couple of times in Wilma's lumpy backyard as I make my way around to the front of her house. Here there's a streetlight down the block that casts an eerie glow, but the extra light helps as I walk to the front door. I pull latex gloves out of my jacket pocket and try the doorknob. Not locked. It opens easily. Huh.

I give Wilma a call before entering the house.

"Yeah?"

"Ms. Parnell? Detective Myers here. I'm standing in front of your house over on Blaine Street."

"What happened?"

"Nothing that I can see, but the door was unlocked. Did you leave it that way?"

"Christ. No."

"When were you here last?"

"Day before yesterday. I've been working on another property. But I locked up the Blaine Street house when I left."

"You sure?"

"Positive. What are you doing there?"

"Wondering if your break-ins have something to do with another case, that's all."

"Has anything else gone missing?"

"Don't know yet. Is it okay for me to enter the premises, Ms. Parnell?"

"Yeah. Go ahead. Jesus."

"Great. I'll be in touch. In the meantime, stay out of the house for a couple days. Can you do that? Just till we look into a couple things."

"I've got other projects going, so no big deal. Maybe you can finally figure out who's been messing around over there."

"We'll try." I end the call.

Inside the place is dark and quiet. I need to keep my eyes on the floor, so I don't fall over the junk that I know is scattered around the first floor. I make my way to the kitchen, to the window over the sink. I look up. From here I can see the Liddle home, lights glowing. I can even see faint silhouettes of the people inside. I blow out a breath. Is there a connection?

We've already dusted for prints here, so that's been done. But no hits on the prints. I'll check all the rooms just in case. Upstairs I feel a cold draft coming from one of the bedrooms. As I approach, I hear noise. Quietly I stash my phone in my back pocket and draw my sidearm as I move slowly toward the room. As I near the door, the noise grows louder. Peering around the doorframe, I see light from the Liddle home. An open window looks directly across the yard and into the first floor of their place. The noise is coming from the window, and I recognize it as a set of blinds pulled halfway up, rattling in the breeze. I lower my weapon and let out the breath that I was holding. I crouch down in front of the window. The Liddle house is lit up like a Christmas tree. I can clearly see the people inside. This is a great vantage point, even better than the kitchen window if you wanted to spy on the Liddles. Now, why would anyone want to do that?

CHAPTER 20
Eve

*T*HE BACK DOOR SLIDES OPEN AND COLD AIR WHOOSHES THROUGH the kitchen. Detective Myers is coming in from the deck. I didn't even notice that she'd gone. One minute we're in the living room talking, the next I'm back at the table. Time seems to be skipping around, and I'm doing everything in my power to keep my mind blank, to not think of Rosewyn or I might start screaming, go raving mad right here on my kitchen floor.

The detective is standing near me, her hand on my shoulder.

"What do you guys know about the house behind you?" she asks.

Nathan sits up straight. "What about it?"

"You know the woman who owns it?"

"We've talked to her a few times over the fence. She's renovating it," Nathan says.

I let him answer her. I can't think to put two words together.

"She's had a couple of break-ins lately," Detective Myers says. I hear murmurs from my mother, sharp demands or something.

"She told us, but you think that could have something to do with our baby?" Nathan croaks.

"There's no reason, at this point, to think so. But I wondered if you had seen anything unusual over there."

Nathan shakes his head. Then clears his throat. "No, wait. I did see something."

"When?"

"New Year's Eve." He jumps to his feet and points. "I saw a light back there in the house, like a flashlight. I've never seen that before. It's usually dark over there at night. Ms. Parnell doesn't work that late. I don't think so anyway."

"That the only time you've seen a light over there?"

"Yeah. But what has that got to do with us? Ms. Parnell thinks it's just some kids."

"Probably. But there's an open window upstairs. It looks directly into your house. I could see perfectly into your kitchen."

I shudder. "You really think there's a connection to us?" My voice cracks. "Someone stole some tools. What would that have to do with taking Rosewyn?"

"Maybe nothing. Maybe a coincidence."

"But maybe not?" I say, my heart pounding against my ribs. "You think someone's been over there *spying* on us?"

"It's possible," Detective Myers says.

"Then why take stuff?" Nathan asks. "That doesn't seem to make sense."

Detective Myers draws a deep breath. "We just don't want to miss anything. Probably no connection."

"But you need to be sure," I say. "Could someone have been back there watching us and they took Ms. Parnell's things to disguise their real intent?"

She doesn't answer, but I see it in her eyes, the slight nod, and I can't seem to catch my breath.

"We just need to be thorough," she says. "I looked around and didn't see anything amiss, other than the open window."

"Why haven't you found anything yet, Detective!" my mother screams. Her voice cuts through my head and I cover my ears.

"We're doing everything we can," she responds. "Why don't you guys order some food?"

"I can't eat," I say. I drop my head down to the table, onto my folded arms. I hear my mother stand, push out her chair.

"I'll do it. We need to keep our strength up."

"That's right," Detective Myers says. "You need to try."

While my mother yammers on the phone, I stand and walk into the living room, collapse on the sofa, and bury my head in a couch pillow. Dark settled in a while ago and my baby's not here where she belongs. My mind wanders to her birth, before that even, when I cried because I hadn't planned on being a parent. Serves me right that someone took her. What kind of a mother am I? I groan into the pillow, trying to blot out my chaotic thoughts. But all I can see is Rosewyn, her chubby pink cheeks, the way she giggles when I tickle her with Elephant. And how she sleeps on my chest when I hold her, perfectly happy and content. The sweet smell of her. My baby. My child, and now she's gone. She trusted me and I failed her.

Nathan is kneeling next to me, his hand on my back. I feel his head next to mine and we cry together.

The house is deadly quiet and dark. Did I doze off? How could I? I roll over onto my side. Nathan is still sitting on the floor next to me. I hear gentle snores from across the room. Rachel is curled up in the armchair. There's a faint light coming from the kitchen. I push to sitting and stagger toward it. Nathan scuffles behind me.

Detective Myers is sitting at the table, writing in her notebook, a cup of coffee at her side. My mother sits at the head of the table sipping her own coffee. Takeout bags from the dinner I missed sit on the counter.

"What's going on?" I mumble. The detective looks up.

"Nothing new, Doctor Thayer."

I nod. "Call me Eve, please." I wander to the kitchen window, gaze out across the backyard. Could someone really have been watching us from the neighbor's house? I wrap my arms over my chest to try to stop my trembling.

"You want some coffee?" my mother asks.

I shake my head, but Nathan walks over to the pot and pours two mugs anyway. He's at my side.

"Please, Eve. Drink this. You're shaking."

I take the warm mug. But I can't seem to force the hot liquid past my lips. The time on the microwave says 2:30 a.m. "So, what's next?" I ask.

Detective Myers looks up. "We've been working around the clock at the station and out in the field, Eve. We won't stop until we find her."

Nathan places his mug on the counter. "I'll be right back," he says and squeezes my shoulder.

I try to sip my coffee, but it's bitter on my tongue. There's nothing I can do to find my baby. I'm helpless. Useless. My daughter has been taken away and I am completely useless. I've utterly failed as a parent. The sound of Detective Myers's pencil scratching against her notebook sounds as loud as a jet engine and I want to scream. I notice that she's drawing. A diagram of some sort.

I decide to look for Nathan. I wander to the back door and see him through the glass, standing on the deck, his back to the house. He doesn't notice as I sidle up beside him. He's enveloped in a cloud of smoke. The scent of burning tobacco fills my nose.

"Sorry, Eve," he says, and crushes out his cigarette.

"I didn't know," is all I manage to say.

"I just started again. Today. I didn't want to." He sniffs and wipes at his cheeks, puts his arm around my waist. The wind that had lashed the house earlier is gone and it's just cold and dark, except for an abundance of stars overhead. I hadn't noticed them before.

CHAPTER 21
Rita

I'M RUNNING ON ADRENALINE AND CAFFEINE AND PROBABLY SHOULDN'T be driving, but after another officer relieved me at the Liddles' house this morning, I headed back to the station. I called Ms. Parnell on the way in and asked about the window upstairs. She was emphatic that she didn't open it. But someone did.

We gather in the conference room, Chief Bob Murphy, Lauren, Doug, Chase, and me. Everyone looks exhausted but wired. There's coffee and a big box of Dunkin' Donuts in the center of the table. Maps and notes adorn the whiteboard.

I stand and look over my notes. The chief wants me to run through everything, so we can come up with a game plan for today. He is going to address the media at noon. I hope like hell we have a break by then.

I turn to Doug. "Anything from the neighbors?"

He shakes his head. "Nada. The couple people who were home didn't see a thing. And we checked the only video we found, a house down the block to the east of the Singletons', and there was nothing there."

"Great." I sigh. "Okay. Nothing new overnight then. Doctor Thayer's mother insists it's a kidnapping. She's pretty wealthy, apparently, but so far there have been no ransom calls." But that was pretty far down on our list. Kidnappings for ransom are extremely rare. "Anyway, this is where we are. Yesterday at approximately three p.m., Rosewyn Liddle disappeared from the Singleton home."

"That's according to Barbara Singleton, though," Chase adds.

"Correct. No one except her, as far as we know, saw the baby after Mr. Liddle dropped her off at seven-forty-five that morning. So, if Mrs. Singleton was involved, she could've taken the baby anywhere at any time up until she called 911 in the afternoon."

I fill them in on what the Liddles said about the baby picture on Barbara's table. "Chase, did you guys find anything on this mystery daughter?"

"Nothing yet. Just the son in college."

"No death certificate?"

"Not that we could find."

The chief sips his coffee. "You think there's something to that? You think the Singletons had a kid that died or disappeared somehow?"

"Possible. I'll ask Mrs. Singleton."

"Oh," Lauren says, "Mr. Singleton is back. He's at his sister's house with Barbara."

"Good to know. I'll take a ride over there." I glance down at my notebook. I go over our visits to Donald Barry, the psychiatric hospital, and the collision shop.

The chief grunts. "Nothing promising then, Rita?"

"'Fraid not. But here's the thing I keep coming back to. If it wasn't Mrs. Singleton, who then managed to slip into her house, unseen, at precisely the time she was in the backyard, sneak upstairs and take the baby, and get away before anyone saw anything? Granted the house is on the corner of a quiet street. But why don't we have *any* witnesses? Lauren, what did you find out from the real estate agent?"

She clicks computer keys. "She sent me a list of the people she showed the house to—three couples and a single man."

"Did you check them out?"

"Working on it." Lauren looks up from her computer screen. "But I did see that there's a virtual tour of the house online."

"So, what does that tell us?" I ask, although I'm already getting the picture.

"Anyone could've looked up the Singletons' address and looked through the house. I watched it and you can easily trace your way through the front door, into the foyer, and up the stairs. The baby's room is the first one at the top. The crib is right there on the video."

"Great. So, anyone who was interested in the Liddle baby would know right where to find her."

"Yup."

The chief lets go a tired breath.

"Technology." I sigh.

Lauren shoves a hank of curly hair over her shoulder. "If it wasn't Mrs. Singleton, then someone planned this. Very carefully. Someone who had scouted out the neighborhood. Someone who was watching and had probably already seen the layout of the house one way or another."

Doug leans back in his chair. "Still. That's a lot to swallow. The most obvious explanation, seems to me, is that Mrs. Singleton killed the baby and drove her someplace and dumped the body. Then she comes home, sets the stage, and calls 911."

We all groan. But he's right. "That is the simplest explanation," I concede, and throw my pencil on the table. I flip through my notebook, land on the page where I'd sketched the Liddle backyard and Wilma's house. "But something bothers me." I tap the page with my finger. "That break-in at the Parnell place. That house is directly behind the Liddles' house."

"Coincidence," Doug says. "Local kids causing trouble. Somebody lifting a few tools. Seems like a stretch."

"Maybe. But I don't know. I searched the place last night and there's a window upstairs, which was open, looks directly into the Liddle first floor. It was like watching a movie. The homeowner says that she never opened that window. Why would a thief do that? And Mr. Liddle recalls seeing someone over there with a flashlight New Year's Eve, and it wasn't the homeowner."

The chief raises his bushy, gray eyebrows. "What are you thinking, Rita?"

I put a hand on my hip. "Either Doug's right, Mrs. Singleton is a psychopath and did away with the baby, or someone is obsessed with the Liddles and has been meticulously planning to hurt them in the worst way possible."

CHAPTER 22
Eve

*I*T'S MORNING AND NATHAN AND I HAVE BEEN UP ALL NIGHT. RACHEL IS in the kitchen talking to the young officer who replaced Detective Myers earlier.

My mother has run home to take a shower and "freshen up." She has her priorities but insisted she'd be back soon. I hope she takes her time actually. I feel calmer without her here. But a numbness has settled into my bones. It's a new day. The sun is shining, and I don't know if my little girl is alive or dead. Nathan and I sit on the sofa together. Even though we haven't had much to say to one another, I feel closer to him than I have in a long time. He's the only person on earth right now who understands how I feel, how we both feel. For whatever problems Nathan and I have, we both love Rosewyn more than our own lives.

Rachel walks into the dark living room and sets two mugs on the coffee table.

"Coffee's fresh and I made toast," she says.

I want to laugh at the thought of food, a hysterical laugh that bubbles up in my chest.

"I'll get it, and I saw you had grape jam in the fridge. I'll get that too." Then she walks away.

Eventually, we stand and wander around the house. Nathan peels off to the bathroom and I stop at the kitchen window, my gaze on the back of Ms. Parnell's place.

I glance down at the sink. There's an empty glass there and the bottle of Jack Daniels we keep in the cupboard is sitting out, half empty. I see Nathan now, out on the deck, smoking. Before I would've been furious, but now nothing matters except our baby.

Oscar winds around my legs. I pick him up and cuddle him, wiping my cheek over his silky fur.

"Eve?" Rachel calls from the kitchen doorway. I turn to face her. "I hate to do this, but my boss called. I've got to go in for a couple of hours." She walks over to my side.

"Okay." I drop the cat gently to the floor and he trots out of the room.

"I wouldn't leave you now, but he's going to fire me if I don't go in. He's such an asshole. And I'd say 'go ahead, fucker,' but my rent's due soon and that freaking hospital bill for when I hurt my back and had to go to the ER right after Thanksgiving . . ."

I put a hand on her shoulder. "It's fine, Rach. There's nothing you can do here."

"I'll only be gone a couple of hours. I think that will satisfy him. He's got some family emergency and God forbid he closes the shop." She sniffs, wipes her nose with her hand. "I'll have my phone in my hand, and I can be here in less than ten minutes if you need me."

"It's fine," I say again. "Really. There's nothing you can do here." And I mean it. There isn't anything my friend can do to bring my baby home. "I'll see you after," I say and walk her to the front door.

Nathan comes in from the deck. "Where did Rachel go?"

"She had to run into work for a little while." He smells of cigarette smoke. It's seeped into his clothes.

Nathan looks at the young officer, who is quietly scrolling through his phone. "Any updates? Anything at all?"

"Sorry, Mr. Liddle. I haven't heard anything from the station. They'll let me know though."

Nathan nods and wraps an arm around my waist. "Have you eaten anything?" he asks.

"No." I had dumped the toast that Rachel had prepared into the garbage.

"Let's have a dish of ice cream," Nathan says.

Everything is upside down. "I couldn't," I say and drop down into a kitchen chair. My head is throbbing. My stomach feels like it's full of glass. But I haven't cried since early this morning. I don't think there's enough fluid in my body to make any more tears.

Nathan sets a dish of strawberry ice cream in front of me along with a tall glass of water. "Please, Eve. You're going to collapse." He knows that strawberry is my favorite and for him I try.

The officer stands and walks into the living room, leaving us alone. Nathan pulls up a chair right next to me and sits.

"We're going to get her back," he says, "and things will be different because I love you, Eve."

I spoon the ice cream into my mouth, swallow over the lump in my throat and rest my head on his shoulder.

CHAPTER 23

Rita

I'M PACKING UP MY STUFF IN THE CONFERENCE ROOM. WE'VE ALL, ALmost, dispersed to the tasks at hand. Chase and Lauren are digging into Donald Barry's work calls and the real estate people. And the chief has put off the press conference until later this afternoon.

I've coordinated with the crime scene team to meet me at the Parnell house. I want to see it in the daylight and have them go over it with a fine-tooth comb.

"You really think you'll find anything there, Rita? The baby disappeared from the Singleton house," Doug says, following me down the hall. He looks fresh and rested this morning.

"It can't hurt, Doug. It bugs me." And he bugs me, but I swallow a snarky reply with my cold coffee. He heads to his office while I walk to the back exit. The tech team should be on the way already and I need to get out there.

The house looks forlorn and dilapidated by day. I see the crime scene van parked out front. Hugo Martinez and his people have gotten started. I shift my van into park and stride up the cracked sidewalk. I'm greeted at the door by a young officer who hands me a pair of booties as I pull latex gloves from my pocket.

Inside, I walk into the kitchen where a tech is busy at work. He greets me with a timid smile. I don't know why I'm so scary. Guess my age and experience. Also, I made it clear that I needed a thorough job, and that the scene was possibly connected to our perp in the missing baby case.

Nothing of note in the kitchen that I can see. Nothing looks different from the last time I was here. I head to the second floor. The cold from the open window in the bedroom greets me as I get to the top of the stairs. Hugo is up here.

"Hey, Rita."

"Find anything interesting?"

"Not yet. I was just checking out the bathroom." He points over his shoulder. "Didn't see anything in there. But we dusted it."

"Good." I follow the cold air into the back bedroom, Hugo on my heels. The room is completely empty and the sound of the blinds shuddering in the breeze fills the room. But they look untouched since I was here, still pulled halfway up. If someone was spying on the Liddles from here, it would make sense that he or she would have crouched down, dropped to their knees probably. I settle on my haunches, not wanting to touch the floor with more than my feet. Again, from here you've got a clear shot into the Liddles' kitchen.

Then I see something.

"Hugo?"

He's at my side. I point at the wooden windowsill. There's a piece of thread, red, caught under a splinter.

With the thread bagged up, I head outside. It's midafternoon and I hear school buses, their pneumatic brakes squealing in the distance. My gaze shifts up the street, looking for the teens that Wilma told me hung out in the neighborhood. So far, I haven't been able to find them, although I hadn't looked very hard with only tools missing, but now, I need to find these guys.

I watch as a bus turns down the street at the far end. It stops, and a girl with a backpack that looks like it weighs more than she does, steps off and heads in the other direction, but after her, three boys start walking my way. One tall, the other two shorter. They slow as they near the house, taking in the van. I meet them in the street.

"Hey, I need to talk to you guys a minute," I call.

They stop, look at one another. The tall one steps forward. "What's going on?" He tips his chin at the house.

I show them my identification. "I'm Detective Myers. We're looking into some missing items. You guys know anything about that? Seen anyone around here you didn't recognize?"

The tall one shakes his head, "We don't know anything about that place." He exchanges glances with the other two.

"Nobody's in trouble," I say. "But it would really help . . ."

The tall one smirks, pulls his beanie over his ears. "We don't know anything."

One of the shorter ones wearing a puffy blue jacket, pipes up. "We don't go near that place. We don't mess with Ms. Parnell."

The other short one chuckles until the tall one glares at him.

"Why's that? You know her?"

The tall one shrugs. "A little. She's kind of a bitch. Sorry. But she is. When she first bought the house, she told us to keep our scrawny asses off her property. That's what she said, so we did."

"Okay, you guys ever see anyone else around here besides Ms. Parnell?"

"No. We have to get going," the tall one says. They start to walk away, then Blue Puffy Jacket stops and turns around.

"We did see *someone.*"

My heartbeat ratchets up. "Wait a minute, guys." I pull my notebook out of my satchel. "Wait just one minute." The tall one glares at his friend, shuffles his weight from one foot to the other.

"We don't want to be involved," he says.

"Well, you are, and you'll cooperate either here or down at the station." They lower their heads and I take their names and contact information.

Blue Jacket's name is Ben. "So, who did you see? When?"

He nibbles his chapped lips. "A person."

"A man or a woman?"

He shrugs. "I couldn't really tell. It was dark."

"When did you see this person?"

"Um. New Year's Eve. We were out here in the street." The tall kid, Jeff, elbows him.

"There were, uh, some people doing fireworks on the next street, so we went over to check it out." His gaze shifts to Jeff. The other kid, the quiet one, laughs nervously.

"I don't care about a bunch of firecrackers, guys. What did you see at the Parnell house?"

Ben wipes a bare hand across his red nose. "Somebody went in there. But I don't know who it was."

"Could it have been Ms. Parnell?"

"No. She never works in there after dark. And her truck wasn't in the driveway. It was somebody else."

"What color hair did the person have? Was it long or short?"

"Couldn't tell. It was too dark. They might've been wearing a hood or a hat, I think."

"Was there anything else you remember about the person? You sure you couldn't tell if it was a man or a woman?"

"Nope. Just a person. That's it."

"Was there a car on the street? How did they get here?"

Ben looks at the other two and they all shrug. "I don't remember seeing one."

"Do you think this person lives in the neighborhood maybe?"

"No idea."

"How about you two? You have anything to add to what Ben said?" I ask.

"Nope. That was it," Jeff says. "That's what we saw."

"What time New Year's?"

Ben furrows his forehead. "Probably around nine or ten, I think."

"You guys ever see anyone besides this person and Ms. Parnell go into the house?"

"Nope."

"Did you see the person leave?"

"No. We walked over to the other street, like we said," Jeff says.

"Okay." I'm scribbling in my notebook. "If you guys remember anything else, you be sure and call me." I hand them each a card, which they look at and then stuff into their pockets.

"Can we go now?" Jeff whines.

"Yeah. Fine. Thanks for your help."

I'm sitting in my van going over my notes when my phone rings and nearly scares ten years off me. It's the chief.

"Rita?" There's all kinds of noise in the background. "We've just had a citizen call 911. He found a baby at Green Hills Park."

My heart is pounding out of my chest as I start my van and slip it into gear. "Alive?"

"We don't know. EMS is on the way. The man who found the baby is still on the phone with the operator, but he's nearly incoherent. Get over there. I've got officers on the way, but you're closest to the scene and . . ." Someone interrupts him.

"I'm on my way," I say, and chuck my phone onto the passenger's seat.

CHAPTER 24
Rita

*G*REEN HILLS PARK IS AT THE EDGE OF GRAYBRIDGE PD'S JURISDIC-
tion. It's a little out of the way and a fairly neglected place consist-
ing of walking and running trails and some basic restroom
facilities. That's it. It's not the kind of park where you take the kids
or that has much foot traffic.

My heart is beating in heavy thumps as I cruise through town
and out the country road that will take me to the scene. I whisper a
quiet prayer that the baby is alive.

Finally, I pull into the gravel parking lot. There's one civilian car
sitting in the corner with a man in running gear leaning against it,
his hands covering his face. I pull up next to the ambulance in the
opposite corner. It's running, lights strobing. I hear police sirens in
the distance.

I jog over near the restroom building where EMTs are bent over
a cardboard box. They don't hear me coming and are laser focused
on what's inside. I peer over their shoulders and see the baby, a
heavy quilt beneath her. She's moving and I start breathing again.
One of the EMTs notices me. He knows me.

"She okay?" I ask.

"Vitals are all normal. She looks to be fine." The young man
smiles.

"Thank you, Jesus," I whisper.

"Is she the Liddle baby?" the female EMT asks.

"She fits the description right down to the pink ruffled top." I notice that she's missing a sock. The one she's wearing is pink with lace trim. "Is the other sock in the box?" I ask.

"We didn't see it," the female EMT says.

I write this bit of information down in my notebook. The baby starts to cry. "You sure she's okay?"

"I think so. She might just be hungry. She's warm, temp is normal, so I don't think she was out here too long."

"That the guy who found her?" I angle my chin toward the man leaning against the car.

"Yeah. That's him. We told him to wait for law enforcement. He's pretty shaken up."

"Did he touch anything?"

"Says he didn't, but we didn't talk to him too long."

"Okay. I'll go speak with him."

I call the chief, and he's relieved as hell, of course. He'll contact the parents. We need them to meet us at the hospital and positively identify their daughter. I feel the weight of the world slide off my shoulders.

"Sir," I call as I approach the man. He scrubs his hands over his face and shakes his head like a wet dog. I introduce myself and he says his name is Gary Moffit.

"Okay, Gary. I take it you found the baby?" I juggle my notebook out of my satchel.

"Yeah." He blows out a breath. "I pulled into the lot to run and I, uh, got out of the car to stretch. I did that right here for a few minutes before I walked over to the trail." He points at where the box sits.

Police cruisers and the crime scene van pull into the lot. That momentarily diverts Gary's attention.

"Was anyone else here when you got here?"

"No. But . . ." His mouth falls open. "There was a car. A dark car of some sort, sitting in the entrance like it was looking to pull out."

"When was that?"

"Right when I got here."

"Make, model of the vehicle?"

"I have no clue. I didn't pay any attention. I didn't find the box until like ten minutes later. The car was long gone."

"Can you tell me *anything* about the car or the driver?"

He shakes his head. "No. Just a dark sedan, I think."

"Okay, so, you got out of your vehicle, stretched, then walked over to the trail?"

"Yes." He taps the side of his head. "The car might have been silver, actually. I can't remember."

Great. Eyewitnesses are notoriously unreliable. "Okay. So, you really don't know what color the car was?"

"No. But it was definitely a car or a small SUV. Not a truck. I don't think."

"Okay, then. What happened after you walked over to the trail?"

"I saw a box. And I thought someone had left trash and I thought 'what an asshole.'" He starts to tear up. "I thought someone had left junk. Then I looked inside, and I saw the baby. And I just about lost it." Gary's lips tremble. "I have a little boy, and I can't imagine anyone being so heartless. To leave a baby like trash. What if I hadn't found her? She would've died of cold eventually."

But that's probably what the person in the car was waiting to see, making sure that someone would find the baby in a timely manner.

"Okay, Gary. So, you saw the baby. Did you touch her?"

"No. I just called 911."

"Did you touch the box?"

"No. I didn't touch anything."

"That's good. All right. Here's my card in case you think of anything else." I take down all his contact information. He seems truthful, but we'll need to look into him just to be on the safe side.

The crime scene team has released the baby to go to the hospital and the EMTs are loading her into the back of the ambulance. Hugo catches my elbow. "Rita, go see what we found on the baby. We took photos and everything but have a look before they take her in."

I stick my head into the back of the vehicle. The male EMT overheard our conversation, so he lifts up the baby's shirt to show me.

CHAPTER 25
Eve

*T*HE HOUSE IS ODDLY EMPTY NOW THAT RACHEL LEFT, AND MY MOTHER, who came back a while ago, has retreated to the guest room to make some "personal calls." Nathan and I stand like statues in front of the picture window in the living room. The drapes are closed but they're sheer enough that we can see shapes through them. Reporters have gathered in front of the house. They'd left mostly overnight, but now they're back like a flock of nervous birds hoping for crumbs.

The young officer hasn't had much to say, and neither have we. Nathan stands next to me, his arm around my waist. What do we do now? How long can we stand this and keep breathing?

I hear a phone ring in the kitchen and the officer walks over to us, phone in his extended hand. "Doctor Thayer? The police chief wants to speak to you."

My knees buckle and I'm sitting on the edge of the sofa. Nathan cuddles next to me.

"Hello?"

"Doctor Thayer? This is Chief Murphy."

Something in his voice has me holding my breath. "Yes," I mumble.

"We found a baby, alive. And she fits the description of your daughter—"

I'm on the floor somehow. Nathan is crawling to pick up the phone that I dropped. I'm sobbing into the carpet, and I hear Nathan speaking, his voice high-pitched and excited. The next thing I know, Nathan is on top of me and we're both crying and shaking.

We pull up to Graybridge General and ignore the middle-aged uniformed man who screams after us that we can't leave our car there. We race into the lobby and the receptionist points us to Emergency. Then it dawns on me. What if she's hurt? What if she's critical? The chief only said that she's alive.

We skid to a stop in the waiting room and move aggressively in front of an indignant woman who was talking to a nurse at the counter.

"We're the parents," Nathan screams. "The baby they just brought in."

Before she can say anything, Detective Myers greets us.

"Is it her?" I ask, tearfully.

"We're pretty sure."

"And she's all right?"

"The doctor is checking her now, but she appears to be okay."

"Can we see her?" Nathan is squeezing Detective Myers's arm. A nurse joins us from the back. She looks at Detective Myers, who nods.

"Come on back," she says, and the three of us follow. I'm shaking like I've been stuck in a snowbank, my teeth chattering. I just want my baby girl back in my arms.

We weave through a labyrinth of counters and curtained exam rooms. A tall woman with a long dark ponytail meets us.

"I'm Doctor Patel," she says. "I've examined the baby, and she appears to be fine."

"What do you mean she *appears* to be fine?" Nathan asks.

The doctor holds up her palm. "We're running tests just to be sure, but we have no reason to believe, based on the exam, that she was harmed."

I wipe my face, smearing tears over my cheeks. "Can we see her?"

"This way," Doctor Patel says, and she pulls the curtain aside.

Rosewyn is lying in a small plastic crib like the kind they put newborns in. Nathan and I stand on either side of her and she blinks her eyes, waves her arms.

"Is it her?" Detective Myers asks. "We need you to make it official."

"Yes. It's Rosewyn," Nathan cries. "Can we pick her up?" he asks the doctor, and she nods. Nathan and I cradle her between us and sob. "When can we take her home?" he asks.

"After the tests come back," Doctor Patel says, "and we'd like to keep her a few hours for observation, just to be on the safe side."

Nathan looks distraught, but I get it. We need to let the doctors do their work. We can stay right here while they do it. I want to see everything. I want to make sure that Rosewyn is perfectly fine. Then fury starts to build in my chest. Who did this? Who would put my baby through something like this?

A nurse comes in and Doctor Patel turns to leave. "I'll be back," she says. Rosewyn starts to fuss, and the nurse holds up a bottle.

"She's probably hungry," the nurse says.

"Wait," Detective Myers says, and we turn to look at her, a crying Rosewyn in my arms. "Before you feed the baby, Eve, Nathan, I hate to do this, but I need for you to see something. We're trying to find the person who abducted your baby and time is of the essence. We, uh, we've got one clue that you need to see."

She seems uncomfortable, and I can't imagine what the trouble is. Rosewyn is safe and that has lifted all the pain and fear from my being. But I do want the culprit caught and feel my cheeks flame with anger.

"Of course, what?"

"First, Nathan, would you step out of the room? I want to show your wife first."

Nathan's brow furrows, but he nods and leaves.

"Would you lay the baby down a minute?" Detective Myers says.

"Okay." I put Rosewyn, who's squalling now, in the crib. Detective Myers lifts up the baby's shirt, and there, written on her stomach in what looks like black Sharpie are the words:

Your husband is cheating on you

Part Two

CHAPTER 26
Nathan

I CAN'T IMAGINE WHY I HAD TO LEAVE THE ROOM, BUT IN AN INSTANT, Eve bolts from behind the curtain. She doesn't stop when I call after her. The young nurse, still holding the baby bottle, looks on with confusion. Then Detective Myers calls me in.

"I'm sorry," she says, "but my job is to find the person who abducted your baby."

I'm filled with dread. Something is definitely very wrong.

Rosewyn whimpers as Detective Myers lifts the baby's top and I see the words that someone has written on her little stomach.

I'm sitting in a consultation room with Detective Myers, my head in my hands. I've done this. This is all my fault.

"Where's Eve?" I ask through my fingers. "Is she all right?"

Detective Myers is sitting across from me at the small table. "I sent someone to look for her."

"And Rosewyn?"

"They're giving her a bottle. Then they'll get her cleaned up. We'll take her clothes into evidence. We've taken photos of the message, so they'll wash it off now."

I heave a big sob. Then clear my throat.

"I need to ask you some questions, Nathan."

"I know." I know that a few minutes ago I was on top of the

world. Rosewyn was back and she was going to be okay. Then, in an instant, I'd virtually lost her again and my wife along with her.

Detective Myers opens her notebook. "What can you tell me about the message?"

"I didn't think she had anything to do with this. Why would she?"

"Back up, Nathan. Who are we talking about?"

"Nicole Clark. The woman I was seeing."

"So, you *were* stepping out on your wife?"

I nod. It's the best I can do.

"Give me the details. All you know about her."

I realize then that I don't know all that much. "She lives with her grandmother, and she works in Woburn."

"When did you start seeing her?"

"A few weeks ago. But I broke it off."

"When?"

"Just after New Year's."

"How did she take it?"

A lump forms again in my throat and I swallow. "She was fine. I had no reason to think she was mad or upset! I swear! I didn't think she had anything to do with what happened."

Detective Myers's gaze meets mine. "She may not have, Nathan. But somebody knew you were cheating. Anyone else who might've known?"

"Are you going to talk to Nicole?"

"Yes, of course. But is there *anyone* else who knew?"

I drop my head in my hands, my mind a blank. "I have no idea."

CHAPTER 27
Eve

*M*Y FATHER WAS A HABITUAL CHEATER. MY MOTHER NEVER QUES-
tioned my dad about the women in his life, and she knew full well
what was going on. I never wanted to be my mother. Except for the
cheating, I always looked to my father as a role model. He was a cardiac surgeon and well known and respected in New England. People came from all over so he could "mend their broken hearts," he
liked to say. He was a tall man, ridiculously handsome well into
middle age. And he provided me and my mother with every material possession, a huge, historic home in Concord, several luxury
cars, and my mother's well-heeled friends salivated over her jewelry
collection. And she just didn't care about his infidelities, or she
pretended she didn't. I always knew when there was a new woman
in his life. He would drive home in a new Cadillac for Mom, or present her with a five-thousand-dollar tennis bracelet, or tickets for a
pricey spa getaway for her and her sister, who was more than happy
to sponge off my dad.

My mother has a relationship with money instead of people. We
all have ways of filling our hearts and hers could be bought. I think
she stayed with him because she didn't want to split his money in a
divorce settlement, and she enjoyed the prestige of being the wife
of the renowned Dr. Theodore Thayer. And I think she was prepared to wait him out.

Ironically, Dad died of a massive heart attack at just fifty-seven while he was away at a conference in Dallas. Doctors are notoriously bad patients, caring for others while ignoring their own health.

There was a little talk when my father died in that hotel room, when people realized that the young nurse who had accompanied him was not his wife. But there was always talk like that about my father. There are some things that can't be hidden and, to be honest, he didn't try very hard to keep his affairs secret. So, Mom inherited everything and still lives in our house in Concord enjoying the fruits of my dad's labor, as she should, I suppose. In her mind, she earned them. Who am I to say she didn't?

And now I'm here. With Nathan. How did I not see it? We haven't spoken since I came racing out of Rosewyn's hospital room. I heard him call after me, but I didn't answer. Couldn't answer him. After I got ahold of myself in the ladies' room, I went back, livid. But he was gone. The nurse, who had Rosewyn on her lap, said that Detective Myers had taken him somewhere. My baby was sucking eagerly on her bottle, oblivious.

I sat and watched, not wanting to let her out of my sight. Then they took her away to bathe her and put her in some generic hospital infant attire and handed her to me. She slept in my arms, her chubby cheeks flushed and content while quiet tears dotted my face.

Hours later we took her home. I hadn't said a word to Nathan, although he mumbled I'm sorry several times. I stole a look at him once or twice and he looked like a wounded animal, hair unkempt, stubble on his chin, eyes that looked sunken like an old man's. But I have no pity for him. I have nothing but anger for him.

I wonder again how I ended up married. I guess because Nathan really did sweep me off my feet, in a way. He was so different from all the other men I had dated. My earlier relationships had all been with men who were like me, professionals who were driven to succeed. There were dinners in exclusive restaurants, getaways to exotic locales, and the conversations always centered on our careers. I dated a hedge fund manager, a prestigious company CEO, and, of course, a high-powered doctor, among a few others. There was always a hint of one-upmanship between us, a desperate competition. I enjoyed the sparring to a point until it was time to move on.

I never once thought of marriage to any of them. But then I met Nathan.

He was so down to earth, so normal. Personable and kind. I got the impression that his job was only something to pay the bills, that he left the office behind at five o'clock and didn't think about work until he arrived the next morning. I relaxed in his company. I felt cherished, and it was a heady feeling. Something that had always been missing in my life. How could I not fall for Nathan?

When we got home, my mother cried all over Rosewyn, which made Rosewyn cry, and I had to take her upstairs. I could hear my mother and Nathan rumbling around downstairs, my mother's sharp, cutting voice, Nathan's low, short replies. Neither of us said a word to her about the message. It's none of her business, and I just wish she'd go home, which I expect she will when she thinks she's done her duty.

I'd called Rachel earlier and left her a message on the way to the hospital, after we knew Rosewyn was safe and before I learned the truth about my husband. She called and left me happy follow-up voicemails. But I don't want to talk to anyone right now, so I don't call her back. I have no idea what to say.

I'm full of anger, to the point that it's probably better I stay away from everyone, and I wonder about the woman who Nathan was seeing. Could she have taken Rosewyn? The thought fills me with rage, at her and my husband.

CHAPTER 28
Rita

I CALLED THE STATION, SPOKE WITH LAUREN, AND SHE FOUND AN AD-dress for Nicole Clark. She's a Graybridge local if we've got the right woman, so I head out to see her. It's nearly evening, so she should hopefully be home from work, but we'll see.

The small clapboard house is painted a light blue. It's well kept on a street of houses just like it. A tiny, gray-haired woman answers the door. I identify myself and there's confusion plainly on her face.

"A police detective?" she asks.

"Yes. I'm looking for Nicole. Are you her grandmother?"

Her brow furrows as if she's not sure. Then I hear a woman's voice behind her. "Nana? Who's at the door?"

The woman appears and I introduce myself again. "Yes. I'm Nicole Clark," she says in answer to my query. She invites me into a warm living room full of chintz and knickknacks.

The elderly woman looks at her granddaughter. "What does she want, Nicole?"

"It's nothing to worry about, Nana. Let's go into the kitchen, so you can finish your tea." Nicole motions for me to have a seat in the living room as she ushers her grandmother away.

"Sorry about that, Detective," Nicole says when she returns. "My grandmother"—she lowers her voice—"has dementia."

I take out my notebook while Nicole sits across from me on the couch. Her hair is long and blond, pulled up in a high ponytail like a teenager. She gives off a young vibe despite being a thirty-something, I'd guess. She's casually dressed in leggings and a long top. She smiles easily. "What can I do for you?"

"You know why I'm here?" I ask.

Her eyelashes flutter down, and her cheeks redden. "Not really, no."

"You heard about the Liddle baby?"

Her blue eyes widen. "Yes. It was terrible, but I heard they found her. Everything's okay."

"Yes. Thankfully, the baby is fine and reunited with her family."

Nicole leans back into the couch cushions.

"But we've learned that you and Mr. Liddle were romantically involved."

She blinks her eyes and grasps her hands together. "What does that have to do with anything? We were briefly involved, but I broke it off."

"Yes. He told me."

"So, that's why you're here. You want to know if I know anything?"

"That's right." I'm letting her talk, letting her fill in the gaps.

"Well, it's not like me to see a married man, Detective. I broke it off last week—before the baby was taken. I really don't know anything about that. I feel terrible for Nathan. He seemed like a good father, but I have no idea who would do something like that."

"Uh huh." I sketch her face in my notebook. The flushed cheeks, wide eyes, the slight cleft in her chin.

"Have you found any clues?"

My eyes meet hers and she breaks our gaze. "We're working on it. Nicole, where were you yesterday afternoon?"

"Here. I worked from home yesterday and today."

"Did you leave the house?"

"No. I was here the whole time. I don't like to leave my grandmother alone if I can help it." She glances toward the kitchen.

"Do you go into the office at all?"

"A couple times a week."

"But not yesterday?"

"No."

"Did anyone see you here?"

"My grandmother."

"Anyone else?"

She shakes her head.

"You make any phone calls?"

"Probably." She puts her hand to her forehead. "Yes, but I can't remember to who exactly."

"Mind if I look through the house?"

"I guess not." She stands. "But really, Detective, I had nothing to do with taking Nathan's baby. Why would I? He's a good guy and *I* broke it off."

I don't know what to think about this woman. She seems sincere, and yet there's something about her. I think about the red thread we found at the Parnell house. I'm anxious to see if I find anything that matches it. She follows behind me as I walk through the tidy but cluttered rooms. I look through her closet but don't see anything that would match the red thread. I end in the kitchen where her grandmother is sitting at the table rooting through a bag of cookies.

"What do you need, Nana?" Nicole asks.

"I was looking for the lemon ones. I know we bought some."

"They're here, in the cupboard." Nicole picks up the bag her grandmother was looking through. "These are ginger snaps."

My hope that Grandma would be able to tell me whether Nicole was actually home all day yesterday and this morning is pretty much shattered. I don't think this woman even knows what day it is. I need to ask her anyway.

"Nicole, you mind stepping out of the room for a few minutes?"

A cross look passes over her face, but she nods and leaves.

"Ma'am?" Grandma's cloudy eyes meet mine. "Was Nicole here all day yesterday?"

She works her mouth like she's chewing gum. Her eyebrows draw together. "I believe she was. Why?"

"What about this morning? Was she here this morning?"

"Why do you ask?"

"Just trying to put together a timeline."

She nods as if that clears it all up. "Nicole is a good girl. My daughter won't lift a finger to help me, you know. She doesn't come near me, never did. Even when she wasn't in the looney bin. But Nicole is a good girl. What did you say your name was?"

"Detective Myers." I glance down at my notebook. "Did Nicole bring a baby home in the last day or so?" It's worth a shot.

"Oh, no. Nicole doesn't have a baby." Her brow puckers. "Nicole!" she hollers. "Did you find the lemon cookies?"

Back at the station, everything has shifted. People are busy, noisy, but with a sense of purpose rather than anxiety. The Liddle baby is safe, but the kidnapper is still at large. The chief has just finished a press conference that I'm thrilled I missed while I was out talking to Nicole Clark.

I close my office door and sit at my desk. The sleep I didn't get last night has finally made itself felt full force. I'm drained and I can't stifle a yawn. My phone rings. My brother.

"Hey," I answer.

"Rita, how are things? I just saw it on the news. That's wonderful that the baby was found safely."

"Yeah. We're thrilled here."

"You sound exhausted."

"I am. Completely."

"You haven't found the perpetrator yet though? That's what they said on the news."

"Right. It's still an active investigation. Still lots of work to do."

"Well, get your rest."

"I haven't forgotten," I say.

"What about?"

"Maureen's."

"Don't worry. We can go any time. I'm in no hurry."

"Thanks, bro." We hang up and I notice several texts from Joe. I'm sure he knows all about the Liddle baby and that we were this close to calling the FBI for help.

But Joe's texts are all personal, asking me if I'm all right. I smile, yawn, and text him back.

CHAPTER 29
Eve

*T*HE NEXT COUPLE OF DAYS PASS IN A BLUR. AT MY REQUEST, NATHAN is staying in the guest room and out of my way as much as possible. Rachel and my mother have both stopped by, offered to help, but I've had little to say to either of them, and nothing to say to Nathan. I walk through the house with Rosewyn in my arms, not wanting to let her go.

I hold my baby close, and she squirms, but I can't put her down. I still shiver at the thought of how close we came to losing her. I never knew that you could love another person as much as I love my daughter. I sigh and know that I'd do anything to protect her. And I know that, despite what he did, Nathan loves her, too.

But Nathan is still drinking, just as he was when Rosewyn was missing. I smell the whiskey mixed with cigarettes on him as we pass each other. He's tried several times to talk to me, to touch me lightly on the arm or shoulder, but I'm not ready to talk yet. The trauma of losing Rosewyn is still too raw. My emotional well is dry at the moment.

But I know that I need to go back to work, and *that* we'll have to discuss. Rosewyn is upstairs in her crib, napping. The baby monitor sits on the coffee table where I can see her. Nathan is in the armchair. I sit across from him.

"I need to go back to work at the end of the week," I say.

He nods. "I'll stay home with Rosewyn. I've got three weeks of vacation time."

We don't have much choice. There's no one else to take care of her, and no matter what I think of Nathan now, he loves Rosewyn. He's a good father.

My gaze meets his. "You can't be drinking and take care of a baby, Nathan."

He drops his head. "I won't. I'm sorry."

"And we need to be careful. You need to have your wits about you. Who knows if whoever took Rosewyn will try again." I glance toward the kitchen and think about the possibility that the kidnapper might have been spying on us from Ms. Parnell's house. Detective Myers said that they were stepping up patrols in our neighborhood. Still, the thought that someone may have been watching us, planning, fills me with trepidation.

"I'll watch the baby like a hawk, Eve."

I sit still on the sofa, glaring at my husband. "All right. That'll have to work until we . . ." I stand. "Figure things out."

I finally agreed to meet Rachel for lunch. She's been texting me nonstop, and I haven't wanted to talk about Nathan and me, but I can't put it off any longer. The restaurant is small, out of the way. I don't want to run into anyone I know. I push Rosewyn in the stroller and park it next to our table.

Rachel reaches down and pats Rosewyn on the head. "You're a little trooper," she says, then looks at me. "She seems okay."

"Yes. She's been fine, so I hope the trauma she went through won't affect her."

Rachel's brow furrows. "At her age? She won't remember it, right?"

"Probably not, but the mind is a complex thing. We don't really know how things we experience as a baby might somehow lurk in our subconscious." I sniff, sip the ice water that our young server brought.

We settle in with our menus. Rachel peeps over hers. "So, you're going back to work soon?"

"End of the week." Which is just a couple of days away.

"And Nathan is going to watch Rosewyn?"

"Yes." Our server is standing by, pencil poised.

"What can I get you ladies?" he asks, full of youthful enthusiasm.

We both order Cobb salads, and he collects our menus and scurries away.

"So," Rachel says, "have they found anything?"

"No. Not yet."

"Do they have any clues?"

I shake my head and reach down to tuck a blanket around Rosewyn.

"They have no idea who would do something like this?" Rachel asks.

"Not that they've told us." I feel my frustration mount with her questions.

She glances around the restaurant, lowers her voice. "Do you feel safe with a kidnapper out there?"

I swallow. "No. Not really. We're having a security system installed next week."

"Well, that's good." Rachel settles her napkin on her lap then glances back at me. "What's wrong, Eve? You should be thrilled to have the baby back. I know you're worried about the kidnapper, but is something else going on?"

I am grateful for Rachel. Through everything since we met as eighteen-year-olds, she's been there for me. Even in that stupid drama class we took together. When Professor Daniels was standing too close, laying a hand on my shoulder, making me cringe, Rachel would say something snarky, divert his attention. After one particularly creepy run-in, she tried to convince me to go to the administration and report him, but I didn't. I didn't know what I'd even say. The semester was almost over by that point, so I let it go.

I fuss with Rosewyn's blanket then glance at Rachel. She's waiting for an explanation, her dark eyes wide. I don't want to get into the whole message thing. The police told us not to tell anyone, but Rachel might as well know the reality of the situation between me and my husband. "I found out that Nathan was cheating."

"What? You're *kidding*." Her face reddens. "The fucker." She turns her head, probably to see if anyone heard her. "When? How did you find out?"

"He broke it off just before Rosewyn was taken." I learned that much as Nathan tried to apologize.

Rachel slumps back in her chair. "Jesus. Do the cops think that she took Rosewyn?"

"They've questioned her, but they haven't made any arrests."

"I'm sorry, Eve." Rachel taps the table with her manicured nails. "What do you know about her? Where did he meet her?"

"I don't know. We haven't really talked about it. I . . . can't. Not yet."

The server arrives with our salads and my stomach is in knots. I wish I hadn't decided to meet Rachel for lunch after all. What was I thinking?

"So, what are you going to do? You're not going to stay with him."

"He's moved into the guest room for now. I don't know what to do. I haven't gotten there yet, emotionally." I feel my face flush, my heart start to pound. "I'm so angry."

"You've been through the wringer. That's for sure." She sips the wine she ordered with her salad. "Men are such dicks. I'm so glad I never got married."

"Gee, thanks." I pick up Rosewyn and put her on my lap. She kicks and babbles and I place my cheek against her soft head.

"Sorry. That was uncalled for." Rachel squeezes my arm. "You've got a beautiful daughter out of the whole deal. Things will get better. Take some time. Take care of yourself and that sweet baby. You don't need to make any big decisions right now."

I nod. Rachel finishes her salad, sips her wine, while I push my salad around on my plate. I actually feel a little better now that I've told someone about Nathan, not that she or anyone else can really help me. But I've got to face this new reality and figure out what to do.

CHAPTER 30
Rita

OUR INVESTIGATION INTO THE KIDNAPPING OF THE LIDDLE BABY HAS shifted now that the baby has been found and the ominous message discovered. We gather in the conference room—Chase, Lauren, and I—our short suspect list on the white board: Donald Barry, Barbara Singleton, and now, Nicole Clark. But, so far, we haven't gotten very far with any of them.

I sip my coffee and take a deep breath. "Ok. Let's think about this. What was the purpose of taking the baby?"

"Not to keep her, possess her," Lauren says.

"Right. She was returned in short order, so the point was to make the Liddles suffer—"

"And to break them up," Chase adds.

"That would appear to be the case," I say. "Let's look at Donald Barry first." I stand and walk over to the white board. "What was his motivation?" My gaze meets Chase's.

"He wanted Doctor Thayer for himself, or he wanted her to suffer. He was angry that she transferred him to another doctor. He finds out that Mr. Liddle was cheating. Sees that as his opportunity to break them up. And," Chase adds, "we know that he is in therapy, but, since we don't have access to his medical records, we don't know why. Maybe he's a psychopath who wouldn't see anything wrong with stealing a baby."

I nod. "Lauren, what did you find in his call records?"

She leans back in her chair, clicks a couple of keys on her laptop. "He had a window between calls that afternoon where he could've gone out to Barbara's and taken the baby."

"How big a window?"

"Almost two hours."

"How far is it to Barbara's from his place?"

"Eleven minutes."

"How would he know that the coast would be clear for him to enter the Singleton house undetected?" Chase asks.

I look at Lauren. Part of my job at this stage of my career is to mentor the young detectives.

She drums her fingers on the table. "Maybe he's been casing the house. He watches the virtual tour online. He's in IT, and he's probably online all the time, so he knows the house's layout, knows where the baby is napping. Then he waits and watches. He sees Barbara go out into the backyard and tries the front door, and it just happens to be unlocked. Maybe he tried a couple of times and this time it worked."

"Okay. That could've happened," I say. "Then what? When we questioned him at his house, there was no sign of a baby."

"He wouldn't have kept her there. Maybe a hotel nearby?" Chase asks.

I tip my head. "You can't leave an infant alone in a hotel room. He was at his apartment, no baby, while she was missing."

Lauren blows out a breath. "He'd need help."

"Right. So, let's look at anyone in his life who might've been an accomplice. Lauren, you dig into that."

Her eyes shift to her computer screen. "Will do."

"All right. Let's look at Nicole Clark. What's her motive?"

Chase leans back in his chair. "She wanted payback. She said the breakup was amicable—"

"Doesn't mean it was," I finish. "So?"

"She's really angry. Here she is, divorced, living with her grandmother while Mr. Liddle lives his perfect life with his doctor wife and their precious baby. She wants him to suffer. When she appears fine with the breakup, it's just an act."

"Could be. What about an accomplice? She'd have to talk some-one into helping her hide the baby." I raise my eyebrows.

"Maybe not," Chase says and gets to his feet, paces. "You said her grandmother has dementia. What if Granny really has no clue whether Nicole was home or not?"

"Could be," I say. "She seemed pretty well out of it when I was talking to her. Okay, but Nicole would also need somewhere to take the baby, with or without an accomplice. Granny said that there was no baby there while Rosewyn was missing. As much as she's out of it, I don't think she'd miss the presence of a baby in that little house. Chase, you start looking at hotels. Start in Graybridge and fan out from there." This will be an arduous task. There are a gazil-lion hotels in the greater Boston area, but there's a chance that this could solve our case in short order. "Talk to desk clerks and look at surveillance video." That's one good thing about hotels, they all have some surveillance video, even the cheap ones.

"Okay, what about Barbara?" I glance at Lauren. "Did you find out anything about a possible daughter?"

She shakes her head. "No. Nothing."

Chase sips his coffee. "But she did tell Mr. Liddle that the baby in the photo was her daughter?"

"That's what he told me." I twirl my pencil in my fingers. "I'm going out to talk to Barbara this afternoon, and I'll ask her about this mystery baby. But okay, what reason would Barbara have for kidnapping the Liddle baby and writing the message?"

"It doesn't seem to make sense, Rita," Lauren says, pausing her computer clicking.

"No. It doesn't. When Mr. Liddle told me about the picture, he and his wife became hysterical wondering if Barbara had a baby girl and she killed her, or maybe the baby died, and Barbara wanted their baby to replace her own."

Chase's eyes go wide. "You think that's possible?"

"Anything's possible at this point," I say.

Lauren clears her throat. "What if Mrs. Singleton coveted the baby. She is certainly attached to her. So, she decides that she wants to keep her, to get her away from the parents. She takes the baby away somewhere and hides her. Then she gets cold feet." Lauren's gaze meets mine. "What's she going to do? She's in over her head, and she's discovered that Mr. Liddle is cheating, so she writes the message on the baby to throw us off, or she figures she'll try to punish the Liddles for being bad parents. What if she lost her own little girl, and she was a devoted mother, and here are two very flawed people and they have a beautiful, healthy baby and she lost it. Wanted to punish them."

"Could be," I say.

"That seems pretty extreme," Chase says.

Lauren shrugs. "I watched the interview tapes, and she seems pretty unbalanced to me."

"Okay. Let's just assume that Lauren's right. Who helped Barbara? She'd definitely need an accomplice, and her husband was out of town."

"She's got pretty much unlimited funds, Rita, being a Torrence. She could've paid someone to help her," Lauren says.

"Do you really think that Mrs. Singleton is that deranged?" Chase asks.

"Remember," I say, "there's a possibility that someone has been watching the Liddles from the Parnell house. That says obsessed to me. And the neighborhood boys saw a stranger go into the house New Year's Eve." The Parnell angle is what bugs me. Maybe it isn't connected, but my gut says it is. "All right, let's back up and look at some other possibilities. What did you find out from the real estate woman?" I ask Lauren.

"She gave me the names of the three couples and the one single man who looked at the house." Lauren's gaze meets mine over her computer screen. "The house has only been on the market for a short time, so not a lot of people have seen it, which is good." She clears her throat. "Anyway, two of the couples are young with small kids. The other couple is older with grandchildren. The man is middle-aged and unmarried. So far, none of them is looking likely. And the agent hadn't noticed anything unusual."

"You look into her?"

"Yes. She's got four teenagers. Didn't seem to fit."

"Still. Keep digging." I lean back in my chair. In any case, you have to go where the evidence leads and so far, it's led us nowhere. "Maybe it's someone connected to the Liddles that we haven't considered yet. Let's make a list of everyone we know that they know. The perp knew Liddle was stepping out on his wife. That's one thing we know for sure."

CHAPTER 31
Rita

WITH THE RECOVERY OF THE LIDDLE BABY, BARBARA SINGLETON has gone down on the suspect list. Despite our wild speculation, Barbara seems to be a weak possibility at this point. Why would she take the baby then bring her back? How did she know about Mr. Liddle's affair? Maybe she did and maybe she wanted to punish the Liddles. Still, it seems like a stretch. But the mystery baby in the photo has to be addressed.

When I get to the well-appointed Singleton home, Mr. Singleton answers the door. He's slim, but solid looking. His graying hair is neatly trimmed, his posture erect, his gaze straight forward, every inch the airline captain. He leads me to their front room while he goes to find Barbara. That gives me time to take a look at the photos on the end table. The pictures are just as Mr. Liddle described them. Lots of nice family shots of the Singletons and a boy, their son apparently, at various stages in their lives. But in the back, in a tiny silver frame, is a newborn girl with a pink bow on her head. What the hell happened to her?

Barbara sits in a chair opposite me while Mr. Singleton busies himself in the kitchen, but not out of earshot. Barbara looks terrible, eyes red and puffy, skin gray and sunken. She clutches a wad of tissues in her hand.

"Mrs. Singleton, so far, we've had no luck finding the person who took the Liddle baby."

She nods, her gaze on her lap where she's twined her fingers together. "I've told you all I know," she whispers.

"Did you know that Mr. Liddle was cheating on his wife?"

Her red eyes dart up and meet mine. "No. I had no idea before I heard that on the news."

"But you think the Liddles are bad parents?"

"I didn't say that. I said that Doctor Thayer didn't spend much time with Rosie. From what I gathered, Nathan took care of the baby in the mornings while his wife went to work. Then he picked Rosewyn up at the end of the day. He said that his wife usually worked late. A baby deserves to have her mother take care of her, at least sometimes. How could she do that and be at that hospital all the time?"

"A lot of women have careers, Barbara. That doesn't make them bad mothers."

She bites her lips and sniffs. "I know. That's not what I mean. That sounds so backwards of me. I just . . ." Her gaze wanders to the big front window. "I just thought Rosie deserved more, you know? I loved taking care of her." Tears trickle from the corners of her eyes. Mr. Singleton comes to the doorway, stands there a minute before retreating back to the kitchen.

"Okay." I turn the pages in my notebook. "I do want to ask you about one more thing. Mr. Liddle said that he saw a picture of a baby girl." I point in the direction of the table. "He said you told him that the baby was your daughter, but no one can find any evidence that you have a daughter."

Her face reddens, and she raises her hands. "Yes. I had a daughter." She wipes at her cheeks. Her voice raises an octave. "When I was young, Detective, I got pregnant. The baby was put up for adoption. No big mystery. It happens. But it's nobody's business. I don't know why Nathan had to bring that up."

"But you've kept her picture?"

Barbara starts to sob, and I'm afraid she's going to fall completely apart. Mr. Singleton comes in and sits beside her and wraps an arm around her shoulders. He glares at me with stern gray eyes.

"I'm sorry, Mrs. Singleton, but I have to ask painful questions sometimes. We have a kidnapper at large."

She nods and leans into her husband.

"Is that all, Detective?" Mr. Singleton asks.

I stand. Barbara's such a mess, there's not much reason to keep at her at this point, but the baby mystery has been cleared up anyway. "For now," I say. "I'll show myself out." But he stands, whispers to his wife that he'll make her a cup of tea in a minute. He pats her shoulder and follows me out the front door.

We're standing on the porch, chilly wind ruffling the strands of hair that have fallen from my messy bun.

Mr. Singleton clears his throat. "Detective, my wife has been shattered by what happened to the Liddle baby, and believe me, she had nothing to do with it, so I would appreciate you leaving her alone."

"I understand, but there were questions that needed answering. We found it strange that your wife told Mr. Liddle that she had a baby girl, but we could find no evidence of a daughter."

He frowns, wipes his hand over his mouth. "You didn't get the whole story about . . . the baby in the photograph."

"Why don't you fill me in then?"

He pulls the heavy front door closed to keep our conversation from Barbara, I assume. "This isn't easy to talk about, but maybe you'll get a better picture of my wife and understand why I'm so concerned about her."

"Okay."

He takes a deep breath. "Back when Barbara was a senior in college, she was walking home from a late class, after dark, to her off-campus apartment, when some low-life pulled her into a clump of trees in a park she had to pass, and raped her." He draws another breath. "I was away at basic training when it happened. Her family was there to support her. She reported it to the cops, but the guy was never found. It went unsolved. We'd just announced our engagement two weeks earlier, before I left. It was some big swanky event at her parents' country club.

"Anyway, I was frantic, but she didn't want me to drop out and come home. Said her parents were taking good care of her." He grits his teeth like he's still regretting his decision to stay away all those years ago. "Six weeks later, she calls me, crying. She's pregnant with her attacker's baby. I told her to end the pregnancy, you know, for her sake. How could she carry the baby from something like that? Her parents totally agreed with me. But Barbara said no, no way. She said she'd have the baby and give it up for adoption, and she was resolute, so she did. Her parents had their big-deal lawyer handle the private adoption when the time came. Barbara insisted on keeping the newborn picture. I don't know why she wanted it, but she did, and she insisted it stay on the table in the front room with our son's pictures."

"I'm sorry she had to go through that, Mr. Singleton. Really sorry. And the perp was never apprehended?"

"No. The case went nowhere, so I guess it's cold, the documents still sitting in some dusty Boston PD basement."

It's a shame, but it happens all the time. Lots of monsters never pay for their crimes. "Well, thank you for telling me, Mr. Singleton. I'll certainly keep all that in mind when I speak to your wife in the future."

"Please do. But that's not all." He glances off to the street where an SUV flies by. "After we got married, Barbara got pregnant right away and miscarried a little girl. Barbara was devastated and she went to therapy for a while. She felt she was being punished for giving away her first baby. Anyway, we didn't have any luck in the baby department for years and then, surprise, surprise, she's pregnant with our son. Everything went great. He was a healthy baby and has grown into a fine young man. Barbara dotes on him, but losing our daughter, and if I'm being honest, the first girl, still weighs on her. So, when the Liddles asked her about watching their daughter, I didn't want Barbara to do it. I think it brought back too many bad memories. She had been all right taking care of a little boy, but a girl, I was afraid it would be too much."

"I understand. Is there any reason you can think of, though, that Barbara would have been involved with the Liddle baby's disappearance? Maybe the memories eventually got to her, and she felt she was protecting Rosie by keeping her away from the parents. Maybe she thought Rosie would be better off with her."

"How could she get away with that?"

I raise my eyebrows. "Was her mental state such that she wasn't able to think clearly? I've seen some bizarre things in my time as a cop, Mr. Singleton. People sometimes act irrationally when they're distressed enough. And it sounds like Barbara has had plenty to distress her."

He shakes his head. "She was in therapy a long time ago. She's been fine for years. And she *was* fine until the Liddle baby disappeared. *That's* when she started to fall apart." He turns abruptly and disappears back into the house.

I start my van. The radio comes on and an old Gordon Lightfoot ballad fills the vehicle. I sit for a minute, listening, my eyes shut. Then I slip the gearshift into drive, peer in my side mirror, and head back to the station, the case filling my head. Even though Mr. Singleton said that Barbara was fine until the baby disappeared, maybe she wasn't. Definitely something to ponder and look into.

CHAPTER 32
Eve

I'M BACK AT WORK, SITTING IN MY OFFICE WITH THE DOOR CLOSED after running the gauntlet of concerned colleagues who don't know what to say, and neither do I. I rushed by, thanking people for their concern, and made it back to my office. My docket is full, patients who've been waiting days to see me have stacked up, and I don't have a minute to myself today, which is just as well.

I can't stop thinking about the kidnapper. Is he or she still out there watching us? Waiting for another opportunity? And why? Why take my baby? I don't understand why anyone would want to hurt us so badly. I shudder and stick my icy hands in the pockets of my sweater. *Get a grip, Eve. Don't dwell on what you can't control.*

The old building is cold and drafty. The day is dark with clouds. I look out my window at the barren trees, a forest stretches past the lawn. A lawn that in the warm weather would be full of inpatients taking the air, just as they've done in the past. Back in the forties they'd have been accompanied by white-clothed nurses in peaked caps instead of the aides in blue scrubs today. There's a knock on my door and I shake myself out of my thoughts.

Brian Tanaka peeps around the door. "Got a minute?"

"Sure. Just."

"I wanted to let you know that I'm here, and I'll help any way I can."

"Thanks, Brian. I really appreciate it."

"I mean, if you need someone to talk to, I'd be glad to listen."

He means therapy. Do I need therapy? Heat rises to my face.

Brian clears his throat. "I know someone in Boston if you'd rather. She's terrific and very discreet."

I clear my throat. "Thanks. I'll think about it." I glance at my phone and stand. "I have a patient who's probably waiting."

"Yeah. I need to get going, too," Brian says, and I follow him out into the hall.

The day flies by, and it centers me to immerse myself into the lives of my patients. I've checked with Nathan off and on, texting just enough to make sure that Rosewyn is okay. I glance out my window. Darkness is setting in, so early in the dead of winter, but at least it's not snowing. In fact, we've had a bit of a warm-up since yesterday.

My last patient of the day sits in my office. Marie Williams looks stunning, as usual, designer blouse and neat slacks, shiny pumps. Her hair is perfect, makeup too.

"I'm so sorry for what you went through, Doctor Thayer," she says, removing her gloves. "But I'm glad that everything worked out."

"Thank you." I've had to endure every patient bringing up Rosewyn at the start of their session, but now, hopefully, we can move beyond that. "So, how was your week?"

"Great," she says. "In fact, this will be my last appointment."

I had a feeling. "That's wonderful, Marie. I feel like you've made terrific progress."

"I have and I am so grateful to you. I mean, my parents' deaths will always be a sad chapter in my life."

"Of course."

"But I'm not experiencing the depression that I was having. I can feel sad occasionally and then move on."

"That's healthy," I say.

"So!" She smiles. "I'm going to Paris for a couple of weeks. When I get back, I'm moving. I found a gorgeous apartment in Boston with a view of the harbor."

"That's lovely."

"I'm so excited," Marie says, then a shadow passes over her face. "I'm sorry. I know you've been through a horrible ordeal."

"Everything is fine now. No need to be sorry."

We run through the past few weeks that she's been coming to see me. Discuss a few things to make sure we've tied up any loose ends. But I'm pleased that I could help her. That's what I got into this line of work to do, help people. Brian's words earlier come back to me. Maybe I need to help myself. It's a grim thought. I always considered myself above needing anyone. Hubris maybe, and we all know what that leads to.

"Doctor Thayer?" Marie is standing, slipping into her coat, and I realize that I had zoned out for a moment.

"Yes? Sorry."

"No need. I was just admiring the painting behind your desk."

"The seascape?"

"Yes. It's lovely."

"My friend, Rachel Chapman, painted it. She's a professional artist. She works at a gallery on Graybridge Square." I like to plug Rachel's work when I can.

"I'll need to stop in. I'm going to need artwork for the new apartment."

I walk Marie to the door, and she gives me a hug. "Thank you again," she says.

I see Glenda walking down the hall toward me. She's here a little early. Marie scoots past her and Glenda smirks in her direction. Glenda isn't the friendliest nurse on staff, and she rarely deals with the outpatients.

"Hey, Doc," Glenda calls, and waves a file folder. "Got a scheduling question."

I take a deep breath. "Sure. What's up?"

Glenda opens the folder. She's printed out the next week's nursing schedule and points out a couple of night shifts where we're a little thin.

"I'm interviewing someone tomorrow, actually," I say. But I know that doesn't help with next week. "Can we pull someone from days in the meantime?"

"I'll talk to Cheryl," Glenda says. "She might be able to cover."

Keeping good nurses has been a challenge. "You've worked in this field a long time," I say.

Her lips thin. "Yeah. I've seen my share come and go. Psychiatric work isn't for everyone. Most nurses don't make it their whole career."

"What keeps you in it? And nights, too."

She leans back against the wall, her gaze down the hall where Marie is talking to the receptionist. "I found my calling. Sure, it's tough as hell." She shakes her head. "I've been bitten, scratched, had two teeth knocked out." Her eyes catch mine. "But that's not the worst part. The howls and the hallucinations and the heartbreak of the patients and families, too. Sometimes they abandon their loved ones. Can't take it." She raises her chin. "Someone has to."

She's right about the challenges. Psychiatric work is difficult and sometimes frightening. "Why nights? With your experience, you could easily get the day shift."

Her eyes wander behind her glasses as if taking in the whole facility. "I like nights. It's quiet. Patients are asleep mostly, and you get left alone." She shrugs. "I got used to the stillness. It suits me. And you don't have to deal with the families. Some of them, as you know, are pretty useless."

I nod. That's the truth. "Let me know about Cheryl. If she can't cover, I'll see what I can do."

"Will do." Glenda snaps the folder shut. "Sorry about what happened with your kid, by the way. Glad you got her back okay."

"Thanks."

Glenda walks back down the hall, and I retreat to my office. I peer out my window into the darkening sky. I think about Marie heading out to her perfect life. She seems to have it all. A great career. No worry about money. She can run off to Paris when she feels like it. No husband. No ties. Her life is her own. I turn away from the window and head back to my desk.

The seascape *is* beautiful. Rachel painted it after we went on a weekend getaway to the Cape two summers before I met Nathan. It makes me smile to remember it. We'd had so much fun and met a couple of handsome stockbrokers from New York to boot. It had been an adventure. And it feels like another lifetime.

* * *

I pull into my driveway. I have a splitting headache as I walk through the door and am immediately greeted by a squalling Rosewyn. She's standing in her playpen, holding on to the rail, tears rolling down her red cheeks. *Where the hell is Nathan?*

I pick her up and she starts to quiet in my arms. Nathan comes running in from the deck, cigarette smoke in his wake.

"What the fuck, Nathan?"

His face falls, his mouth hangs open a minute. "I'm so sorry. She was fine. We, uh, I just gave her a bottle. I fed her dinner first. And I was getting ready to give her a bath—"

"But you had to have a smoke first, right?"

"She was fine, Eve, in the playpen. I was just out on the deck for a minute. I swear."

"Jesus, Nathan." I move past him and hurry up to my room. I don't want to be near him, and he seems to get the message. He doesn't follow me or call out as I slam the door of the master bedroom. I pace with Rosewyn on my hip. I wipe her little face and dry her tears. I'm so angry, I can't think straight, and I don't want my little girl to feel that. I turn on the TV to a kid's station. She's too young to care about that, but the bright colors and jaunty music help dispel the angry atmosphere that seems to surround me like a cloud.

I sit on the bed and play with Rosewyn. Her natural good nature surfaces, which should soothe away my pain, but instead, it makes me feel more worthless. I've failed. I thought I could be a great mother, wife, psychiatrist, but my life has crashed around me.

I decide to give Rosewyn her bath and put her down for the night. I have no idea what Nathan is doing, and I don't care.

The baby is sleeping in her crib with Elephant looking on from the dresser. I shut her door and creep downstairs. Nathan is in the kitchen, pouring himself a whiskey from the nearly empty bottle. He said he would stop drinking, so that infuriates me further. But from what I can tell, he only drinks at the end of the day, after Rosewyn is in bed. Still.

He turns to face me, and I've never seen him look so bad, eyes bloodshot beneath drooping eyelids. Unshaven, hair sticking up like he hasn't combed it in a week. His oxford shirt a rumpled mess.

"I'm so sorry, Eve," he says, and places the glass in the sink.

I raise my palm. "I don't want to hear it, Nathan." But my anger bubbles to the surface. We haven't spoken about the message, not yet, but now I can't contain my emotions any longer. "How could you do that to me?" I whisper through gritted teeth.

He spreads out his arms, like an appeal for understanding. "I'm so sorry. I'm a piece of shit. I wish it had never happened."

"You knew about my father, what I went through as a kid. You knew that cheating was something I'd never tolerate. Why did you do it? And what about Rosewyn! I don't want her to grow up like I did with people talking, laughing about her father. Did you stop to think about how it would affect her?"

He hangs his head. "I never wanted to hurt you or her."

"Well, you did!" My voice breaks. Tears tremble on my cheeks. "You broke my heart, Nathan. Did you enjoy that? Enjoy her? What's her name?"

"Nicole. Nicole Clark."

"How did you meet? I want the whole fucking sordid story!"

He leans back against the counter, his hand over his eyes. "At a bar, across from work."

"*Lucia's?* Where we first went out together?"

He nods. "I was there with some of the guys. You were working another late night."

"Don't make this my fault! You knew what my hours were like when you married me. You were more than okay with my job then."

"I didn't mean that. It wasn't your fault, Eve. It was mine, totally. I fucked up and I'm so sorry."

"When? Nathan. When was it going on?"

"Sometime after Thanksgiving. Then I broke it off right after New Year's."

I stagger back toward the table, rest my hand there to steady myself. "What if it was her? What if she'd hurt Rosewyn?"

"We don't know who took Rosewyn, Eve. Detective Myers said it could've been anyone who knew about . . . the affair. If it was Nicole, why haven't they arrested her by now?"

"Don't you dare try to defend her!"

"That's not what I'm doing."

"So, who else knew then?"

"I don't know."

"Jesus, Nathan. I can't believe you did this to me! To Rosewyn!" He starts to walk toward me, but I put my hand up. "Don't come near me! Don't! I could kill you."

I turn and run up the stairs. Inside my room, I shut and lock the door. I lay on my bed and scream into the pillow, balling my hands into fists.

Part Three

CHAPTER 33
Nathan

Now

I'VE BEEN ABLE TO FIGURE OUT A FEW THINGS. I'M DEFINITELY IN THE hospital. I'm awake but I can't see anything. They've bandaged my eyes and there's an oxygen mask over my mouth. Maybe I can signal someone by raising my arm. But I can't move anything on my right side. I'm in so much pain. I try to move my fingers, but I think they're in a cast. Did I break my arm? My bones feel heavy, like they weigh a thousand pounds. And my leg is immobilized. Another cast? *Jesus.* I must've broken every bone in my body when I fell down the stairs.

Fear creeps up my spine. Where's Eve? She could be in the room at this very moment, but I don't smell her perfume, so maybe I'm alone. I hope so. I knew she was strong, willful, but I never thought she was violent. That's crazy, but she must've hit me. I felt the blow to the back of my head. And she was so angry and, again, I don't blame her, but how else did I end up at the bottom of the deck stairs? I've been out there a million times and I've been just fine. Sure, I've been drinking too much, but I wasn't that drunk that night. Whenever that was. Shit, I wish I knew what day it is.

My thoughts turn to Rosewyn. I can't die and leave my little girl.

This brings tears to my eyes and the throbbing in my head grows like a jackhammer.

"Mr. Liddle?" a faraway voice calls. "Mr. Liddle? Can you hear me?"

It's not Eve. I try to rise to the surface. I lift my left arm and the woman clasps my hand.

"You can hear me. Wonderful. Lie quiet now." She places my arm back on the bed. "You're in the hospital. You've had a bad fall, but you're getting better. You need to rest now. I'll let your doctor know that you're awake. Lie still." She pulls the blanket up over my chest and gives me a couple of pats that are supposed to be reassuring.

I want to ask a thousand questions. I reach for the oxygen mask, but she intercepts me and places my hand back on the bed. "Leave that alone for now. Try to relax. Everything is all right."

I hear the door close. She's wrong. Everything is *not* all right. My wife tried to kill me and who knows if she'll finish the job. I start to panic. My heart races.

I'm listening closely, waiting for my door to open again, and hoping like hell it's not Eve. Time ticks by and finally the door *does* open, and I hear people, plural, come into the room. I relax. Even if Eve is with them, she can't do anything when others are around. I feel a large presence near the side of the bed. A man?

"Mr. Liddle?" Definitely a male voice. "I'm Doctor Mintz. We hear that you're awake."

I start to grab for the oxygen mask again. "We'll remove that for a few minutes so we can chat, but it'll need to stay in place after, for a little while anyway."

I use all my strength to nod as someone pulls the mask off. I move my mouth and it feels like I've been chewing sawdust.

"How do you feel?" he asks.

It takes a minute for me to form words. "I hurt," I manage to mumble in a husky voice.

"Okay. We'll check your pain medication. Do you know what happened, Mr. Liddle?"

"Fell down the stairs," I say. I don't want to say that my wife hit me in the back of the head and knocked me down the stairs because Eve could be standing right there. She'd deny it, of course, and they'd believe her. She's one of them.

"That's right. You have a skull fracture and there was some bleeding on the brain. You were in surgery for that. You also have broken ribs on your right side along with a broken right arm, the humerus, and a couple of broken fingers. You also damaged ligaments in your right ankle. You had quite a fall, Mr. Liddle, but you're healing. It's going to take a long time, but the good news is, you survived, and you'll get well."

Easy for him to say. I already felt broken and battered and hearing my injuries described in detail only makes it worse. "How long have I been here?"

"Six days."

I can't believe it. It feels like it just happened.

"You've been in a medically induced coma to help you heal, but we backed off that medication so you'd wake up. You'll need to start regaining your strength."

"What about this bandage?" I try to raise my left arm to my eyes, but I'm so weak, it flops down on the bed. "I can't see anything." I sense an air of tension in the room. It sounds like Doctor Mintz is clicking computer keys.

"We still have tests to run. That bandage needs to stay on for now." He clears his throat. "The nurses will try to sit you up later today and we'll see if you can start tolerating a liquid diet." It sounds like he's wrapping up, moving on, but I have so many questions.

"Wait!"

"Yes?"

"Where's my wife? Where's Eve?"

A female voice pipes up, "She was here this morning, Mr. Liddle. She usually stops back in the evenings as well. I'm sure she'll be thrilled that you're awake. I'm Chloe, by the way, your nurse."

A shudder runs through me as Chloe places the oxygen mask back over my mouth.

CHAPTER 34
Rita

*I*T'S BEEN A ROUGH WEEK, AND WE'RE STILL NO CLOSER TO FINDING THE Liddle baby kidnapper. Lauren sits in my office across from me, her computer on her lap.

"Any updates on Mr. Liddle's condition?" I ask.

Lauren shakes her head. "Still unconscious as of yesterday," she replies.

Some people have no luck. He gets his baby back only to have an accident that puts him in the hospital in bad shape. "That sucks. Hopefully, he'll get better soon." I clear my throat. "How's that list coming?" Lauren's been compiling a list of everyone who we know is even tangentially in the Liddles' circle. It's a big task as she runs down all the employees at the collision shop and Doctor Thayer's hospital, as well as any friends and acquaintances that we know of.

"I've come up with dozens of people, Rita."

I nod. I'd hoped to talk to the Liddles again to get their take on the people on our list, but then he ends up in a coma. I'll talk to her anyway. It's going to be a monumental task to weed through all the names, but I don't think we have any choice. "Well, prioritize them by their closeness to the Liddles. If we know one thing about this case, it was personal." To write that message on the baby would seem to exclude any random person taking her.

"Right." Lauren sticks a pen behind her ear.

"I'm going to go out and talk to Barbara again," I say, getting to my feet.

"It can't hurt," Lauren says.

Something needs to pop. "Maybe she's thought of something she hasn't already told us."

Lauren's gaze meets mine. "Or she slips up and tells you something she meant to keep to herself."

"I don't know any more than I've told you, Detective," Barbara says, working her fingers together.

Still, I need to circle back with the people most closely connected to the case. "I appreciate that, Mrs. Singleton, but sometimes a memory surfaces later on."

She shakes her head. "I don't know."

"Have you ever been to the Liddles' home?"

"No."

"But you know where they live?"

"Well, yes. Just a few blocks from here. I know the neighborhood."

"What do you know about it?"

"Well"—she glances out the window—"it's a short walk from here. I like to walk in the mornings before Rosie . . ." Barbara starts to tear up. "So, that's how I know where they live, but I've never been in their house, Detective."

"But you regularly walk in their neighborhood?"

"Sometimes. Yes."

"Okay." I decide to change gears. I glance at my notebook, where I've started a sketch of her face. "Have there been any offers on your home?"

Her brow furrows. "No. There's been an uptick in requests to see it recently. But my agent is trying to weed out the serious people from the gawkers." Her tired blue eyes meet mine. "I can't believe people would be such ghouls."

I believe it. "We've noticed that you and your husband have been looking at homes in Calgary, Canada." This is something we discovered in the last week.

She seems surprised that I know this. "My husband is from Canada. He has dual citizenship."

We'd already found that out as well. "Does he have family there? It's an awfully long way to go. Quite a change from here."

"We're looking for some solitude, and now we figure we won't find that here." Her gaze shifts to the little end table with the photos of her son and the one of her daughter. "It's time for a change."

"You were looking at Calgary before the Liddle baby was kidnapped. Isn't that right?"

"We were considering it." She shrugs. "Is that important?"

I return her shrug. "You tell me."

She frowns. "It has nothing to do with what happened. Why would it?"

I nod, add to my sketch. She's uncomfortable. Her eyes dart around the room. I think back to the Liddles and their wild speculation that Barbara wanted to take their daughter to replace her own. Was this possible? Was Barbara thinking of taking the baby to Canada? It seems like a pretty outrageous idea, but there's something desperate about this woman. And knowing what I know now of her past, did she learn of Mr. Liddle's cheating, Eve's shortcomings, as she sees them, and have a breakdown of some sort? Did she in her mind feel like she needed to save the baby?

I notice Mr. Singleton in the doorway.

"How's it going in here?" he asks with a forced smile. After my last visit, I understand why he is protective of his wife and why he's ready to pounce if I cause her any pain.

"Fine," I say. "Would you join us?" I have a few questions for him too.

He sits next to his wife and claps his hand on her knee.

"Mr. Singleton, we hear that you two have been considering homes in Calgary."

"That's right," he says. His eyes are stern and direct.

"Why are you moving so far away?"

"I'm taking early retirement. We're looking forward to a change of scene."

I turn my attention back to Mrs. Singleton. "Were you planning to tell the Liddles that you wouldn't be able to care for their daughter much longer?"

She takes a big shuddering breath. "We'd only made the decision fairly recently. At first, we had planned to downsize and stay in the area where I could still babysit."

"What changed your plans?"

She throws up her palms in an I-don't-know gesture. "Things change. I was starting to get a little too attached to Rosie."

Her husband clears his throat. He didn't like that answer. "Really, Detective, we made the decision after our son decided to transfer to the University of Montana. We'd be closer to him there, and it was always my plan to retire in Canada."

And now, with what's happened, he wants to get her as far away from Graybridge as he can.

Mrs. Singleton nods, her gaze on the floor. "Yes. We want to stay close to Mark."

Her husband stands. "Well, we're headed out to spend a few days at our lake house, Detective. We'd like to get going."

Barbara smiles slightly. "It's my favorite place. I'll miss it if we move to Canada." She wipes tears from her cheeks. Mr. Singleton sits again and wraps an arm around her shoulders.

"Her dad bought us the house on Graybridge Lake when we got married," he explains. "We spent a lot of time there when Mark was growing up."

Barbara sniffs. "It's my happy place. I used to take Rosie there sometimes. I'd sit out on the deck with her on my lap and we'd watch the ducks. It was so peaceful."

"Canada will be peaceful, Barb," Mr. Singleton says and gives her a squeeze.

But this is interesting. Did Barbara take the baby out there the day she disappeared? Pay someone to watch her while she figured out her next move? But then she got cold feet? Again, it's a stretch, but who knows?

CHAPTER 35
Eve

*M*RS. FRASER SITS PRIMLY ON THE LIVING ROOM SOFA. SHE'D BEEN highly recommended by the agency I'd contacted. Nathan's been in the ICU for six days, and I need to get back to work soon after taking time off for his accident.

"When was the last time you took care of an infant?" I ask, looking over her resume.

"A year ago." She's wearing a purple sweater and slim black pants. Her gray hair is cut in a neat bob. She's probably in her seventies but gives off a younger vibe. "I tried retirement, and it was for the birds." She swishes her hand. "I've been taking care of kids since my own started school, and you can imagine how long ago that was. Then my husband passed about ten years ago, and I started working for the nanny company. I've been working in peoples' homes instead of taking kids in at my place. But a year ago, the family I was with moved to Florida, so I figured it was time to retire. But I don't know what to do with my time. I miss the babies." She smiles.

"I see. Mrs. Fraser—"

"Call me Joanne."

"Okay, Joanne." Rosewyn starts to cry, her voice coming through the monitor on the end table. "Let's go up and you can meet the baby."

She follows me quickly up the stairs. No problem with her mobility. That's a plus. Rosewyn is standing in her crib, holding the rail. Her tears stop when she sees me. I pick her up and she looks over my shoulder at Joanne. I turn. "You want to hold her?" I'm not sure that's the right thing to do. I still feel a little awkward around babies, even my own. Nathan always knows what to do somehow. I banish him quickly from my thoughts. I can't think about him now.

"I'm still a stranger," Joanne says. "Let her get used to me and my voice first."

"That's prudent," I murmur. I show Joanne around the room, pointing out the changing table and supplies. I outline Rosewyn's routine as we head downstairs.

When we're back in the living room, Joanne reaches for a toy in the playpen, a plastic set of keys. I sit with the baby on my lap and Joanne smiles at her.

"Hi, Rosewyn," she says, and hands her the toy. The baby takes the proffered keys and watches Joanne intently.

I need to settle a few more things before we conclude the interview. I need to know how she feels about the kidnapping. Everybody in the greater Boston area knows, and I assume the agency would've filled her in as well. "You'd be comfortable here with all that's happened to us?"

"Things happen," she replies, and there's something in her brown eyes that makes me believe her. Life is unpredictable and sometimes cruel, and I get the impression that Mrs. Fraser is of the unflappable sort. Someone who's been through her share, and that's what I want, not some wide-eyed college girl.

"Yes. We've installed a top-of-the-line security system, and the police are patrolling the neighborhood." I clear my throat and my gaze meets hers. "But the kidnapper is still out there."

"I'm not worried," she says. "I was an Army nurse in Vietnam."

I nod. Tears start to gather in my eyes, and I blink them away. She's perfect.

Joanne is going to start Monday and that takes a lot off my mind. My mother has been watching Rosewyn when I've run up to the hospital in the mornings and then Rachel has stepped in when I go up in the evenings. I make my visits short. He's unconscious anyway and doesn't know that I'm there. But I want to check on his treatment, talk to his doctors.

I'm not totally comfortable leaving Rosewyn. My mother isn't thrilled about watching her and has grumbled that it's been too many years since she's cared for a baby and doesn't know what to do. And Rachel is willing enough but is totally clueless about babies. I don't have a choice. I'm relieved that I've finally found a nanny who knows what she's doing.

The weather has turned wintry this week after a warm spell, which was fortunate for Nathan. He might've died of hypothermia otherwise. The full brunt of January chill is back and sleet pings against my face as I make my way to the hospital doors. Rachel is with Rosewyn now, as has become our evening routine. The hospital is quiet as I exit the elevator on the second floor. A nurse is coming out of Nathan's room. Chloe.

"Oh! Doctor Thayer. Doctor Mintz was supposed to call you."

My blood freezes. "What happened?"

"He's awake. We cut back on his medication. We told you that, right?"

"Yes." I do remember that, but I haven't been thinking straight these past few days. I haven't even been thinking about the possibility that Nathan would wake up soon. I've been so laser focused on Rosewyn. "That's great."

Chloe walks with me over to the nurses' station and pulls up Nathan's chart on the computer. That has been our routine as well these past few days.

"You just missed Doctor Mintz. I think he left for the day. Do you want me to call him?"

"No." I check my phone. "He left me a message." Then my eyes sweep over Nathan's chart. "I'll, uh, go check on my husband and catch up with Doctor Mintz in the morning."

"Okay," she says and closes Nathan's chart.

My heart is beating in rapid little thumps as I enter Nathan's room. It's dark and I snap on the light next to his bed. He turns his head at the sound.

"Hello, Nathan," I say. He moves his lips beneath the oxygen mask, but I have no idea what he's saying. He reaches weakly for the bandage over his eyes. I gently clutch his arm and place it back on the bed. "Leave that alone for right now. I hear you're awake. That's good." I want to say how glad I am, be cheerful and upbeat, but I just can't. I'm as kind as I can be, but my emotions are still too raw where my husband is concerned.

I see the heart monitor start to ratchet up as I sit in the hard chair next to the bed. "Relax, Nathan. You need to rest." I don't know what to say to him. I need to meet with his medical team to go over his latest tests and see what the next steps are. He's got a long way to go and it's a miracle that he even survived.

And I wonder what he remembers.

CHAPTER 36
Rita

*C*HASE, LAUREN, AND I ARE SITTING IN THE CONFERENCE ROOM. We've eliminated the real estate people, and so far, nothing has turned up in Chase's hotel search. I fill them in on what I learned from Barbara earlier, which wasn't much.

"What if they had planned to take the baby to Canada?" Lauren's eyes are wide. "Do you think they might really have tried that?"

I lean back in my chair. "Maybe in Barbara's mind that was possible, but the husband seems pretty sharp. I think he would've shut down any crazy plan. While Barbara seems to have some mental health issues, the husband seems okay. I'm pretty confident he wasn't involved in any big scheme."

Chase sips a soda. "She said she was getting too attached to the baby?"

"Yeah."

Lauren shakes her head. "Creepy."

"I think Mr. Singleton just wants to get her out of here, up to Canada for a change of scene and away from the baby. Their son's move just provided a destination. Bring her someplace where they can visit him. Maybe he was thinking that would ground her."

Lauren twirls a curly hank of hair that's fallen out of her braid. "If she did take the baby, but got scared and returned her, the husband might know that and want to prevent her from trying some-thing else."

"Could be," I say.

"But so far, we haven't found anyone who could be an accom-plice for Barbara," Lauren says, "or Donald Barry either."

Chase sets his phone on the table. "And Nicole Clark's grand-mother has vouched for her being home when the baby was ab-ducted and returned, right?"

"But I'm not sure we can trust the grandmother's memory," I say. "While I think she'd know if there was a baby in the house, she might not be so certain that Nicole was home when the baby was missing."

"How out of it was she?" Lauren asks.

"I'm not an expert, but she seemed pretty far gone to me. What did you find in Nicole's background?"

Lauren clears her throat. "She and her husband divorced two years ago. Her ex's name is Alex Clark, a local businessman. She's been living with the grandmother since. She works in Woburn."

"What's the name of the company?" I write it down as Lauren spells it out. "I'll take a ride out there."

"But she already told you she was working from home those days, right?" Chase asks.

"Yes," I say, "but maybe they heard her talk about something, or they noticed something when she *was* there." I throw my pencil on top of my notebook. "Grasping at straws here."

The office building is shiny with windows that reflect the weak winter sun. At least it's not snowing, I think as I climb out of my van. The receptionist is young and shiny like the building. She is a little discomfited when I introduce myself and show her my ID, but she calls someone she says is the manager in Nicole's department.

I'm sitting in the lobby for at least ten minutes when a stout middle-aged man in a dark suit approaches.

"How can I help you?" he asks after introductions. He remains standing, so I get to my feet.

"I'd like to ask you a few questions about Nicole Clark."

His gaze darts to the receptionist. I figure Nicole's been the talk of the facility since she was identified on the news as a person of interest in the kidnapping.

"She no longer works here, Detective."

Hmm. We didn't hear about that. "Why?"

"I can't go into that sort of personnel issue."

"Okay. Let's back up then. How long did she work here?"

"About two years."

That would coincide with her divorce. "Was she a good employee?"

"Fine. Did her work."

"She work from home a lot?"

"I'd have to check the records, but most of the employees in our department work from home a couple days a week."

"But you don't know which days she was home in the last few weeks?"

"Not without checking the records."

"Okay. Was she close to any of her coworkers?"

He shrugs. "I don't know how close she was. They all went to lunch occasionally."

"You go with them?"

"No, not usually."

This is getting me nowhere. "How well did you know her?"

He clears his throat. "Detective, I don't get chummy with the people who work for me. I know that Nicole is under suspicion in that kidnapping case. All I can tell you is when we heard about it, no one I talked to had any idea she was capable of something like that, so I guess she pretty much kept her personal life to herself. We were all really surprised."

"Okay then. You sure there isn't anyone here she was close to?"

"No. Sorry." His gaze shifts to the elevator bank. "I really need to get back to work, Detective."

"Okay. I need you to check your records. I need to know when Nicole was in the building the week the baby went missing." I hand him my card. "Call me with those details."

He smirks, looks at my card and stuffs it in his pants pocket. "Sure. I'll get that information to you." He gives me something that looks like a salute and strides quickly away and disappears into an elevator.

I stop at the receptionist's desk. "Do you know anything about Nicole Clark?" I ask. Worth a shot. Receptionists are often a wealth of information.

She looks a little uncomfortable, brushes her long, shiny dark hair over her shoulder. "I didn't really know her," she says. "But what I heard is she kept to herself. No one I know was really friends with her. We were all surprised when we heard on TV about what happened."

"Okay. Thanks." I stuff my notebook in my satchel and start for the door.

I'm halfway across the lobby when the receptionist calls me back. "Detective?"

"Yes."

"I did hear *something* . . . about Nicole," she whispers. "But it has nothing to do with the baby."

My eyes meet hers. "Tell me anyway."

"I heard that she got fired for harassing a woman in her department."

"Harassing how?"

"Social media stuff. You know, really juvenile crap. I overheard someone talking about it in the cafeteria. The woman Nicole was harassing went to HR and they fired Nicole."

"What's this woman's name?" I ask as I dig for my notebook.

The receptionist shakes her head. "I don't know her. It's a big company." She bites her lip and her gaze shoots to the elevator bank. "I shouldn't have said anything. I just overheard someone talking. I don't want to get in trouble."

"I understand." She hasn't told me anything I can really use anyway, but it's interesting just the same and adds to what we know about Nicole, if it's the truth. It's about two steps beyond hearsay.

"I thought I should tell you. It's awful what happened to that baby."

"Thank you. Don't worry, I won't tell anybody what you said."

She smiles and nods and I stuff my notebook back in my satchel.

CHAPTER 37
Nathan

*I*T'S MORNING. I FEEL THE SUNSHINE FROM THE WINDOW. EVE WAS HERE last night, but I couldn't talk to her since they won't take this freaking oxygen mask off. What would I say to her anyway? Maybe she's sorry for what she did. Maybe she's not angry anymore. But I don't want to let my guard down yet.

My door opens and there are several people in the room. I can feel it, hear their footsteps.

"Mr. Liddle? It's Doctor Mintz and Doctor Goldberg. Your nurse Chloe and your wife are here as well. We're taking off the oxygen mask for good now. Your numbers have come up enough for that."

Chloe, I think, gently removes it.

"How are you feeling?" he continues.

I stretch my jaw. "Okay. A little better. Can someone take the bandage off my eyes, though?"

"In a minute. First, we want to go over the next steps." He clears his throat and something in his voice has me on alert. "We're moving you to a rehab facility and fortunately there's one here in Graybridge, right next to the hospital where your wife works as a matter of fact." He chuckles. Why is that funny? "So, it'll be convenient. Over there, they'll work on getting you back on your feet. Helping you manage your physical recovery. Also"—he clears his throat again—"they'll do some cognitive testing over there as well."

My stomach clenches and I catch my breath. "Do you think my fall caused brain damage?" I stammer.

"We don't have all the answers yet, Mr. Liddle. You did have substantial intracranial bleeding."

"So far, our tests indicate that any damage may be minimal or reversible," another man says. Must be Doctor Goldberg. But I shudder at this news.

"Like what kind of damage?"

"Memory issues. Perhaps some cognitive difficulties."

I think Eve nears the side of the bed. I can feel her next to me. I grab at the bandage over my eyes and cold slim fingers stop me.

But then Doctor Mintz says, "Chloe, go ahead and remove it." She's standing on my other side. I feel the tape pull at my skin and cold air flit across my brow.

"Is it off?" I gasp.

"Yes," Doctor Mintz says. He's leaning over me. I can smell the coffee on his breath. I feel the warmth of a light in my eyes. He stands back, light gone. "What can you see, Mr. Liddle?"

I swallow. Panic fills my chest. "Nothing."

CHAPTER 38
Eve

*J*OANNE SHOWED UP BRIGHT AND EARLY THIS MORNING. I WAS STILL GETting ready for work, glancing at the clock every couple of minutes and second-guessing myself. Should I go back already? But I want my life back, some semblance of it anyway. Between the kidnapping and now Nathan's accident, I hardly recognize myself anymore. My life had been on such a calm, linear plane before my husband. Work and fun, and both pursued with a vengeance. Since I met Nathan, nothing has gone according to plan. It all went crazy after someone ran me off the road, which caused the damage to my car, which led me to Nathan. It's been two years that my life took on a direction of its own and I feel out of control.

Standing in the powder room, I close my eyes a moment. I hear Joanne talking to Rosewyn and hear the baby giggle. I try to drink in that normalcy, but I'm afraid. Maybe for the first time in my life. My mind seems to want to delve into places I'd rather not go. I've never questioned my own mental health, but I'm thinking about what Brian said at work. Do I need to talk to someone? I feel like I might break into a thousand pieces, fall apart and never get back up if I let it out.

I slick on lipstick and run a brush through my hair one more time before heading into the kitchen. Rosewyn is sitting in her highchair. She smiles when she sees me and I almost cry. I've got to keep it together if only for my little girl.

There's fresh coffee in the pot. Joanne hands me my travel mug. "Black," she says. "That's how you take it, right?"

"Yes. Thank you. Do you have the list I gave you?"

Joanne pats the countertop. "Right here." She sits next to Rosewyn and places a small plastic bowl with diced bananas in it on her tray. "We'll be fine, Eve."

"You remember how to set the alarm?"

"Yes."

"You have your phone nearby?"

"In my pocket." She smiles. "Don't worry."

But I do as I drive into work.

They're moving Nathan to the rehab center this morning. He isn't taking the possibility of permanent vision loss, perhaps nearly complete loss, very well, as is to be expected. While some of his sight might return, we don't know at this point. He had little to say when I visited him over the weekend. I didn't have much to say either. I have no idea how this new life is going to work. I guess we'll figure it out. I shouldn't project. Take it one day at a time.

Even though it's my first day back and my schedule is full to bursting, I manage to sneak out for a quick visit with Nathan just before lunch. I want to make sure that he's settled in at the rehab center.

The room is small. I imagine the space was originally designed for two people back in the forties and was divided during the remodel. People today expect a degree of privacy that old facilities didn't have. The walls are painted gray and there are several cheap prints hanging there. The room has a medicinal smell over the slight smell of mold. Nathan's in bed, which is raised until he is nearly sitting, his eyes closed, and I don't know if he's asleep. On the bedside table, a dull pink plastic pitcher sits next to a plastic cup and a small square box of tissues. It's a dreary room, very hospital-like, and I sigh. Corporate seems to have skimped on this building's remodel maybe even more so than on my building.

"Nathan?" I call softly.

He opens his eyes, but they remain unfocused, and I feel my stomach clench. No matter what I think about my husband, I didn't want this for him.

"Eve?"

"Yes. I wanted to see that you were settled in."

He nods. "Yeah. Here I am," he says flatly. "You found me."

"When did you get here?"

"I don't know. A couple of hours ago."

"Can I get you anything?"

"No."

"Have the doctors been in?"

"When I first got here."

"What did they say?"

"Not too much."

He obviously doesn't want to talk. I glance at my phone. I need to hurry back. There's a clatter in the hall and a round-faced, cheerful aide walks in with a tray. "Lunch, Mr. Liddle," she calls.

He doesn't respond as she places the tray on his bedside table.

"I'll be right back to help you," she says. "Unless your wife . . ."

"She's got to get back to work," he snaps. "I'll manage."

The aide's face reddens. "Okay. I'll come back and check on you."

After she leaves, I walk over to the table. "I can stay a few minutes, Nathan. Are you sure you don't want help?"

He shakes his head. "How is Rosewyn? That's what I want. I want to see my daughter."

"I'll bring her by. I'll have Joanne meet me here sometime this week when I can get away."

"How's the new nanny working out?" I'd told him over the weekend about Joanne.

Rosewyn is all we talk about.

"She's amazing so far. But it's the first day. I'm keeping close tabs."

"You're keeping the alarm set?"

"Of course."

"Are the cops patrolling the neighborhood like Detective Myers said they would."

"Yes. I'm being careful, believe me."

"That's good." He turns his face toward the window and closes his eyes.

"Well, I do need to get back. Get some rest, Nathan."

CHAPTER 39
Rita

MR. LIDDLE WANTS ME TO STOP BY THE REHAB CENTER WHERE HE'S been moved. It was great news that he regained consciousness, but I guess he's still pretty banged up. Some people can't catch a break and it looks like the Liddles are some of those people. I pull into the lot in front of the low-slung building that sits a stone's throw from the psychiatric hospital where Doctor Thayer works. Convenient.

I pull up my collar against the cold wind as I walk to the sliding glass front doors. I sign in and follow the hallway down to room 116.

He's sitting in one of those generic, vinyl-covered armchairs that are about as comfortable as a slab of concrete. He looks a little better actually than the last time I saw him, back after the baby was found. He looks like someone has washed him up, given him a shave. He has that baby pink look of someone who's been tended and recently scrubbed. He's wrapped in a flannel robe.

I knock on the open door. "Mr. Liddle?" He appears to be gazing out the window. And I see that while he has hair on the front of his head, the back is shaved and there's a row of stitches like train tracks across the back of his skull.

"Yes?"

"Detective Myers."

"Come in," he says. "Thanks for coming." He clears his throat and runs his good hand over his eyes.

I start to sit in a chair that's across the room when he says, "Would you shut the door?"

"Sure, no problem." I thought he wanted an update on the kidnapping, but now I'm wondering. Something seems off. "How are you feeling?" I ask as I sit.

He licks his lips. His eyes seem to wander, to focus on nothing.

"Just so you know, Detective, I can't see you. You're alone, aren't you?"

"Yes." This isn't good. I knew he was in bad shape. I didn't know his accident had left him *blind.*

"Good." He sniffs. "I'm in a rough spot here, Detective."

"I'm sorry about that."

"What progress have you made on my daughter's case?"

"Well, we're working it with every resource we have, but there isn't any news since I talked to your wife yesterday."

"You are providing protection in case the kidnapper tries again?" His voice is hoarse.

"Yes. We have a cruiser in the neighborhood on a regular basis."

"Good. What's next?"

"We're going to look at everyone the two of you know, expand our circle. I did want to ask if you thought of anyone we should prioritize, anybody we haven't talked to so far?"

He shakes his head. "I can't think of anyone."

"So, what else can I do for you?"

He grimaces. "I haven't told anybody this yet. You're the first, but I want this on the record, in case."

"Okay." I reach for my notebook, pull it out of my satchel. "What do you want to tell me?"

"I didn't just fall down the stairs, Detective," he says quickly, as if trying to get the words out fast. "My wife knocked me down the stairs. She hit me in the back of the head with something."

I lean back in my chair, dangle my notebook over the armrest. I wasn't expecting *that.* "Are you *sure?*"

"Yes, I'm sure," he snaps. "I wasn't that drunk!"

I open my notebook to a fresh page. "Let's back up. What do you remember from that night?" I scribble down the date when the accident occurred.

"I was out on the deck. It was morning. I think, but really early, still dark. I was having a cigarette. We'd been fighting the night before. Well, she'd been fighting. I just stood there and took it. Apologized. Tried to explain."

"How did the argument start?"

He tips up his head as if looking at the ceiling, blows out a breath. "She came home from work and Rosewyn was in the playpen. I'd only been out on the deck a couple of minutes. But the baby was crying and Eve exploded." He runs his hand over his mouth. "We hadn't really talked, Detective. In the days after we got Rosewyn back, we didn't talk about, you know, the message. I didn't know what to say except sorry. Eve didn't want to hear it. She didn't want to hear anything. She told me to move into the guest room, which I did. Then we decided that I would take care of the baby while she went back to work. But we didn't discuss . . . what I did. I didn't know what to say and Eve just closed up. I knew she was furious, and I didn't blame her. But we needed to talk, and that wasn't happening. That night when she came home and the baby was crying, she went crazy. She took the baby upstairs and put her to bed. Then Eve came back down. She wanted to know all about Nicole and how we met and all that. She was livid."

His unfocused gaze swings in my direction.

"Detective, she said she could kill me."

Okay. Many a wife has said those very words to an erring husband. "Then what happened?"

He shrugs. "I stayed downstairs. She went back upstairs. I fell asleep on the couch. Then I woke up, but it was still dark. I went out on the deck for a smoke. Then next thing I know she hits me in the back of the head, and I fall. I remember falling and the pain. Then I wake up in the hospital six days later." He whooshes out a breath.

"There was nothing unusual in the police report," I say. I'd looked at it when we'd heard about Mr. Liddle's fall. "It was listed as an accident." But I'll pull the report and give it another read.

His face reddens. "Who wouldn't believe my wife? The well-respected Doctor Eve Thayer."

Okay. This is possible and needs following up. I admit, we as a society aren't quick to look at women in spousal abuse cases. "I'll need to speak to your doctors, Mr. Liddle. I'll need to see your medical records."

"I'll sign whatever damn forms you need. I just feel vulnerable now that I can't see a fucking thing. I wouldn't be able to see her coming."

"Okay, Mr. Liddle. We'll look into it."

"Thanks," he says. "Oh, and I don't want her to know. Eve. Just keep this between us for now."

"Okay. But I'll have to see where it leads."

"Yeah. I know. Just don't tell her I accused her, okay? Not yet anyway."

"All right."

"I'll call my nurse to get whatever release forms you need to see my records."

"Good deal," I say.

Back at the station, the afternoon flies by. I look over Lauren's list and we try to figure out a game plan for how to attack it. Doctor Thayer hadn't been any more help than her husband had been when I'd asked her about prioritizing the people on it.

But Mr. Liddle's latest revelation sits in the back of my mind like a snarling beast. I reread the report our officers filed on the accident. They didn't see anything at the scene that aroused their suspicions. No evidence that this was anything other than an accident.

Near the end of the day, I get a call from the rehab center. Mr. Liddle's doctor can meet with me on my way home.

We're sitting in a small consultation room that is cold as hell. The walls are painted gray and there's a framed print of two happy penguins on the wall. Seems out of place in this dreary building.

Doctor Lassiter looks to be about eighty years old. His thick glasses keep riding down his drooping nose and I'm antsy, worrying they're going to drop onto the file folder he has open on the table.

He goes into medical-speak, detailing Mr. Liddle's injuries.

"I'm interested in his head injury, Doctor." Then he launches into more medicalese. "Was it consistent with the fall that he took?"

Doctor Lassiter peers at me quizzically. "Yes. His injuries are all consistent with someone having fallen down twelve steps and hitting concrete below. Also, his blood alcohol was twice the legal limit."

Hmm. "What about his vision loss? Is that permanent?"

"We don't know at this point. He had bleeding on the brain."

"What about his memory? Was that compromised?"

"Could be. Most patients don't remember what actually happened to them in a case like this."

"What about cognitive function?"

"Too early to tell." He looks at his watch, a big gold piece like you might get at a retirement party.

"I need your opinion, Doctor. From a medical standpoint, is there any reason to believe that Mr. Liddle might have sustained a head injury right *before* he fell down the stairs."

Doctor Lassiter leans closer to the folder on the table. His glasses slide. He shuffles through a couple of papers. Then he sits back in his chair. "There's nothing here that indicates that, Detective. But we can't say for sure either way."

The doctors wouldn't have been overly concerned about how their patient was injured. They would've been focused on treatment. The how would be up to law enforcement. Did we drop the ball? If Mr. Liddle had died, an autopsy might have given us the information we needed, but since he survived, that, of course, didn't happen. That makes our job, especially days after the fact, much more challenging.

I head back out to my van. Could Doctor Thayer have been so angry that she hit her husband and caused him to fall down the stairs? I didn't get that impression when I spoke to her afterwards. No vibes from her that this was anything other than an accident. I think back to our conversations. She's a bit of an enigma. Quiet. Austere. Emotions usually well hidden. Even when their daughter was missing, she seemed to hold up much better than her husband. But am I speculating? Reading too much into this? Mr. Liddle has been through awful trauma. Sometimes it's hard for people to admit that their misfortunes are just damn bad luck. They want to assign blame. It's a common human reaction.

I sigh. I need to get home, have some dinner, and pour myself a glass of wine.

CHAPTER 40
Eve

ON MY WAY HOME, MY PHONE RINGS, AND I STIFFEN. WHAT IF IT'S Joanne? What if something has gone wrong? I picture a shadowy figure circling the house, watching through the window, his eyes on my baby. Joanne calling in a panic.

I dig my phone out of my purse at a red light. Rachel. I sigh and put her on speaker.

"Hey. How was your first day back?" she asks.

"Fine. Busy."

"Well, I'm standing on your porch, but the new nanny won't let me in until she checks with you first."

That's good, I think to myself. "Hang on. She's calling now." I switch lines. Peep up in my rearview mirror to make sure there aren't any cops around to see me on my phone.

"Hello, Joanne? Is everything all right?"

"Hi, Eve. Yes. But I wanted to double check with you. There's a Rachel Chapman at the door. She says she's your best friend, but I wanted to talk to you before I let her in."

"That's fine. She can come in. Thank you for checking." I switch back to Rachel. "You've been cleared."

"Thanks. I'll see you when you get here."

* * *

The house is clean and Rosewyn is smiling in Joanne's arms. I let go a breath of relief. Joanne gives me a quick run-down on their day as she gathers her purse and jacket. I walk her to the door, feeling some sense of calm that day one went so well.

In the kitchen, I set Rosewyn in her highchair where she picks up a small plastic horse and starts banging the tray with it. Rachel is sitting at the table with a glass of wine.

"So, everything went okay today?" Rachel asks.

"As good as can be expected. I was really busy, but I had a few minutes, so I ran over to see that Nathan was okay. They moved him to the rehab center this morning."

"Why do you give a shit, Eve? Let him take care of himself."

I sit next to Rosewyn. "What am I supposed to do? His mom's dead. His brother is in California. His dad is almost as useless as my mother is."

"Still. He's a grown man. Let that skank he was seeing take care of him."

Annoyed, I stand and go to the fridge. "He's blind, Rachel. Maybe permanently."

"That sucks. Really?"

"Yes. Really," I say as I pour myself a glass of red.

"Well, you could help out with getting him set up with resources. Caretakers. Whatever. Then I'd cut him loose. You're not going to stay with him after what he put you through?"

I sit back at the table and drop my head in my hands. "I can't think about this now. It's too soon."

"Sorry. I'm here anyway. I'll do what I can to support you, Eve."

But I hear it in her voice, the contempt for Nathan.

It's after eight o'clock when Rachel finally leaves. She sat at the table drinking wine while I fed Rosewyn her dinner and then got her ready for bed. Rachel prattled on about work and her dull social life until I finally started yawning and made excuses about my early day tomorrow.

I glance out the sliding glass door. I don't see any lights on over at Ms. Parnell's. Everything sits in darkness over there and I relax a little. The baby is asleep and the house is quiet. I remember that I had no dinner and search the fridge. I pull out a container of fried rice and sit in the living room with it and a glass of water. I click on the TV for company, but I'm not really watching it.

I know Rachel means well, but something has shifted between us. We were great for each other back when I was single. But I didn't want to be one of those people who gets married and turns her back on her single friend, so we've managed to stay close. But now I'm starting to realize that we've moved in different directions. I don't feel the same sense of closeness that we once had. She's starting to drain my energy. But we've been friends forever. Shared so much. I don't want to lose her friendship. So, what to do? I put on my therapist thinking cap. Redefine the friendship. Tell her how I feel. My need for different social activities. Maybe invite her to go with me and Rosewyn to the zoo when the weather gets warm. Ask her over with other friends for a casual evening at home. All the normal things people our age do.

But what about Nathan? Where does he fit into my life? *Does* he fit into my life?

My eyes keep shifting to the kitchen and the sliding glass door. I can almost see Nathan standing on the deck and I admit to myself that I miss him. The house seems so empty. I knew we had grown apart. I knew my marriage wasn't healthy, and I wonder now how it had gotten so off track. Maybe because we didn't take enough time to get to know one another before we got married. Then the pregnancy. Then my promotion. It was too fast. Too much. And we let our relationship get lost in all the drama.

I sigh. Nathan's infidelity hurts almost like a physical pain in my stomach, something sharp and acute. Different from what I felt from my parents' neglect when I was growing up. That pain was slow and burning and grew as I grew. When I was a child, there was no real nurturing, no feeling that I was important in my parents' lives, so I turned to accomplishments for reassurance that I was worthy. Then to friendships and to fleeting relationships. But sitting here in my midthirties, I feel entirely lost. Nothing in my life seems to have filled that void left by my parents and I wonder if I *should* talk to someone. Would it help? We know that damage done in childhood is often there for good although there are ways to cope, of course, to live with it and still be happy. And I wonder if I have been coping in a healthy way. But I know the answer to that. When the going got tough, parenting, work, I pulled away from Nathan instead of growing closer to him, confiding in him. I think I figured he'd let me down just like my parents. And then he did.

I tip my head back, close my eyes. What do I do now?

CHAPTER 41
Nathan

*F*IGURING OUT WHAT DAY IT IS HAS BEEN HELL. BUT A COUPLE DAYS have passed since I got here, and I've been put through the wringer with PT. They've got me up with a walker and they take me up and down the hall like I'm a dog out for a stroll, a therapist with a hand on my shoulder instead of a leash. They've also run a bunch of tests, but the one I'm most worried about concerns my vision. If I only could get that back, I'd be a happy man. I can deal with a few broken bones. But what am I going to do if I can't see? How am I going to take care of my daughter? I start to tear up thinking of Rosewyn as I sit by the window in my room. I sit here every day like a potted plant.

A wave of anger washes over me. I can almost feel the chemicals in my brain rushing through the passageways there, releasing a tide of fury. But at whom? Eve? Nicole? Myself?

My dinner, such as it is, sits on the bedside table. I'm managing to eat on my own okay. I've refused any help in that department. I don't want to be fed like a baby. If I spill and make a mess, that's the way it goes. I switch on the TV to have some noise in the room, and to hopefully drown out the voices in my head. Voices telling me I'll never see my daughter's face again. I've just about mastered the remote by feel. I can turn it on and off, adjust the volume. I leave the channel on 24-hour news. I started messing with that yesterday and ended up on some women's show where they were discussing menopause, so once I found the news again, I left it there. So I've gotten a steady dose of all that's wrong in the world. At least it helps keep my mind off my own problems.

Eve is supposed to bring Rosewyn by sometime this week. About damn time, but she says that she's super busy at work since she'd been out so much. At least she can go to work. I'll probably get fired. They can't legally do that now because I'm in the hospital, but they'll let a few months go by and find a reason to let me go. Corporate America for you. Then what will I do? Live off the government, I guess.

I take a deep breath. I don't like what I'm turning into. My nurse says it's normal to have some depression after a head injury. They're giving me something for that, but I don't know that it's working. I'm either wallowing in self-pity or biting someone's head off, and I can't seem to stop myself. I was never that guy. I need to do better. Be better. If for nothing else, at least for Rosewyn.

"Knock, knock. Nathan?"

It takes me a second, but I finally recognize the voice. "*Nicole?*"

"Yes. It's me. I heard . . . what happened."

She moves close to my chair. I don't know why she's here and it makes me anxious. But it's not like she's a secret anymore. It was on the freaking news that I was cheating on my wife. Like that is anyone's business. But still, I don't want Eve to run into Nicole and give her more reason to finish me off.

"Mind if I sit?" she asks.

"Fine. Sure." I hear her drag the visitor's chair near me.

"I'm so sorry, Nathan, about it all. How are you feeling?"

"Okay."

"Well, I wanted you to know that I was thinking about you, praying."

"Appreciate it."

"And I'm moving. I got a job in New York. I didn't want to leave without stopping by, and, I know, um, you can't see a text right now."

"Yeah. It's been tough, Nicole." I'm uncomfortable with her here. Who knows if she was the one who took Rosewyn? I don't think so, but she is a suspect.

"What are they saying, you know, about your vision?"

I shrug. "How did you hear about that?"

"I overheard the nurses talking."

Great. So much for privacy. "They don't know right now. It might get better." I hear her sniff. But I really don't want her pity. "So, you're moving on?"

"It's for the best. I need a change of scene."

I take a deep breath. "Did the cops talk to you about the baby?"

"Yes. But I couldn't tell them anything."

I try to gauge her tone. Would she be here talking so nonchalantly if she was the kidnapper? "They asked me all about you," I say. "Somehow, they found out about us."

"Who knew, Nathan? I didn't tell anyone."

"Me neither." But the message written on Rosewyn proves that someone knew.

We fall silent. I'm waiting for her to say something that might implicate her. She'd have to be a psycho to have taken Rosewyn, and I didn't get that impression when I was with her, obviously. She seemed so normal. But you never can tell. Eve says that people are awfully good at hiding their true selves.

"Do they have any clues?" she asks. "Do they have a suspect yet?"

"I don't know. They haven't told us much."

"Well, I'm glad you got the baby back safely. And I really hope that you're good as new soon." I hear her get to her feet.

"Thanks."

"I remember this place," Nicole says, her voice soft, reflective.

"What do you mean?"

"It was years ago." She sighs. "It was part of the mental hospital. Creepy. But it's nicer now. They've remodeled."

"How did you know about it?"

"Just local lore. And when I was a teenager, it was vacant. The state closed it down. My friends and I used to drive over here to party. Stupid things teenagers do."

I nod. I don't have anything more to say to her. I really wish she'd leave.

"Well, I'll let you eat your dinner," she says. "I just wanted to say goodbye."

I thought we'd already done that a while ago, but, whatever. "Have a good one," I say for lack of anything better.

I'm a little sleepy. They had me walking the halls forever today and that's the most exercise I've had since before I got hurt. But I better eat before my dinner gets cold. It's unappetizing enough when it's hot. I pull my rolling table over to my chair and start on what I think is Salisbury steak and mashed potatoes.

After a while, a nurse comes in to get me settled for the night. I still need help getting into the tiny bathroom, brushing my teeth and all that. Finally, I'm in bed and she snaps off the light and I'm alone again. Funny that they still turn the light on and off every day. Not like I need it. Oh, well, I guess they do.

I'm drifting in a dark dream land. I think I'm dreaming. My life has become one bad dream and it's hard to tell when I'm awake or asleep sometimes. I'm out on the deck. I can smell my cigarette, but I'm not the one smoking. Eve is smoking, leaning against the railing, looking at me like I'm the most despicable thing she's ever seen. She takes a long drag, then exhales the smoke between her red-painted lips. *Where's the baby, Nathan? What have you done with the baby?* But I can't speak. I don't know where Rosewyn is, and panic fills my chest. I try to run, to look for her, but I can't move. My feet are cemented to the deck and Eve starts walking closer.

I feel a gust of air rush over me. A cool hand touches my fore-head, brushing back my hair. I'm awake. I shudder. A nurse wouldn't touch me in so intimate a way.

"Who is it?" I call into the dark. "Eve?" I can barely speak. "What are you doing here so late?" I think it's late. I feel for my call button, my fingers tangling in the sheet, but I can't find it, and my heart starts thumping so hard I think she can hear it. Her hand slides smoothly down over my cheek and I try to grab it, but I'm still so awkward with my left hand that I miss, and she pulls her hand away and touches my chest, leans on it a moment, as if she's thinking of smothering me. I'm panicking, sweating, trying to yell, but I can't seem to make a sound. But then she moves away.

I hear her walking around my room, picking up bottles on my bedside table, putting them down again. What's she up to? I try to sit up. I need to get out of here and into the hall where someone will see me. They are short staffed, especially at night, but there should be someone around.

She's by my side again and pushes me back into bed. I flail my good arm around trying to catch her, but she's like a will-o'-the-wisp, here and gone in an instant. I hear the door open and close. Did she leave? I flop back down on the bed. I'm sweating like a pig. Did she come back to kill me? Will she try again?

I struggle to my feet. She could come back. I need to get out into the hall and call for help. I stagger toward where I think the door is and bang into a chair and nearly fall over. *Fuck. That hurt.* I reach out and feel along the wall until my hand brushes against the door-knob. I turn it and I'm through. It's colder out here and I hear footsteps in the distance. *Eve?* I shudder.

"Mr. Liddle?" It's the older night nurse.

I exhale. Safe. "Is she here? Did you see her?"

"Who?"

"A woman. A woman was in my room."

"There's nobody here. You were dreaming. Let's get you back into bed." She grabs my arm and walks me back inside. I don't know whether I believe her or not. *Was I dreaming? Am I dreaming now?* I don't fucking know.

Back in my bed, I stay wide awake in the dark. In my perpetual darkness for the rest of the night. Or maybe the rest of my life.

CHAPTER 42
Eve

I'VE ONLY BEEN BACK AT WORK A FEW DAYS AND I'M ALREADY EX-
hausted. My last appointment canceled, which helps, but I'm prac-
tically seeing double as I work at my computer and my head is
throbbing. I don't get a lot of headaches, but when I do, they're
brutal.

"Eve?" Brian is leaning in at my door.

"Yeah?"

"Just wondered how you were doing."

I sigh. I want to lie and say I'm terrific, but I don't have the
strength. "Fine if it weren't for this headache from hell."

He walks inside and shuts the door. "You need something for it?"

"I just took two ibuprofen. That should help, hopefully."

"How's Nathan?"

"Coming along okay."

"That's good." Brian fidgets with his collar. "Mr. Jacobson was
talking to me about a new inpatient coming Monday. I told him
that based on the patient's records, you'd be a better fit, but he
wants me to take him." Brian looks at me sheepishly, like he's
stabbed me in the back or something.

"That's fine. I can consult if you'd like."

"That would be great."

I think Brian feels guilty. Since I've been out so much, he's been taking over the lead medical position duties, *my* duties, holding meetings, supervising staff. In the past, I'd have been angry. I worked too hard for the top spot to let it slip away, but now, things are different. Now I can't run my personal life, let alone my professional one. "Don't worry about it, Brian. I really do appreciate all you've done since I've been out so much. It's fine." I glance at my phone. It's just after four o'clock.

"You need to go home?" he asks.

"I don't have another appointment this afternoon." I shouldn't leave now, but I feel terrible.

"I can do your evening rounds."

I lean back in my chair and rub my eyes with my palms.

"Really, Eve. Go home and get some rest. You've had more on your plate these last few weeks than anybody should deal with in a lifetime. Amanda and I were talking about that the other day. We're in a good spot right now. Her mom's here from Ohio, so we've got plenty of help at home. Look, there might come a time when I need *your* help."

I nod and swallow. "Thank you. When my life gets straightened out, you can count on me for anything, Brian. I really appreciate it."

"No problem."

He leaves and I tidy my desk. I grab my purse from my drawer and hesitate. Should I just tough it out? How is it going to look when the staff sees Brian checking on my patients? I glance at my office door. Brian is so nice, such a good colleague. But I wonder. Is he maybe after my job? Is that possible? For all his kindness, I've never met a doctor who wasn't ambitious. You don't last long if you're not at least somewhat driven. I shake my head. *Get a grip, Eve.* There's no reason to think that Brian is anything but a concerned friend. I flick off my office light and head out.

My headache does start to ease off as I drive toward home. I'd texted Joanne to let her know I was on my way, so she isn't surprised when I walk through the door more than two hours early. She and Rosewyn are in the living room, toys scattered over a colorful blanket on the floor.

"Are you feeling any better?" Joanne asks as I pick up Rosewyn.

"Yes."

"I can stay if you need to lie down."

"No, thank you though. I'm fine." We walk out into the kitchen where Joanne starts gathering her things.

I stand at the sliding glass door when I notice something in the yard. "What is that?"

Joanne walks to my side. "I saw it earlier. I thought it might be one of Rosewyn's toys."

I hand Rosewyn to Joanne. "Stay here. I'll go take a look."

I turn on the flood light and gingerly make my way down the steep deck steps and traipse through the patchy snow. About halfway between the deck and the back fence I find a doll lying on its back. I stop and catch my breath. Its white dress is covered in what looks like blood. And someone has scribbled over its eyes with what looks like a black Sharpie. I step back, reach into my pocket for my phone, and call Detective Myers.

She says she's on her way, not to touch anything. I'm shivering, my arms clasped around my stomach. I hear noise from over the fence.

"Ms. Parnell?" I call.

She appears at the fence in a spot where the boards have fallen away.

"Hey, Eve. What's up?"

"I found something in my yard and wondered if you knew anything about it."

She leans over and squeezes through the fence. "What is it?"

I don't answer, just point, and let her look for herself.

"What the hell? Not your kid's, I take it?"

"No. It's not ours."

"Is that blood or just mud?"

"I don't know. I hope it's mud."

Ms. Parnell turns and glances back at her house. "Wonder if it was those boys."

"The teens you think are breaking into your house?"

"Yeah. Those delinquents. I wouldn't put it past them. Or maybe it's someone else who's been breaking in."

I shudder, thinking of the kidnapper. "Has anything else gone missing?"

"Not that I've been able to tell."

"I called the police. Detectives are on the way."

"Good. Can't be too careful." Ms. Parnell's brows draw together. "Sorry about all the trouble you've had. You think this is related to that?"

"I don't know. The cops are looking into it."

Ms. Parnell puts her hands on her hips. "Geez, I hope not. You've got cameras up now, right?" She shades her eyes, peers up at the back of my house.

"Yes."

"Maybe it was just those boys," she soothes. "The video ought to tell. I wouldn't put it past those hooligans."

I hope she's right, but my gaze wanders to her upstairs windows, the ones that face the back of my house.

CHAPTER 43
Rita

*C*hase and I make our way across the Liddle backyard. Eve and Ms. Parnell are standing over the doll that Eve told me about on the phone. Don't know if it's anything, but we'll see.

"When did you notice it?" I ask Eve.

"Just a little while ago. I called you as soon as I came out here and saw what it was. But my babysitter said she'd seen it from the window this morning and assumed it belonged to my daughter."

The doll looks like someone dripped blood all over it and scribbled over its eyes with black marker. Creepy. "Nobody's touched it?" I ask, and Ms. Parnell and Eve say that they didn't.

"Chase, take pictures, would you?" He's better at that than I am.

We all step back while my partner pulls out his phone and snaps away. When he's finished, I pull on latex gloves and lean over the toy.

"Is it blood?" Ms. Parnell asks.

"Looks like it, but we'll know for sure after it goes to the lab. Would you two mind backing up?" I say, not wanting either Eve or her neighbor to see what I might find as I examine the doll. The head, arms, and legs are plastic, but the body is stuffed with a soft material. I gingerly lift the doll's dress, and it appears that something is written on its stomach. I turn on my phone flashlight to get a better look. Written in black ink are the words:

Watch Your Back

Same person. No one but law enforcement and the parents know that a message was written on the Liddle baby. I pat the dress back down; I don't need anyone to see that right now. This changes things.

I turn to Ms. Parnell. "You ever get those cameras?"

"Not yet. Haven't had time."

Eve pipes up. "We have cameras, Detective. We just had a whole security system put in." She moves next to me and points up at the back of her house. "That camera should've caught whoever was back here."

This is good news. "Chase, call the crime scene team to come out and make sure no one comes into the yard while Eve and I go into the house and look at the video."

Eve huffs out a tearful breath. "Why would someone do this? Do you think it was the kidnapper?" she croaks.

"I don't know, but we'll do everything we can to find out." Maybe this whole case can be wrapped up in short order if the video captured the perp. "Ms. Parnell, I'll need you to stay away from the scene." Her brow furrows. "But keep an eye out for anyone hanging around your place."

She nods. "I'll keep a look out." She reluctantly heads for the open spot in the fence. "Let me know if you guys need anything, Eve," she says as she steps over into her own yard.

The babysitter is standing in the kitchen holding the baby. "Everything all right?" she asks.

Eve says, "Hopefully, it was just a prank."

But she doesn't know about the message yet. We sit at the kitchen table and Eve pulls up the video on a laptop and runs it back to last night.

The yard is eerie in the darkness, and I wait eagerly to see a figure approach, but that's not what we see. At 12:54 a.m., all is quiet. No one around. Then the doll comes flying through the air from

Ms. Parnell's yard and lands in the Liddle backyard. The fence shields the perp from view.

"He or she must've known about the cameras," Eve says. "They knew that we have cameras now." Her voice is breathy, worried.

"Maybe," I say, and stand, pull out my phone. I walk into the living room and call Chase, let him know that Ms. Parnell's yard is also part of the crime scene.

Back in the kitchen, Eve is at the window. "Maybe it *was* just those boys that Ms. Parnell said hang out on her street. They might've seen my cameras. Kids are nosey and they can be cruel, not realizing how badly they can hurt people."

I hesitate. I don't want to scare her, but she needs to know. "Eve, that's not all." She turns to face me. "There was a message written on the doll's stomach."

"You're *kidding*?" She hits the counter with her fist. "What did it say?"

I clear my throat. "Watch your back."

"Who is doing this, Detective? What did we ever do to deserve this?" Her voice has grown hoarse, just this side of frantic.

"We're going to find out and arrest the culprit, Eve." I put my hand on her arm. "In the meantime, we'll have a cruiser in front of your house, and we'll step up our patrols of the neighborhood."

"It must be the same person, right?" She blinks away tears.

"Unless news of the first message leaked, that would be my guess. Let's see what forensics finds. Maybe there's something else out there that can help us."

"Do you want me to stay?" the babysitter asks Eve.

"No." Eve squares her shoulders. "We're fine, Joanne. You might as well go home. I won't let whoever is doing this impact our lives if I can help it. I'll see you in the morning."

Eve takes the baby and walks Joanne to the front door.

I walk over to the sliding glass door and see that Hugo and his team have just arrived and are setting up lights.

Eve returns to the kitchen and sets the baby in her highchair.

"I'll be outside lending a hand," I say.

"Let me know if you find anything," she says, her lips trembling.

* * *

It's cold as hell and our breath lingers in the lights as bursts of steam. But we need to get this done. Chase is dogging Hugo's steps, watching and learning. Then a tech calls from the side of the Liddles' yard.

We gather around a basement wall where a neat pile of firewood is stacked. A young tech shines his flashlight behind the pile.

I step forward, Chase at my shoulder. There's a crowbar wedged behind the wood.

"Is that hair?" Chase asks.

"Move your flashlight closer," I tell the kid.

"It's hair," I say. "And maybe blood as well." I step back, blow out a breath. How did the guys miss this when Mr. Liddle fell? I squeeze my forehead with my hand. "He was right."

CHAPTER 44
Eve

*I*T'S NEARLY NINE O'CLOCK AND THE COPS ARE STILL IN MY BACKYARD. I wonder what's taking so long. I put Rosewyn down an hour ago and I've been pacing the kitchen ever since. Then a knock on the sliding door startles me. It's Detective Myers.

"Eve, we need to talk," she says, and my heart pounds.

We sit at the table, and she pulls out her notebook, flips through a few pages, her eyes skimming her notes. Voices in the backyard punctuate the silence. Then Detective Myers turns to a fresh page and her gaze meets mine.

"I want you to tell me about the night that your husband had his accident."

I wasn't expecting that. "Why?"

"Just run through it for me."

"Okay. I came home from work. Nathan and I talked, well, we had a disagreement, so I went upstairs with the baby. I put her to bed. Then I went to bed a while later."

"You didn't come back downstairs before you went to sleep?"

"I did. I wanted to speak to Nathan. We talked about . . . the affair, finally." Why is she asking me this? Did they find something in the yard implicating Nathan's mistress?

"What did you talk about, exactly?" Detective Myers's gaze is direct, stern. She seems very different than she's been in the past when we've talked, and I'm starting to sweat.

"The woman he was seeing."

"Did that make you angry?"

I stand and pace the kitchen. "Well, of course it did, Detective."

"How angry, Eve?"

I shrug, feel tears clog my throat as I relive that night in my head. "Pretty angry," I croak.

"Did you say that you could kill him?"

My stomach drops. "I might have said that." I turn around to face her. "What is this all about? What does this have to do with the doll?"

"Maybe nothing."

"Why all the questions about Nathan?"

She takes a deep breath. "Your husband asked to see me the other day. He thinks someone hit him in the back of the head and knocked him down the stairs."

The breath flies out of me. "Oh, my God. Did he see someone?"

"He did not." Her eyes meet mine.

I clutch my hands over my mouth. Understanding hits me like a lightning bolt. "He thinks it was *me*?" I cry.

"Was it?" she asks quietly.

I drop down into a chair, tears seep from my eyes. "Of course not. As angry as I was, I would never . . ."

"We've uncovered some evidence in your yard that backs up your husband's claim that *someone* hit him, Eve."

"What did you find?"

"You own any tools?"

I shake my head. "Not really. We have a hammer and a few screwdrivers. But that's about it. Neither of us is very handy. Why?"

"You have a crowbar?"

"No. Is that what you found?"

"We'll get into that later. But we'd like to search your house."

"Really? Is that necessary?"

"I'm afraid it is."

"Fine. Okay. But I didn't hit my husband, Detective, I swear to God."

"Then you have nothing to worry about."

My heart is thumping so hard I'm afraid it will burst. I drop my head in my hands. Detective Myers gets up from the table.

"Wait!"

She turns to face me. "What is it?"

"Maybe someone *did* hit him. Maybe this is all connected." I'm gulping for breath, my insides shaking. "What if it was the same person who took Rosewyn?"

"Could be," she says, and walks out the back door.

CHAPTER 45

Rita

*I*T WAS A LATE NIGHT AT THE LIDDLE/THAYER HOME, SO I'M PRETTY
sleepy this morning. I head into the breakroom to get a coffee refill and hope the caffeine helps. Lauren is standing there holding
the coffee pot like she's not sure what to make of it.

"Good morning," she says. "Should I dump the rest of this down
the sink and make a new pot?" Neither of us is very handy in the
kitchen. And there's always that dilemma, do I take the rest of the
coffee and hope someone else will make a new pot, or do I do
the right thing and make it myself?

"I vote to chuck what's in there. Looks pretty heinous. Let's brew
a new pot."

She nods. "You guys had a pretty late night. Chase still isn't
in yet."

"Yeah. I didn't get much sleep. Chase called me. He's on his way.
Traffic's a nightmare on 495, as usual."

"You think Doctor Thayer really knocked her husband down the
stairs?" I had filled Lauren in on my visit with Nathan earlier, and
she heard about the crowbar last night when we finally got back to
the station. I don't think the girl ever goes home.

I rifle through a basket of creamers and sugar packets as the coffee pot starts to burble. "I don't know. I don't think so. But it appears someone did. We didn't find anything when we searched her

house. No bloody gloves or anything. She swears she didn't do it and I think as smart as she is, she wouldn't have hidden the crowbar in pretty much plain sight. And she said that they don't own a crowbar if she was telling the truth."

Lauren rinses her mug at the sink. "You think the crowbar was the one stolen from Ms. Parnell's house?"

"Ms. Parnell thinks it is." I'd sent a picture of it to Wilma, and she thought it was hers.

Lauren pours coffee into each of our mugs. "Why would Doctor Thayer have stolen her neighbor's crowbar, hit her husband, then hidden the tool in her own yard?"

"Exactly." I raise an eyebrow. Let Lauren think it through.

"And it sounds like the argument they had was spontaneous and then she tells him she could kill him. Why would she say that if she planned on trying to kill him? And she would've had to plan it to steal the crowbar weeks earlier, when she didn't even know about the cheating. That doesn't make sense."

"No. It doesn't. Unless Eve was lying about owning a crowbar, but I just don't think so. I didn't get that feeling when I was questioning her. She was totally surprised."

Lauren dumps a buttload of sugar into her coffee. "It makes much more sense that someone has been spying on the Liddles from the Parnell house. He or she takes the crowbar anticipating using it on Mr. Liddle at some point. And the doll is just another way to terrorize the Liddles."

I sip my coffee. "That's what I'm thinking." I grimace. "Coffee's terrible."

Lauren laughs. "It is. Oh, well, we did our best. At least it's hot." She throws a coffee stirrer into the trash. Her brow puckers. "This case is getting pretty scary, Rita."

"Yeah." I blow out a tired breath. "It looks like someone is targeting the Liddles. I just wish I knew why."

CHAPTER 46
Eve

I'M SITTING AT MY DESK, EXHAUSTED, BUT I NEEDED TO GO TO WORK. Joanne showed up bright and early and I filled her in on what took place after she left. We discussed this development and, luckily, she didn't flinch, didn't hand in her resignation. She was appalled to learn that I'm apparently a suspect in my husband's attempted murder. Luckily, she believes me and now thinks that the cops are bumbling idiots. But, obviously, someone tried to kill Nathan. We sat together at the table and talked while Rosewyn had her breakfast. We've got this, Joanne said. We'll be vigilant.

As much as I want to ask Nathan if he told Detective Myers that I hit him, I decide to wait, see what the cops figure out. Nathan is still healing from very serious injuries, and I don't want to jeopardize his recovery by getting into something so fraught with emotion. What good would it do at this point? He's had a head injury. If he did accuse me, it might be paranoia; it's sometimes another complication of brain trauma. And I don't want to keep Rosewyn from Nathan any longer. I had promised to bring her by today at lunchtime and seeing her might help him heal.

They didn't find anything to incriminate me last night because there wasn't anything to find, so I'm a free woman, at least for now. I close my eyes. This is a nightmare. My mind winds back through all that's happened, my anxiety causes my stomach to clench and sweat to sprout on my back.

Get a grip, Eve, and get to work.

I've finished my morning rounds and am heading back to my office. With limited success, I've tried to switch my brain from my own problems to those of my patients. Janet, our daytime nursing supervisor, stops me in the hall.

"Eve, you have a minute?"

"Sure. What's up?"

"Frances. She was mumbling this morning about a woman she heard overnight in her room."

"One of the nurses?"

"No. Some woman who Frances said was taunting her. Laughing."

I sigh. "Another hallucination. She didn't say anything to me when I checked on her just now."

"It was earlier. Maybe she forgot about it."

I pull up Frances's chart on my laptop. And there's the notation added this morning. I missed it. "I see the note now." I glance up at Janet. "No one documented this last night?"

"I asked Glenda this morning and she said that Frances didn't say anything to her."

"Okay. I'll see what I can do with her medication. Let me know if she has any other instances."

"Will do." Janet tries to smile, but we're all a little frustrated. Frances should be doing better, and her setbacks leave me feeling inadequate.

It's quiet on the outpatient side of the building. As usual, the lights are dim in our hallway, something we've complained about. I near my office and pull up short. My door is ajar. Did I forget to close and lock it? Probably. My brain is mush from fatigue and worry. I glance up and down the hall, but no one's around. I enter my office tentatively and it's empty, so I shut the door behind me. As I sit at my desk, a figure steps out from the shadows in the corner. I cry out, stumble to my feet and grab for my phone.

Don.

"What are you doing in here?" I croak.

"Sorry, Eve. Hey, I didn't mean to scare you. I have an appointment with Dr. Tanaka and wanted to stop by to see if you were okay."

I inch toward the door. "How did you get in here?"

He licks his lips, smooths back his nest of hair. "The door was open, partway."

My heart is hammering. "Well, I'm okay. I think you better get on your way."

He blinks, his eyes bore into me. "I'm worried about you. Your worthless husband in the hospital. I heard about him on the news. A cheater. How could he have cheated when he has someone like you?"

"It's none of your business, Don. Now please leave."

"You need someone to protect you, Eve, before things get worse."

Could he be behind it all? Could he have taken Rosewyn? And it would be only too easy for Don to spy on me from the Parnell house, to throw the doll over the fence. To heft a crowbar and knock Nathan down the stairs. I'm trembling. Sweat is dripping down my back. I draw myself up. "What do you know about what's going on in my life?"

He smiles and shakes his head. "Only what you've allowed me to see."

What the fuck does he mean by that? He steps in my direction, and I run for the door, nearly knocking Brian over in the hallway.

"What's going on?" Brian grabs my arm and braces me. His gaze shoots over my shoulder. "Don, what are you doing?"

"Nothing. I just wanted to check on Doctor Thayer. I haven't seen her in a while, and I wanted to make sure she was okay."

Brian looks at me. "What happened?" he whispers.

"Tell you later. I need to see Mr. Jacobson." And I need to call Detective Myers.

I met with Mr. Jacobson, filled out a report on the incident. Now they'll handle it. Don should be banned from the facility and referred elsewhere.

I meet Joanne in the rehab center parking lot at lunchtime. I'm still shaky from my run-in with Don this morning, and from the trouble last night. But I decided to go ahead with our plans despite everything.

Joanne carries the car seat where Rosewyn is buckled in and bundled up against the cold. I glance behind me, looking to make sure that no one is following us. Brian told me Don was angry when he was escorted from the building.

Joanne sits in the lobby while I lift the baby into my arms. Rosewyn kicks and babbles as I walk with her on my hip to Nathan's room. He's sitting by the window again and I stop in my tracks. I can't believe this is my strong, handsome husband. He looks smaller, thinner in his gray sweatpants and top. But at least they are getting him dressed now.

"Hi Nathan," I call as I nudge the door open with my elbow.

He swings his head in my direction. "Eve?" His voice is throaty, like he's got a cold.

"Yes. It's me and Rosewyn."

His face crumples and his hand closes over his mouth as if to stifle a cry. Then he opens his arms. "Let me hold her, please."

I settle the baby on his lap, and he nearly crushes her in an embrace, his cheek against her soft head. He cries silently, tears wetting Rosewyn's dark hair, and I look away.

How did we come to this? And does my husband truly think that I tried to kill him?

I walk to the window, look across the lawn to my building. I'll need to get back in about twenty minutes. Nathan talks to Rosewyn, promises her he'll be home soon and that he loves her more than life. She doesn't understand his words, of course, but it's important for babies to hear their parents' voices.

I sit and watch Nathan and Rosewyn. Luckily, she's in a good mood and giggles as Nathan plays with her. Finally, I pick her up, and Nathan is reluctant to let her go. "I'm sorry, but I have to get back to work." I guess I could have Joanne come in and they could stay longer, but Nathan doesn't ask. I think it's too soon to have a stranger sitting with him.

Nathan turns his face to the window and wipes his cheeks. "Of course."

"I can bring her by again tomorrow," I say, "so we can stay longer."

"I would appreciate that."

I start to leave the room when Nathan speaks up. "What were you doing Wednesday night, Eve?"

I turn. "What do you mean?"

"Were you out?"

"No. Why?"

"Just wondering."

"I went home to Rosewyn right after work." He falls silent and I shut his door behind me. Why did he ask me that? Where did he think I was? I had talked to his doctors about cognitive and memory issues, and they said that, so far, there were some issues, but nothing significant.

A young nurse who has been taking care of Nathan stops me in the hall.

"Doctor Thayer?"

"Yes."

"I wanted you to know that your husband is doing all right. A little depression, which is normal, and the doctors are addressing that."

"Yes. They told me."

"The night nurse did find him out of bed the other night and he was agitated, but we think he was having a bad dream."

I nod. Hike Rosewyn up on my hip. The nurse reaches out and touches her cheek.

"But I bet a visit from this little angel cheered him up," she says.

"Yes. He was really happy to see her."

I head to the waiting room where Joanne is sitting reading a magazine. Nathan must've been dreaming about me. Maybe that's why he asked where I was Wednesday night. Brain injuries can do that. They can also affect personality and we'll see if that is the case as time goes on. I sigh. We just don't know what Nathan's future holds.

I walk Joanne and the baby to the car. "How'd it go?" she asks.

"Good. Nathan was thrilled to see her."

"That's good."

I blow out a breath, glance back at the rehab center. "I'm not sure what's going to happen to Nathan when it's time to discharge him."

Joanne clears her throat. "I was thinking about that. You know, if you're going to bring him home, I could help with his care. I'll be there anyway."

I consider. Nathan coming home is just another one of those unknowns. And how will he feel about that now that he thinks I might've knocked him down the stairs? I shake my head. That must be his brain injury creating paranoia. He'll see reason, eventually, I hope.

"That would be super helpful," I say, and slide the car seat into the back of Joanne's sedan and buckle it in. "And I guess I could hire a home health aide as well."

"It wouldn't be a problem for me, Eve."

I start to get teary. If I'm arrested for attempted murder, Nathan will have to step up somehow and be there for Rosewyn. I push that thought away. It won't come to that. "You sure, Joanne? You haven't done any nursing in a long time."

I hear her sigh. "No, I haven't. But you don't forget all that much. Maybe I'm not up on the latest and greatest medications and so forth, but you don't forget how to take care of wounded young men." She sniffs. "And I've seen my share of head injuries."

We fall silent, each to her own. My mind filled with my broken husband, and I hate to even imagine what's going through Joanne's mind. More than any civilian could comprehend, I'm sure.

CHAPTER 47
Eve

SATURDAY MORNING, I'M RUSHING AROUND, PICKING UP THE HOUSE, tending Rosewyn. I'm going to take her back to the rehab center after lunch, after her nap. She's sleeping upstairs and I have the monitor in my pocket as I gaze out the window wondering if the mailman has been by when I see a woman standing in front of the house. When the baby was missing there had been reporters out there all the time, but they're gone, thank God. But who is out there now? I lean closer to the window. I catch my breath.

Barbara.

I make sure the alarm is set and hurry out my front door. The cold wind shoots through my thin top as I sprint across the lawn. She looks up and starts walking down the sidewalk.

I grab Barbara's arm and pull her around to face me. She's wearing black yoga pants and an oversized red sweatshirt. Her hair is pulled back in a stubby ponytail and her thin face is devoid of makeup. She looks terrible.

"What are you doing?" I ask, my hair fluttering over my eyes.

"Hi, Eve," she stammers. "I'm walking. Exercising."

"In front of my house?"

Her eyes dart to our upstairs windows. "I sometimes walk over here."

"Well, I don't think it's a good idea for you to be on my street, in front of my house."

She wipes her mouth with a gloved hand. "How is Rosie? I can't stop thinking about her. What she must've gone through."

"She's fine. But I don't think you should be over here. The cops are still investigating." I wonder where that police cruiser is that's supposed to be in front of my house.

Barbara appears unfazed by my remark about the investigation. "You can't be too careful with a baby, Eve. Anything can happen. They can be gone in an instant."

"Rosewyn is my daughter and I'll take care of her. You don't need to be involved with us anymore."

"What about Nathan? I heard he's in the hospital. A child needs a father."

"He's going to be fine. We're going to be fine. Now I think it's best you move on." Her eyes flicker up to Rosewyn's window. Does she know that's where my baby is sleeping? How could she? Could she have thrown the doll over the fence? Is she strong enough to have hit Nathan with a crowbar?

"I hope you're all going to be fine," Barbara says finally. "I really hope so, Eve."

I watch her walk away, down the sidewalk in the opposite direction of where her house is. I open the mailbox and pull out a stack of mail that's accumulated for several days. I keep forgetting to check it. Bringing in the mail was another of the many things that Nathan always took care of.

I throw it on the kitchen table and walk upstairs to check on Rosewyn, but she's still asleep, safe in her crib. I go to the window and press my nose against the cold glass. I stand there for a while and then I see her. Barbara's back, looking up at the house.

CHAPTER 48
Rita

I WENT IN TO WORK THIS MORNING EVEN THOUGH I'M SUPPOSED TO BE off. Too much is going on for me to sit at home. Doug is in his office. It's his and Lauren's weekend. I stop at Lauren's cubicle and tell her about Eve's run-in with Donald Barry. Eve had called me and filled me in yesterday.

"Wow, Rita. Looks like Mr. Barry is in the lead again."

"Looks like it. I've been trying to get ahold of him, his ex-wife, too, but so far neither of them has returned my calls. I'm hoping the ex might know something about him that might be enlightening."

"Worth a try. Oh, what about the list we made of the other people?" Lauren asks, turning to her laptop. "You still want me to work on that?"

"Yeah. Let's stay on it. Until we get a solid lead, everyone is still a possibility."

"Right."

"Speaking of the list, I think I'll take a walk over to the square and see if Rachel Chapman is working today."

"Good idea."

I know Eve thinks her best friend is beyond reproach. She scoffed when she saw that Ms. Chapman was on our list, but a best friend is sometimes a wolf in sheep's clothing. I've found that out over the years. I've seen it be the case more than once. And the walk will do me good. The weather isn't too bad, cold, but the sky is bright blue. I walk past André's Café. Maybe after I talk to Ms. Chapman, I'll stop in, say hello to Collin, and pick up a coffee.

I stride down the sidewalk, a cool wind in my face until I reach The Gallery. Clever name. I chuckle. I've never been in here. Danny's bought a couple things from them though. Too rich for my taste. Anyway, the place is squeaky clean, minimalist I think they'd call it. Smells slightly like incense and oil paint. Canvasses hang on the walls, some modern looking with swirls of bright color, while others are more traditional, landscapes and even a couple portraits.

Rachel comes out from a back room probably having heard the bell on the door as I came in. Her dark eyes open wide.

"Detective Myers, what brings you by?"

She pulls up in front of me, flips her long hair over her shoulder setting the bangles on her wrist clinking.

"Hello, Ms. Chapman. You have a minute?"

"I guess. What's up?"

"Can we sit?" I peer around the room. Doesn't look like there's a table or anything nearby.

"Sure. Nothing's wrong, is it? Eve and the baby are okay?"

"Yeah. Fine."

"Okay. Well, we can sit at the counter, I guess." We walk over to where the register sits. There's a tall stool behind it. Rachel looks around. "I'll get another chair from the back."

She returns in a minute with another stool. I sit across from her, the thin counter between us, and pull out my notebook.

"So, what's this about?" she asks.

"Just getting some background on everyone who knows Eve and Nathan. You and Eve have been friends for a while?"

"Best friends. We met in college. Eve was a little quiet. Smart as hell, but she spent most of her time with her books." Rachel smiles. "I had to nudge her out of her shell."

"You're very protective of Eve," I say, tapping my pencil against my notebook.

"Yeah. Her parents were worthless. They kept her sheltered and so busy with school and extracurriculars, she didn't get out much, have much fun."

"You kept up the friendship after college. Both stayed right here locally?"

"Yes. Well, Eve went to medical school, so she was gone for a while, but I went to work here in town after undergrad. But we stayed in touch while she was getting her medical degree. She works really hard, Detective, she did then and she does now. She didn't manage to hang on to many friends, and neither did I, so we depend a lot on each other."

"You ever get married?"

She blinks her eyes. "No. I like the single life. Eve did, too, until Nathan. I was totally surprised when she told me she was getting married."

"What do you think about Nathan?" Her face changes, lips thin. Her gaze shifts over my shoulder.

"He's okay, I guess, or I thought so until Eve told me he cheated. The idiot."

"You have any idea that was going on before Eve told you?"

"Well, I—no, I had no idea."

"Not an inkling?"

She shakes her head. "No. I really don't know too much about Nathan. He and I aren't close."

"Has Eve changed since she's been with him?"

Her face reddens. "Well, she's super busy now with a baby and a husband. We used to have more time for each other."

"You miss the old days?"

She shrugs one shoulder. "Of course. I don't have any unmarried friends left, Detective. Eve was the last."

"And she's your best friend?"

"Yes."

I make notes, take my time. She starts fidgeting with her bracelets. "Where were you the day the baby was taken?"

She bats her eyes. "At work."

"Here?"

"Yes. Then I was at Eve's. You were there."

"Uh huh." I sketch her eyes in my notebook, the sharp arches of her brows. She tries to see what I'm doing.

Then she fills the silence. "You can't possibly think I'd take Eve's baby? Put her through that?" Her mouth hangs open. Her bottom lip trembles. "Why would I do that to my friend?"

Ends justify the means, maybe. Would Rachel be that desperate to get rid of Nathan? I sink back in my chair. But why not just tell Eve about the cheating? Why take the baby? But maybe putting Eve in that emotional state suited Rachel for some reason. I add to my sketch and can feel Rachel's anxiety increase. She's jiggling her leg, picking at her skirt.

"Really, Detective. Eve and I are like sisters!"

"No need to get upset. We're just trying to figure out where everyone was the day the baby went missing. What about the next day when the baby was recovered?"

"I was with Eve!" she shouts, then looks over at the gallery door as if someone were there and heard her.

"All day?"

"Well, no. I came into work for a couple hours. My boss insisted. Ask Eve."

"Okay, Ms. Chapman. Nothing to get worked up about."

She jumps down from her stool and crosses her arms over her chest. "I'm just as upset as anybody about what happened. Eve didn't deserve any of this."

"No, she didn't," I agree, and shut my notebook.

The bell tinkles at the door and an older man, well dressed in a tweed jacket over a turtleneck, comes in.

"Mr. Woodward," Rachel says, wipes her eyes and smiles. "I have your canvas in the back, all wrapped and ready to go."

"Thank you," he replies, and sticks his hands in his pockets and strolls over to a wall covered in small paintings.

Rachel turns to me. "Is that it? I need to get to work."

"Yes. Thank you," I say, stuffing my notebook in my satchel. "I'll be in touch."

I head down the sidewalk. Rachel Chapman seemed awfully nervous, and I want to look a little deeper. She certainly has an emotional connection to the people involved in this drama. Would she go so far as to hit Mr. Liddle in the head? And what would she gain from further terrorizing Eve with the doll?

I'm standing outside of the café, a wintry breeze fluttering my hair. A hot cup of coffee would be nice, but I have a good angel/ bad angel talk with myself.

You know it won't be just a cup of coffee, Rita. You know you'll end up with an éclair or a cookie to go with it.

But Collin is working today. I can see him behind the counter, and since this Liddle case has been open, I've barely had time to speak two words to my upstairs neighbor. And Collin is so good to me. I really should go in and say hello. See how he's been.

Better be prepared to work off that pastry on your bike tonight.

I can do that.

I open the café door.

CHAPTER 49

Nathan

ANOTHER MONDAY AND I'M STILL HERE. THERE'S A NOISE IN THE hall, the squeaky wheel on the meal cart. Must be lunchtime. I'm sitting by the window, resting after a morning of PT. I'm getting stronger. I can feel it in my legs. If only I could get this damn cast off my arm. But overall, I'm feeling better in large part due to the weekend with Rosewyn. Eve brought her up both Saturday and yesterday and having my little girl on my lap made all the difference.

Eve and I didn't talk much. We mainly talked about the baby and the new nanny, who is turning out to be a godsend, according to Eve. She told me one of my nurses told her about them finding me out of bed the other night. The night someone was in my room. Eve said that I was probably having a bad dream. And now I'm not sure. Is that possible? I've been so worried about Eve that I'm having nightmares? What if Eve *didn't* hit me and knock me down the stairs? Maybe that was just my guilt talking. And Detective Myers told me that my medical records were inconclusive. My injuries could very well have come from the fall.

In any case, Eve doesn't seem mad anymore. I don't know what she seems.

I hear a car engine thrum out in the parking lot. A V8, sounds like. Maybe a Mustang. I lean closer to the window, feel the sun hitting me. Then a shadow slips by my face and I swallow, reach out my hand and it bumps against the cold glass. I wave my fingers in front of my eyes, and I see something! My heart starts to hammer. I close my right eye. Nothing. Then I try closing my left and I definitely see a shadow and then something red. The car maybe? I hear the engine rev again then the vehicle exits the lot, I think. But I damn well see a red blob as it goes.

I'm giddy and lean back over my bed searching with my fingers for my call button. I press it repeatedly. I need to tell someone.

"Mr. Liddle?" a cheerful voice calls. It's just the aide with my lunch. I recognize everyone's voice by now. "Turkey sandwich and vegetable soup today."

"Great. Did you see my nurse out there?" I'm trying to zero in on her, see her. And I do see a gray shape.

"No. You need her?"

"Yeah. Please. Right now."

"Okay. Let me drop off a tray next door and I'll look for her."

I'm tapping the fingers of my good hand on the armrest of my chair. Someone needs to get in here and tell me this is for real. Am I getting my sight back? If only I could see again, I can deal with the rest.

Finally, someone comes in. "What's the trouble, Mr. Liddle?" It's the older day nurse. She's trying not to sound too annoyed. I know she's super busy, but this is important.

"I'm seeing something out of my right eye!"

I hear her approach and the blue of her scrubs materializes in front of me. She tips up my chin. I feel her breath against my forehead.

"Huh." She stands back. "How many fingers am I holding up?"

Try as I might, I can't tell. "I don't know, but I can see something that looks like a hand."

"Okay. Anything else?"

"You've got on blue." She chuckles. "Yeah, I know, everyone here is wearing blue. But I can see it. And a minute ago I was looking out the window and I saw a red car."

"That's great, Mr. Liddle. Let me write that on your chart and let your doctor know."

"Thanks."

* * *

Lunch is over and my doctor still hasn't been in. And I'm antsy as hell. I keep looking around the room, trying to identify things. Then I get paranoid and worry that I'll strain my eyes, or eye. I lean back in my chair and let my lids close. Rest.

"Nathan?" I jerk awake. Must've dozed off. Sounds like Eve. I blink. I see her blond hair.

"Hi. What are you doing here?"

"I just ran over for a quick sec. I've got to be back to see a patient in ten minutes." She clears her throat. "Mind if I come in?"

"Fine. Nothing's wrong, is it?" I decide to keep my new-found vision to myself for now. I'm still not sure I trust her.

"No. I just wanted to talk to you about a couple of things. I've been wondering all weekend if I should say anything since you've got so much to deal with, but you're getting stronger, and I think we need to talk."

"I'm not incompetent." I grit my teeth.

"I know that." She starts pacing. "Has Detective Myers called you?"

"Not in a while, why?"

"Well, she told me that you thought someone had knocked you down the stairs."

My insides turn cold. I hope like hell she didn't tell her I thought it was Eve. "Yeah. It's possible, don't you think? I don't remember stumbling or anything."

"Well, with a brain injury, you're not going to remember everything."

So, she's going to use that excuse. I hope she's not going to walk over to me. But then she sits down.

"Nathan, they searched our yard and found a bloody crowbar behind the firewood. What if someone *did* knock you down the stairs?"

"For real? The cops think that's what . . . the person used to hit me?"

"Yes."

"Where did it come from?"

"I don't know. It might be the one stolen from Ms. Parnell's house."

I take a deep breath. Close my eyes. Someone did try to kill me. It's not my imagination. I peep in Eve's direction. Would she be telling me about it if *she* was the one who hit me? I swallow. "Who do they think did it?"

She shakes her head. "Someone is trying to ruin our lives, Nathan. First, they take Rosewyn. Then they hurt you. Then . . ."

"What? Did something else happen?"

She tells me that she found a bloody doll in our backyard with a warning on its stomach.

"Jesus, why didn't you tell me that when it happened?" She never brought any of this up over the weekend.

"I'm telling you now." She wipes her face with a white tissue plucked from a box on my bedside table. "What if someone's been spying on us from Ms. Parnell's house? What if they've been planning this?"

"Who would do that?"

"I have no clue."

I tap my fingers against the armrest. Maybe Eve didn't knock me down the stairs. But *someone* did. Who would hate us that much? "Cops are investigating the doll and everything, right?"

"Yes. That's how they found the crowbar."

I shudder, twist in my chair, frustrated at my own helplessness. "Are they providing protection for you and the baby?"

"There's a cruiser in front of the house twenty-four seven now."

"That's good." And I hope it's enough.

"Anyway, I need to get back to work."

"Okay. Eve?"

"Yes?"

"Don't keep things from me. And be careful."

"I will. I'll bring Rosewyn back sometime this week when I have a long enough lunch hour to make it worthwhile."

"That would be great."

The thought of seeing my little girl's face makes me weepy. With Eve gone, I settle back. My fall wasn't just an accident. I know for sure now. Maybe it was Eve, or maybe she's right, someone has targeted us. An uneasiness slides through me. It sounds crazy. What did we ever do to deserve this? But now that I've regained some vision, I don't feel as vulnerable. I feel like I might come out of this okay after all. I might be able to fight back. And my worry shifts to my family. What if whoever it is tries something else and I'm not there to protect them?

CHAPTER 50
Rita

*I*T'S MONDAY. THE WEEKEND FLEW BY. I COULDN'T GET AHOLD OF Mr. Barry, so I drove over to his apartment yesterday, knocked on his door, but there was no answer. I looked through the parking lot and didn't see his vehicle either. I wondered if he'd left town maybe. After his incident with Eve at the hospital, maybe he decided to get out of Dodge for a while.

I try again to contact him but no luck. I join Lauren in the conference room and give her the rundown on my conversation with Ms. Chapman.

"What do you think, Rita?"

"Maybe. It's possible. I need to follow up on a few things before I cross her off the list. She certainly thinks her best buddy would be better off without the hubby. But we'll see."

Chase comes barreling through the door, a file folder in his hands. "I'm headed out to Graybridge Collision to finish my interviews there." His gaze flickers down to his paperwork. "Only three more to go."

"How's it looking?" I ask.

"Nothing promising. And so far, not a whiff of gossip that Liddle was sneaking off with his lady before the kidnapping. They were all surprised when they heard about it on the news. At least that's what they're saying."

"Let us know what you find out."

"Will do."

Chase takes off and I turn to Lauren. "You find a number for Nicole Clark's ex?" Despite the list, Nicole, Barbara, and Don are still our main focus.

"Yes. I sent you all his contact information this morning."

"Right." I scroll through my phone. "Thanks. I'm going to head down to my office and give him a call."

I push my office door shut with my hip and punch in the number. It rings several times before he answers. "Mr. Clark?"

"Yes. Who's calling?" he grumbles.

Sounds like I woke him up, but it's almost lunchtime. "This is Detective Rita Myers with the Graybridge Police Department."

"Has something happened?" That woke him up.

"Nothing to worry about."

He blows out a breath. "That's good. You'll have to excuse me. I'm in San Jose." I probably did wake him up then. "On business. I've been out of town for six weeks, Detective. What can I do for you?"

"We have a few questions about your ex-wife."

"Nicole? What's she done?"

"Nothing that we know of. Someone she knows had his baby abducted."

"That's terrible." He pauses. "I heard about that. I was talking to a colleague in Boston the other day. The baby was found unhurt, right?"

"That's right." I fall silent, let him talk.

He clears his throat. "Well, I don't know anything about it other than what my friend told me. And I can't imagine Nicole being involved in something like that. I had no idea she knew anyone connected to the case."

"Uh huh. How long ago were you divorced?"

"Two years."

"Amicable?"

He clears his throat again. "No. Not really."

"Who filed?"

"It was mutual, Detective."

"But acrimonious?"

"Yes."

"Why was that?"

"I'd rather not get into personal matters if you don't mind."

"Well, I need to get to the bottom of this kidnapping, Mr. Clark. I need to know if Nicole could've been involved. I need to know more about her. So, what happened between the two of you?"

There's silence for a second. "I had an affair, okay? And I travel for work a lot and that didn't sit well with Nicole. She wanted to know where I was every minute. I felt smothered. Look, we hadn't been married all that long, no kids. It wasn't working out and then I did what I did, and we divorced. I gave her a pretty good settlement, but she was still really angry."

"How angry?"

"Pretty livid."

Could Nicole have wanted to wreck someone else's marriage? Her husband cheated on her. She couldn't make him pay, so she decided to make someone else pay? Then when Mr. Liddle broke it off, she flew into a rage and wanted him to suffer? "What do you know about her background?"

"She has a grandmother in Graybridge she takes care of. She moved in with her after the divorce. At least she did at the time. She might've moved someplace else since. I don't keep in touch with her. But I really don't see her kidnapping a baby, Detective. For all that we had our problems, I don't see that as something she would do."

"When was the last time you saw her?"

He draws a deep breath. "God, it's been a while. A year or more, I'd say. I bumped into her at a coffee shop in Graybridge. I'm not there often, but I was meeting a client and that was halfway."

"Where do you live?"

"Hopkinton."

"How did she seem when you saw her?"

"Fine. She didn't have much to say to me, of course. She was sitting by herself, with her laptop. It was awkward, as you would expect."

"Okay. Anything else you can tell me about her?"

"Not really. Oh, she's a demon on a computer."

"What do you mean?"

"I told you I felt smothered. Well, she hacked into my phone, all my accounts, and they were all password protected. If you'd told me she was involved in cybercrimes, I'd have believed it, but a baby? She doesn't even like kids."

This sets my senses tingling. A hacker can come up with all kinds of useful information. And the fact that she would go to those extremes to spy on her husband is interesting. "All right, Mr. Clark. Thanks for speaking with me. Might have to circle back if we think of anything else."

"Fine, Detective. Glad to be of help."

I check my voicemail and email, hoping that Donald Barry or his ex has gotten back to me. But neither one has. I need to talk with the ex-wife. I've left her several messages, but so far, I haven't heard anything. I'm anxious to see what she has to say. I have a work address for her, an office in Boston, so I grab my jacket and head out the back entrance.

After fighting traffic for an hour, I find a spot in one of the older parking garages and make my way down the busy city block. Too cold still for many tourists, but the sidewalks are filled with office workers bundled up and scurrying back to their buildings after lunch. I check my phone to make sure I've got the right address and head inside a beige-colored building. The man at the lobby desk points me to the elevator bank. I step inside and push the button for the fifth floor.

Gail Barry works for one of those nondescript companies whose name you've never heard of, in one of the myriad businesses you can't describe. I open the glass door and approach the receptionist desk. A fortyish woman with short, dark hair and a slightly plump chin, smiles.

"May I help you?"

I introduce myself, show her my identification and the smile slides off her face. Her made-up blue eyes flicker down to her desk.

"I'm looking for Ms. Barry," I say.

"That's me," she replies.

"Do you have a minute?"

Her eyes dart around the empty reception area. "I guess," she says under her breath.

I pull my notebook out of my satchel and wonder if she's going to offer me a chair. She doesn't.

"I'm sorry, Detective, that I haven't returned your calls. I've been super busy and"—she clears her throat—"I really don't want to be involved with anything that has to do with my ex-husband."

"I understand, but this is important. I just have a few questions for you." She nods. "What can you tell me about him?"

"We weren't married very long. We met on a dating app. I'll never do that again. Anyway, he was nice at first, so attentive. Then, after we got married, he got, I don't know, possessive. 'Where were you? Who were you with?' That kind of thing."

A man in a blue suit walks over from an inner office.

"Gail, I need these faxed. Excuse me," he says in my direction.

"I'll get right to it, Bill," she says and smiles, takes the papers from him. Bill gives me the once over then heads back through the door.

"Anyway, I know he's a person of interest in that kidnapping case." She sighs but keeps talking in a semi-whisper. "I don't know what to think. I assume he knew that doctor, the baby's mom, from seeing her professionally. It didn't say on the news. I guess they can't say that."

"No. They can't. When was the last time you saw Mr. Barry?"

"Not since the divorce was final. About six months ago."

"Have you heard from him in that time?"

She smirks. "Yeah. He calls and texts me, Detective, all the time. I've asked him not to, but he won't listen. I've thought of getting a restraining order. Can you do that for calls and texts, or does it have to be a physical thing, like he's showing up at my house?"

"Has he shown up at your residence?"

"No. I live up in Andover. It's a bit of a commute to work, but I didn't want to be anywhere near him."

"But he's been obsessive about letting you go?"

"Yes. I keep hoping he'll find a new girlfriend."

"Did he ever do anything that frightened you other than the calls or texts?"

She shakes her head and sips from a fast-food take-out drink. "Not really. I always thought Don was all talk until I heard about the kidnapping."

"So, you think he *could've* taken the baby?"

She shrugs. "I don't know."

"Does he have any friends or relatives that you think would help him if he did take the baby?"

"He doesn't have a lot of friends, or he didn't anyway. His family is all in Connecticut and there aren't too many of them left. A few of them came for the wedding, I remember."

"Did you hear from him over the weekend?"

Her lips thin. "He left me a text that he was going out of town."

"Did he say where he was going? When he'd be back?"

"No."

"Okay, Ms. Barry. I appreciate your help." I'm about to tuck my notebook back in my satchel when she puts her hand on her chest. "Wait a minute."

"Yeah?"

"His cousin Paula. I wouldn't put it past her. She lives in Hartford. She was at the wedding. She's a little older than Don and he really looks up to her. She came to live with them when she was a teenager. The first time I met her, we stopped by her condo. She was showing me around and opened the closet in her master bedroom. It was full of designer clothes." Gail grimaces. "Shoplifted. And she bragged about it, like I should be impressed. I was appalled. And last I heard she sued some woman who rear-ended her. Just a tap, didn't even damage her car, but she found some smarmy doctor who testified that Paula had severe back pain, and she got a big settlement. Don laughed it off, said she had a really rough childhood, like that makes it okay to hurt other people. Anyway, I wouldn't put it past her to be involved in something underhanded." Gail purses her lips like she's said too much. "But I don't want to accuse her, Don either, of *kidnapping*. I just don't know, Detective. But she's the only person who comes to mind."

"What's her last name?"

"It's Barry, too. Paula Barry."

On my way back to the station, I call Lauren and have her do a search on a Paula Barry from Hartford.

CHAPTER 51
Eve

I SIT AT MY DESK AS THE AFTERNOON DRAGS ON, MY EARLIER CONVERsation with Nathan running through my mind. Could someone have seen him from the house behind us, seen him outside having a smoke and hit him? How would he or she have managed that without Nathan seeing them? It *was* dark back there. The deck light hadn't worked in months. And he was hurt the week before we put the security system in and fixed the lights. Maybe it was Don. He would've been strong enough to do it. Maybe he's behind it all. Maybe he blames Nathan for the bruises he saw on my arm. And he wanted to scare me with the doll, so that I'd look to him for protection? I swallow and try to slow my breathing. I need to stop. I need to let the detectives handle this.

I finish my evening rounds and head to the lobby on my way back to my office. Glenda is just arriving, unzipping her puffy jacket.

"Hi, Doctor Thayer," she calls, slipping her jacket over her arm.

"When did it start snowing?" I ask, noticing a few flakes clinging to her short, iron gray hair.

"Just as I was heading in. We could get a couple inches they were saying." She stamps her feet on the large industrial doormat. "Have a good evening," she says, brushing past me.

"Wait. How's Frances been? Janet told me that she complained about hearing things in the night."

Glenda shakes her head. "Frances hasn't said anything to me about it. She's been sleeping through. No problems that I noticed. She was probably dreaming. Or maybe she heard Sabrina next door. She wakes up and makes a racket occasionally."

"Okay. I'll ask Dr. Tanaka about Sabrina." She is his patient.

"Yeah. He's adjusting her meds. Maybe that'll help keep her quiet." Glenda marches off toward the patient wing.

In my office, I gather my things, slip into my coat, and leave for the day. I'm meeting Rachel for a drink on my way home. Joanne said she could stay an extra hour, and I checked that the police car is out front. She said it was. I really need to unwind and get my mind off my troubles for a little while at least, and Rachel's been wanting to get together.

Hartshorn's Brewpub is pretty busy. The parking lot is nearly full. I look around before I get out of my car, the words printed on the doll never far from my mind. Two women are walking toward the front door, so I follow behind them.

We're in the doldrums of winter, but inside, the restaurant is warm. The place smells like cheeseburgers and beer, but not in a bad way. Pearl Jam is playing over the sound system. Rachel is already sitting in a booth with a martini in front of her. She waves when she sees me.

"Great idea," she says, and raises her drink. "It was a shitty day."

I slide out of my coat and hang it on the hook on the beam at the end of the booth. "Yeah. Here too. I can't stay long, but I needed to relax a bit." Our server stops by. I order a Cabernet and she hurries away.

"So, tell me about *your* shitty day," Rachel says.

"Where to start?" I run my hand through my hair. It's getting so long, but the last thing I've been thinking about is a salon visit. I tell Rachel about the doll but not the message. The cops want that to be kept quiet like the first message.

"Jesus, Eve. This is getting fucking scary. Why didn't you tell me last week when it happened?"

I shrug. "Sorry. I've just been so focused on keeping my head above water lately."

"What did the cops say?"

"They're looking into it."

"That seems to be their standard answer. They need to look into a certain whack job with the apropos initials, BS."

"Barbara's still in the mix. Anyway, there's more. When they were searching the yard, they found a crowbar with hair and blood on it." I lean toward her. "Rachel, someone tried to kill Nathan. Someone hit him and knocked him down the stairs. He didn't just fall."

"Are you fucking kidding?" Rachel covers her mouth with her hand.

Our server drops off my drink and scurries away. "I wish I was. I think someone is trying to ruin our lives."

Rachel huffs. "This is crazy, but my money's on Barbara. The baby disappeared on her watch. Everything started then."

"Would she have been strong enough to knock Nathan down the stairs?" I sip my wine.

"With enough adrenaline flowing, I bet she could've done it. She's a nutcase. Or maybe it was Nathan's skank. They're still looking into her, right?"

"Yes." My mind is churning. "But *I* think it was a patient of mine."

"Who?"

"I can't say."

"Right."

Rachel furrows her brow. "That guy they named on the news?"

I shouldn't have mentioned a patient. "You know I can't say." This isn't what I wanted to meet Rachel for. I wanted to forget my crazy life for an hour. But try as I might, I can't think of anything uplifting to talk about. I sip my wine and close my eyes a moment.

"Look, Eve. Leave the detective work to the detectives." Rachel squeezes my arm. "You've got someone competent to take care of the baby. You've got a top-of-the-line security system. Nathan is being tended, so you don't have to worry about him."

I nod. "Right. So, tell me about your shitty day."

"Not worth reliving. The same old crap. Aaron is being his usual overbearing self. As if the gallery were the Louvre." Rachel leans forward, smiles. "I know what we should do. Let's take a weekend trip, like we used to in the old days. Well, not quite like we used to. You could bring Rosewyn. Let's head up to Maine, do some shopping, hit the craft breweries up there. What do you think?"

"Sounds nice, but I don't think so." I glance around the restaurant, examine the faces. Could the kidnapper be here in the crowd? "I'm a little wigged out. I wouldn't feel safe taking off right now. I think I need to stay in town where the cops are keeping an eye on us."

Rachel drains her martini then chases the olive around with her drink stirrer. "Yeah, I guess I don't blame you. You are being careful, right?"

"Yes."

"Well, when this whole thing is sorted out and they catch the asshole, we can take a trip and unwind then."

"Sounds like a plan." I try to smile, but my eyes shift toward the door, watching everyone who comes in.

CHAPTER 52
Rita

*T*UESDAY MORNING, I GET A CALL FROM THE LAB. TURNS OUT THE blood on the doll was beef blood, so someone could've bought a package of hamburger and used that. It's a relief that it wasn't human. And, as suspected, the hair and blood on the crowbar belong to Nathan Liddle. I look back over my other forensic files from the case. There was nothing found on the baby's clothes, no fingerprints or DNA on anything so far. The perp must've been super careful.

I tap my pencil against my notebook as I sit at my desk. Snow is falling softly outside my window. I check my phone for the millionth time to see if Don Barry has returned my calls; he hasn't. But I can't sit here another minute, so I grab my jacket and head out to my van.

I don't know if Don is working from home today or not, or if he's even back in town, but I stop at his apartment complex anyway, circle the lot and see his vehicle parked there. Great.

When he opens his door, he frowns when he sees me. "Detective, what brings you by this morning?"

"Well, Don, I've left you half a dozen messages, but for some reason, you haven't called me back."

"I've been busy."

I walk into his living room. He shuts the door and follows me reluctantly.

"I've got a lot of work to do," he says.

"Just have a couple questions. Won't take long."

He sits on the couch, and I plop down in a chair across from him. Take out my notebook. His eyes keep darting to the breakfast bar where his laptop sits open next to a mug.

I ask him where he was the night the doll was thrown into Eve's yard.

"Here. Home."

"All night?"

He rubs his chin. "Yeah. Why?"

"Just answer the question."

"Where else would I be?"

"You tell me."

"What happened, Detective? Is Eve all right?"

"She's fine. But I hear you paid her a visit at her office."

"So?"

"I heard you weren't supposed to be there. Scared her."

He shakes his head. His lips thin. "With all that's gone on, I was worried about her."

"What do you know about what's gone on?"

His eyes meet mine. "Just what I've heard around the hospital and on the news. Her husband's in bad shape, and he can't protect her."

"Protect her from what, Don?"

"I don't know. The maniac who kidnapped her daughter maybe." He looks at me as if he thinks I'm an idiot.

"Okay. But Doctor Thayer has made it clear to you that she doesn't need your help, right?"

He shrugs. "Doesn't mean she won't get it."

"Mr. Barry, you need to stay away from Doctor Thayer."

"Why should I? It's not illegal to talk to someone."

This is getting me nowhere. I can clearly see the obsessiveness that his ex was talking about. But is he dangerous? "You ever meet Doctor Thayer's husband?"

"No."

"You've seen him around?"

"Can't say that I have."

"You been by Doctor Thayer's house?"

He shifts in his chair. "I could've driven by it at some point. It's a small town."

"You know where it is though?"

"No." He glances at his laptop. "I need to get to work. I have a conference call in ten minutes."

"Okay. But you need to stay away from Doctor Thayer. We've got police security for her and if they see you near her, you could be charged with harassment."

"Sure. Fine." He smirks and stands.

I stuff my notebook in my satchel. "So, where were you last weekend?" I ask as he walks me to the door.

"Visiting my cousin."

Hmm. "She ever come here to visit you?"

"Sometimes." His brow furrows. "Why?"

"Just wondering."

On my way back to the station, the Liddle case goes round and round in my head. It certainly looks like someone is out to get them. How could they—a psychiatrist and a collision shop manager—have such a dangerous enemy? Well, my bet's on Eve. In her line of work, she'd be the one most likely to encounter someone that deranged. But is it Don Barry? He's certainly looking good for it about now. If only we had a fingerprint or DNA, something.

I sigh as I pull into the back lot of the police station. I promised Danny I'd go with him to Maureen's on Saturday. Not something I'm looking forward to, but it's the kind of thing you have to do for family. I sit in my van a minute. My thoughts turn to Joe. He hasn't called in a couple of days, and I miss talking to him. I jump out of my van, hike my satchel over my shoulder. Best get to work.

CHAPTER 53
Eve

*T*HE LAB RESULTS ON THE DOLL AND CROWBAR WERE A MIXED BAG. A big relief that the blood on the doll wasn't human, but the dark hair and blood on the crowbar are definitely Nathan's. I know we suspected that, but hearing it confirmed gives me chills. It's unnerving proof that someone did try to kill my husband.

My after-lunch appointment canceled, so I know I don't have to hurry back if I run over and check on Nathan.

I don't see anyone at the nurse's station as I trek toward his room. That's okay. I know they were taking off the cast on his arm and that, physically, he is making good progress, so I don't need an update.

He's sitting near the window again, face turned toward the parking lot.

"Nathan?"

"Hi, Eve." He swings his head in my direction. "Everything okay?"

"Fine. I had time, so I thought I'd come over."

He nods, lets me continue.

I sit in the visitor's chair. "I've been talking to Detective Myers, and it looks like you were right."

He grimaces. "Yeah. She called. Pretty scary to think that some-one wanted to kill me." His eyes seem to fasten on me. Did he *really* think it was me?

"Oh, Nathan. You can't think . . ."

He lifts his chin. "I just need to hear it from you, Eve. I need to be sure."

I stand, pace. "As mad as I was that night, as much as you hurt me. I would never. I'm not violent, Nathan." I run my fingers through my hair, tugging as if this will help me think. I need to re-member, he's had a brain injury. That can skew a person's think-ing, muddle their thoughts and memories.

He clasps his hands on either side of his head, closes his eyes. "You swear, Eve? It wasn't you?" His voice cracks. "You swear!"

"Of course not, Nathan." I stand still in front of him. My heart aches. Aches that he cheated and hurts that he would think this of me. "It has to have been the same person who took Rosewyn, who threw the doll into the yard."

He nods and sniffs. "Okay." He lowers his head a moment, wipes his eyes. "I just needed to know for sure, Eve."

Silence falls in the room. Like something has shifted between us and we need a minute.

Finally, Nathan says, "You're being careful?"

"Yes."

"The cops have someone at the house?"

"There's a cruiser parked out front twenty-four seven. I told you that."

He nods and slowly gets to his feet; his eyes meet mine.

Then it occurs to me. "Can you *see* me?" I whisper.

His lips twitch. "Out of my right eye, yes." He takes a step away from me, his hand on the back of his chair. "I can see you now, and I needed to know the truth. I needed to hear you say it." There's saliva dotting his lips; his face is red.

"That is the truth. I would never. As much as you hurt me."

He rubs his forehead. "I've been so . . . fucking scared, Eve. The thoughts just roll around and around in my brain sometimes. And I have headaches. I don't always know what's real and what isn't."

This squeezes my heart. Head injuries can be life changing. I walk to him, and it hurts when he recoils. I touch his arm gently anyway. "It'll get better, Nathan." And I hope I'm right. "You need to give yourself time to heal."

He drops back down into his chair and leans over, his elbows on his knees, his gaze on the floor.

"Hey," I say in a near whisper. "Concentrate on the improvements you're making. Getting your sight back is amazing. This is great news."

He nods and wipes his nose. "Will I ever be the same?"

The look in his eyes goes straight to my heart, but I won't lie to him. "We don't know." I place my hand on his shoulder. "But you're still the same person you were before. You're Rosewyn's wonderful dad and you're . . . my husband." I feel him trembling.

"I need to see her," he says. "When can you bring her up?"

"This weekend, for sure."

I pull the visitor's chair over and sit beside him. He slowly winds his hand in mine, and I choke back tears. We were happy once. Is it possible that we could get back to that?

"I'm so sorry, Eve," he says. "I'd give anything to go back in time and change what I did."

"I know."

"No matter how lonely I was, I had no right to do that to you. It'll never happen again."

And I believe him. Maybe I shouldn't. Maybe the expression "once a cheater . . ." is true. But my training tells me that's not always the case. People are individuals with their personal demons and their life stories. I believe that Nathan is, despite everything, a good man. And good people sometimes make horrible mistakes. Above everything, he and Rosewyn and I are a family. One worth fighting for.

I squeeze his hand. "We'll work this out, Nathan," I whisper.

"I need to get home. I need to be there for you and Rosewyn."

I let his hand go and brush his dark, damp hair from his forehead. "You need to heal. That's your job right now. Rosewyn and I will be over to see you soon."

I stand. Brush tears from my cheeks.

Nathan nods. "Okay. See you soon."

CHAPTER 54

Rita

*I*T'S SATURDAY AND DANNY'S COMING BY TO PICK ME UP ON THE WAY TO Maureen's. He wants to see what's ours in the attic, and he wants to look through Ricky's boxes for some reason. There are boxes there that belonged to Jimmy as well. But neither of us has had the courage to even acknowledge that they exist. Ricky was so much older than we were, his memory is more approachable somehow, but Jimmy is another matter. Just a year older than Danny, Jimmy was our constant companion. Losing him at eleven from leukemia still seems impossible.

I need a break from the Liddle case, although I'm not sure a trip to the old house is the answer, but Danny wants to go, and I figure I might as well get it over with.

I see his car pull up in front of my building and I head out the door. Danny's dressed in jeans and a sweatshirt, about as casual as he gets, like he's going on an archaeological dig. He drives toward the highway and soon we're on the Mass Pike, headed into Boston.

We walk into Ma's kitchen, and the scent of fresh soda bread hangs in the air. Maureen's got tea stuff on the table. She moved in with Ma after her husband died six years ago, which was good because Ma had started to fail, and she died a year and a half later.

Maureen's red hair has mellowed to a rosy white. She's the only kid who inherited Ma's color. The rest of us got Dad's dark hair. As Maureen pours tea, slices the soda bread, I can't help but see Ma standing there so great is the resemblance.

"So, what's up?" she asks, settling herself in a chair.

"We want to take a look at the boxes in the attic," Danny says.

"Why?" Maureen's lips thin.

Danny clears his throat. "I want to see what's in Ricky's boxes."

Maureen stands and goes to the counter. She reaches for a bag of sugar and sighs. "Why? You two barely remember him. You were little kids when he left for Vietnam."

My insides shudder. "We remember him, Maureen." But we *were* little. Like most big families, there was a generation between the oldest and the youngest. But Ricky's last letter was actually written to me. I finally got it away from Maureen a while ago and read it, one time.

Hey Squirt! Are you being a good girl? . . .

I close my eyes a moment. I can still hear his voice, especially here in the old house.

"Fine. They're in the corner by the window." She sits and stirs her tea, adding more milk from the carton. We talk about the neighborhood, which families are still here, which ones have died or moved away. Maureen talks about her daughters. One lives in Florida, the other in Vermont. She wishes they were closer. We run through our siblings, and Maureen complains that Debbie still hasn't sent her the money she owes her for the Christmas wreaths she put on Ma's and Dad's graves. Ricky's and Jimmy's too.

"I appreciate you doing that," Danny says. He's been uncharacteristically quiet.

"Well, I'm here in town. No big deal."

"Should we stop over there on the way home?" He's looking at me. The last thing I want to do is go to the cemetery.

"If you want."

"Another cup?" Maureen asks, getting up.

"No thanks," I say.

"You want to take some of the soda bread home? I can't eat it all."

Again, I'm reminded of Ma. We never left without food in Tup-perware or covered in foil. I'm about to say no. I don't need any more carbs in the house, but the look on her face has me relenting. "Sure. I'll take a chunk."

"Me too," Danny says. "It's almost as good as Ma used to make." He winks at her.

The attic is chilly. But the clouds have cleared, snow stopped, and the sun is shining weakly through the window. I see two card-board boxes sitting nearby. Ricky's name is scrawled on their sides, faded from the years. I follow Danny and we sit cross-legged on the floor. Dust covers everything and he clears his throat before pull-ing apart the flaps on the first one, sending motes drifting through the sunlight.

Looks like clothes. Who would've kept those? They're musty and wrinkled. Danny pulls out a pair of jeans with a peace sign drawn on the knee in Magic Marker.

I clear my throat and sniff. "Nothing worth keeping in there," I say.

"Well, wait a minute." Danny gets up on his knees and fishes around in the bottom. "Maybe not." He sighs and sits back on his haunches.

He pushes the box away and pulls the other one to him. We hear clanking, definitely not clothes. Inside, an old, tarnished basketball trophy catches the sunlight. Danny sets it on the floor. Next he pulls out a couple of what look like yearbooks. Danny's gaze meets mine.

"You want to look through these?"

I shake my head. I don't want to look through any of this stuff.

"You care if I take them home to look at later?" he asks.

"All yours." I lean back anchoring myself with my hands. I look up at the rafters as Danny rummages through stuff that probably sat on Ricky's dresser. I glance at him out of the corner of my eye occasionally. Finally, he pulls out a stack of 45s. Those small two-song records they don't make anymore.

"Here's something you might like, Rita."

I swallow. My favorite memories of Ricky are all about music. I credit him with my life-long love of rock. The Beatles, The Rolling

Stones, The Yardbirds, and so many others. He'd blast music on his record player whenever he was home. I'd slip into his room and sprawl on his bed and listen. We'd sing together, oblivious to the other nine people in the house. After she'd had enough, Ma would knock on the kitchen ceiling with a broom handle and yell at him to turn it down, and we'd giggle together.

I turn away, scramble to my feet. "Damn it, Danny. I don't want to do this."

Leaving my brother in the attic, I head down the rickety wooden stairs. I sink down on Ma's couch in the front room. It's fairly new. She bought it after Maureen moved in. The room is the same, but different, the way things from your childhood are.

Maureen stands in the doorway, her hand on her hip, and chuckles.

"What's wrong with you?" she says.

"Nothing."

"With your arms crossed and your bottom lip sticking out you look just like you did when you were eight."

"Thanks a lot!" I suck in my lip, uncross my arms.

"So, what did you two find up there?" Her eyes shift to the ceiling.

"Just . . . stuff. Clothes." I blow out a breath. "I don't know why Danny had to drag me down here." As hard as I try, I can't suck up the tear that's started to wend its way down my cheek. I swipe at it angrily.

Maureen sighs. "You know, Rita. Some people live a long time. Some people don't. But Ricky was the happiest person I've ever known, and he spread that happiness around to more people in his nineteen years than most people do in a lifetime."

"Is that supposed to make me feel better?"

"No." She swishes her hand. "I can't control how you feel, but it seems to me that you can choose to be happy or miserable. What good is living a long time if you're just going to make yourself miserable."

"I'm not miserable, Maureen."

"Didn't say you were. You want another cup of tea? I just put the kettle on."

* * *

I sit at the table while Maureen puts out another round of tea. Danny pokes his head around the doorframe, a box in his arms.

"Do you mind if I take this?" he asks Maureen.

"Fine." She snorts. "You want a cup before you go?"

Danny sets the box on the floor by the back door. "Sure."

We sit and drink together, Maureen filling us in on the new neighbors, a young couple from New York. She's not sure about them yet being from out of town and all. Danny tries to catch my eye, but I'm not ready. Maybe when I finish my tea.

We have little to say in the car on the way home. Sensing my mood, he doesn't bring up the proposed cemetery visit. I hope he feels guilty for dragging me down to Maureen's. I sigh. That's not fair. I agreed to go, and I knew how it was all going to turn out. Handling Ricky's possessions was going to unleash a whirlwind of emotions, and I hate that. Isn't living through something awful one time enough?

But maybe this will be healing for Danny. They say stuff like this can be. Dealing with emotions head on. I think of Doctor Thayer. This is her area, not mine. I deal in facts and evidence and the law. And I like it that way. Less complicated than people's inner thoughts. I don't care what kind of mixed-up childhoods my suspects have. I just want them to pay for their crimes. That's fair.

"You okay?" Danny asks, pulling up in front of my building.

"Yeah. Fine."

He reaches over and takes my hand. "Thanks, Sis."

"No problem."

"You want to have dinner sometime soon?"

"Sure. Give me a call." I jump out of the car and open the backseat door. The box sits there like a menacing beast. Well, Danny can take it home with him. I grab my satchel off the seat. Don't know why I brought it along with my purse. It's full of work stuff, file folders and my notebook. But you never know when something will hit you when a difficult case is open.

Inside, my apartment is chilly. The building is quiet, and I wonder where everyone is. I set my satchel on the couch, and it shifts and makes a strange noise. I rip open the flap. Damn, Danny. There's the stack of 45s from Ricky's box. My first thought is to chuck them in the garbage, but I can't do it. I hear Ricky singing "Nowhere to Run" by Martha and the Vandellas. I walk over to my stereo cabinet and stash them on the bottom shelf. Then I head into the kitchen for a glass of wine.

CHAPTER 55
Eve

I'M BACK AT WORK MONDAY MORNING DETERMINED TO FIGURE OUT who is behind all that has happened to us. No matter what he's done, my husband didn't deserve this and neither did our little girl.

I'm walking one of my outpatients to the lobby desk when I see a man striding toward the front sliding doors from the parking lot.

Don.

My breath catches. "What's he doing here?" I whisper to the receptionist.

"He has an appointment today with Doctor Tanaka," she says.

"I'll see you next week," I say to my patient and walk quickly down the administration hall.

Mr. Jacobson's door is partly open, and I hear him talking on the phone. I burst through the door and his eyes meet mine; his eyebrows draw together.

"I need to speak with you," I say, my heart hammering.

"Excuse me a moment," he says into the phone, then covers the receiver with his hand. "I'm busy, Eve. Can it wait?"

"No, it can't." I try to keep my breathing even.

"I'll need to call you back," Mr. Jacobson says cheerfully into the phone.

"So, what's so urgent?" he asks, setting the phone down with a thump.

I can't sit, but pace instead. "I just saw Don Barry arriving for his appointment!"

"Yes?"

"I thought we had let him go? Referred him to another facility."

Mr. Jacobson leans back in his chair. "Eve, I meant to tell you last week, but I was terribly busy, and it slipped my mind."

"Why is he back?" I ask through gritted teeth.

"Your complaint went through HR. They reviewed it, spoke with Mr. Barry, but we had no grounds for banning him from the facility."

"What do you mean, you had no grounds?"

"Did he touch you?"

"No, but why does that matter?"

"Did he verbally assault you? Threaten you?"

I can't believe this. They just don't want a hassle or a possible legal issue with Don. To hell with me. "I *feel* threatened, Mr. Jacobson. I'm afraid of him." Tears claw at my eyes, and I blink them away. "He's a suspect in my daughter's kidnapping, for God's sake!"

"He hasn't been charged. We have no grounds." Mr. Jacobson draws a deep breath. "Eve, we know you've been through the wringer in your personal life, but you've been a psychiatric physician for a long time. You know the problems our patients face. You've got an impressive resume dealing with all types of psychiatric issues. You should be able to handle Mr. Barry." He sits up and points to the chair opposite him. "Why don't you have a seat?"

I want to bolt from the room. The last thing I want to do is sit here and talk to him calmly about this. But I sit while my temper boils.

"We've been very happy with your work here, but . . ." Oh, my God. Am I about to be fired? "It's plain to see that your personal life has interfered with your ability to perform your duties at the level we need. Now, Doctor Tanaka has stepped in when we've needed him to, and we've discussed making him our medical lead *temporarily*." Mr. Jacobson raises his palm as if to ward off my objections, but I'm too numb to care at this point. "We're only thinking of you, Eve. Do you need some time to sort out your life? I can get the paperwork started with HR so that you can take a leave of absence. I think that might be the best course of action for all concerned."

I don't want to admit this might be a good idea. It goes against everything that I've believed my whole life. I can handle anything that comes my way. My father did. Nothing stopped him from carrying out his professional duties. He always challenged me to be the best. To work hard. To be number one. And who knows if I will be the sole breadwinner after Nathan's injury. I need my paycheck. I take a deep breath.

"Let me think about it, Mr. Jacobson." I want to buy myself some time. I want to straighten out my life and get back the control I feel slipping through my fingers.

"All right. Let's see how things go the next week or two." His phone rings.

The meeting is at an end. I stand and shut the door behind me.

CHAPTER 56
Rita

I GOT TO WORK EARLY. DIDN'T DO MUCH OVER THE WEEKEND AFTER the trip to Maureen's, and I'm feeling irritable. This Liddle case needs to be solved and put in the books. I sit in my office, old sweater gripped around my chest, drinking coffee to keep warm.

Lauren raps on the doorframe.

"Come in," I say, my eyes on my notebook.

She sits. "Chief wants to meet with the detectives after lunch in the conference room. I just ran into him."

"Great." I drop my pencil on my notebook. "You have anything new on the Liddle case?" I ask, hopefully.

She shakes her head.

"Nothing more from the lab either," I say. After we'd found out that the blood on the doll was animal and that the hair on the crowbar was Mr. Liddle's, nothing else had been discerned.

"Whoever did this was very careful, Rita, to not have left any trace of him or herself. No fingerprints. No DNA. Nothing physical."

"Except a red thread, maybe. And that has led us nowhere." I lean back in my chair. "Yeah. They knew what they were doing."

"Nothing on the people Chase interviewed at the car place?"

"Nope. That's gone nowhere. Just like the hotel search went nowhere," I say.

"And I haven't found anything more on the Singletons, but she does have a lot of money at her disposal," Lauren says.

"Right. She's got pretty much unlimited funds if she needed to pay someone to help her. Did you find anything on Don Barry's cousin?"

Lauren's face brightens. She glances at her laptop. "A little. She's got a rap sheet. Mostly misdemeanors. I'm still trying to trace her movements about the time the baby was taken."

"What about Nicole Clark? Her ex is pretty wealthy and did say he gave her a good settlement, so she might have the wherewithal to enlist help and hide the baby someplace. Maybe she decided to target the Liddles after Mr. Liddle dumped her. Maybe she took out her anger on him instead of her ex."

"You think she'd hit Mr. Liddle with a crowbar?"

"Who knows?" I lean forward, pick up my pencil. "I'm going to do some more checking up on Rachel Chapman since we're getting nowhere with everybody else." I stand and pick up my satchel. "I think I'll run by the gallery."

I park on the square and make my way down the sidewalk. Not too many people out this early. The shops are all just opening up. Don't know who I'll find at the gallery. Maybe Rachel, or maybe someone who can tell me a little more about her. We'll see. I'm up for either scenario.

The bell tinkles as I walk in and an older man in a fastidiously neat suit complete with red pocket square walks toward me.

"May I help you?" His eyes are owlish behind dark-framed glasses.

I introduce myself, show him my identification, and his smile fades. His eyes dart around as if his clientele, should they walk through the door, might be unnerved by a cop standing in his showroom.

"I'd like to ask you a few questions Mr. . . . ."

"Benson. Aaron Benson. This is my gallery. What is this concerning?"

"I wanted to ask you about your employee, Ms. Chapman."

His brows draw together. He must know about the Liddle baby and Rachel's friendship with Eve.

"How may I help you?"

I remove my notebook, turn to the page where I chronicled my interview with Rachel. "How long has she worked for you?"

He clutches his chin. "Several years. Let me see. Five at least."

"Has she spoken about her friend Eve Thayer?"

"Not that I've heard. I don't concern myself with my employees' private lives, Detective. Has Rachel done something I should know about?" He glances at the paintings hanging in various places around the room as if Rachel might be an art thief rather than a kidnapper.

"No. We are just trying to get some background on everyone who knows the Liddles. Maybe she heard something helpful."

He smiles. "Well, maybe you should ask her."

I nod, look over the timeline I've noted. "So, Rachel was at work the day the baby was taken?"

"I don't know. I'd have to pull her timesheet from the file cabinet."

Guess he still does his business the old-fashioned way, on paper. I can appreciate that. "Would you mind, Mr. Benson? It would be helpful."

"Let me get it." He seems anxious to get me on my way, which is fine, as long as I get the answers I'm looking for.

I wait while he disappears into a back room. He waves a file folder as he returns. "Here it is. Now which day are we talking about?"

I give him the date, and he runs his finger down a page in the folder. "Why yes. Rachel worked that day from open to close."

"All afternoon?"

"Yes. Well, except for lunch. She takes her time some days." He raises his eyebrows.

"Does she clock in and out at lunchtime?"

"Yes." His brow furrows. "She was gone almost two hours that day."

Hmm. "Okay. What about the next day?" Rachel had been at the Liddles' overnight. I had been there too. And she was there when I left in the morning.

"She was off that day. I remember now. She called me early and said that she had a family emergency, or a *friend* emergency as it turns out."

My pulse starts to quicken. "She didn't come in that day?"

"No."

"Not even for a couple hours that afternoon?"

He taps the timesheet. "She took the whole day off, Detective. Why?"

"No reason. Thanks for your help." I turn on my heel and head for the door.

I start my van and dig for my phone. Rachel answers on the third ring. "Hello?"

"Ms. Chapman, Detective Myers here."

Silence. "Has something happened?"

"No. I was wondering if I might talk to you again."

"I guess. When? I'm getting ready for work now."

"I can swing by your place," I say, looking over the address I have for her in my notebook, which sits open on the passenger's seat.

"Like right now?"

"Shouldn't take me more than fifteen minutes to get there."

"Can't it wait? I've got to be at work in a half hour."

"Won't take that long."

"Fine."

I end the call and throw my phone on the seat. I could've asked her to come into the station after work, but I want to catch her off guard, and I want to get a look at her apartment. Luckily, rush hour traffic, such as it is in Graybridge, is going in the opposite direction. I pull up in front of an old Victorian that's been divided into apartments like so many have.

Rachel lives on the second floor. I jog up the wide, shiny mahogany staircase. She opens the door right away as if she'd been waiting for me. She looks ready for work, long dark hair neatly combed, makeup on. She's wearing a long, royal-blue dress and a chunky knotted necklace.

"What can I do for you, Detective?" she asks as she swings the door wide. I walk into a large front room with a bay window looking out on the street. There's a colorful throw, looks like a shawl, over the back of a worn red couch. Art books and magazines are piled on a flea market coffee table. The place smells like patchouli and coffee. There's a half full pot sitting on the counter of the small, open kitchen.

"I've got to leave in like five minutes." She frowns.

"Won't take long." I open my notebook. "On the day the baby went missing, you were at work except for a two-hour lunch."

"That's right." Sounds like she's tapping her foot under her long dress.

"Where were you during that lunch?"

She bats her eyes and blows out a breath. "I went to lunch with Eve! You can't possibly think that I had lunch with my best friend and then went and stole her baby!"

"Trying to figure out where everybody was that day."

"I thought we already did that."

"Just following up." I look up from my notes. "So, you were with Eve the whole two hours?"

She tosses her long hair back over her shoulder. "I did a little shopping after, walked around the square. I was in no hurry to return to work that day. My boss was being an ass. More than usual."

I nod. "Okay. What about the next day?"

She glances off toward the kitchen. "I told you. I was at Eve's house. Then I got called into work for a couple of hours."

My eyes meet hers and she breaks our gaze. "I don't know what else you want me to say," she says to fill the silence.

"Well, I just spoke to Mr. Benson. He says you never went in to work that day. You told him you had a family emergency."

Her mouth drops open and her cheeks blaze. She takes a step backwards.

"Ms. Chapman?"

Her gaze is on the floor. "All right. That wasn't the truth, okay? I just needed a break. You know what it was like at the house. Eve was a mess. Reporters outside. Nathan crying and hanging all over Eve. I had to get out of there and clear my head. And I couldn't tell Eve that."

"So, where did you go?"

"Here. Home. I took a shower. Then took a nap on the sofa. Had something to eat. I just couldn't take it over there another minute, Detective. I was planning to go back in a little while. Then Eve called. They were on the way to the hospital. Rosewyn had been found."

"Where were you when Eve called?"

"Here!"

"Anyone see you?"

She shakes her head, lips trembling. "No. I don't think so. *Jesus.* I didn't take the baby."

"Didn't say you did, Ms. Chapman, but we need the truth. It doesn't help to lie, especially if you have nothing to hide."

CHAPTER 57
Eve

ALL OF NEW ENGLAND IS UNDER AN ICE STORM WARNING. USUALLY it's snow, which we are used to, but ice is another beast. But no matter the weather, I have to be at work. I don't want to give Mr. Jacobson one more reason to insist I take a leave of absence. Joanne packed an overnight bag and is prepared to stay at the house with Rosewyn if I can't get home tonight.

I'm sitting in my office and the wind is howling, the sky dark with those roiling gray clouds so common in the winter in the northeast. The window rattles, and I feel a cold breeze right through the old panes. Icy rain pings the glass. All the afternoon appointments have been canceled. I try to keep my mind on my computer, filling in endless pages of paperwork, but the lights keep flickering and I curse corporate for their lack of doing a proper remodel.

"Here it comes." Brian is standing in my open doorway. He almost looks excited, like a kid who is anticipating a snow day.

I shiver and wish I'd worn another layer under my sweater. "I hope it's not as bad as they predicted," I say. "I really want to get home tonight." I hear car engines starting in the parking lot.

Brian walks over to my window. "Administration is sending people home."

"Not us though."

"Nope. Clerical, office guys." He walks back to my door and peers down the hall. "A few nurses, but most of the medical staff will need to stay."

"Just hope we don't lose power. I have a ton of work to do."

"Generator will kick in." He clears his throat, lowers his voice. "How are you doing, Eve? How are you coping?"

"I'm fine. Nathan is improving." At least physically. I don't meet Brian's eyes. Is he wondering if I'm going to be able to hold onto my job?

He's standing near my desk now. "Are they going to discharge him soon?"

"Yes. Not too much longer."

Brian nods. "That's good." He doesn't know what to say, but he's probably thinking: are you going to take him back? Because everyone knows that he was cheating. It had been on the news. The reporters had found out, of course. You really can't keep any secrets these days, although the message had somehow stayed hidden.

"You know you can count on me if you need anything," he says, stopping at my door.

"Thanks. Appreciate it."

After Brian leaves, I dive back into my work, concentrating, trying to shut out the weather and all its implications. After an hour, I stand and stretch. My muscles are cramped and my back pops when I arch it. I decide to walk over to the cafeteria and get a cup of coffee. I can't seem to warm up.

The hallway is deserted, and my heels make an eerie tapping sound as I head toward the lobby. It feels like I'm the only person on this side of the building, besides Brian, I might be. I see him leaning on the reception desk, talking to the young woman who works there. I'm surprised she's still here.

"Is the cafeteria open?" I ask.

Brian straightens. "Most everyone went home after the patients had their dinner."

"I was hoping for a cup of coffee." I cross my arms over my chest trying to stay warm.

"There might be some left, but you'll have to get it yourself probably."

"That's fine. I'll give it a try," I say, and walk up the other hall. The patients are quiet behind their closed doors, and I wonder how Frances is tonight and hope she sleeps peacefully through the storm.

The cafeteria is strangely still, lights low. No one is around. The coffee pots are empty, clean, and ready for the morning. But I can make some tea. That will have to work. I rifle through the basket of tea bags on the counter and choose an Earl Grey. I fill a paper cup with water and put it in the microwave.

I hear footsteps behind me. They echo in the quiet space. I turn. Glenda.

"You're here early," I say.

"Wanted to get in before the weather got too bad." She searches through bagged pastries at the counter, selects one, and throws two dollars next to the cash register. "I figure we'll be short-handed tonight."

"How are the roads?"

"Getting slick." She huffs. "We had a wicked blizzard years ago when I was working here the first time. We couldn't get home for two days."

The microwave dings. "You worked here before? Before it closed?" Before it was shut down for patient abuse and neglect. This is news to me. I'd pictured that long-ago staff retired, or at least out of the profession. I'd heard that a couple of the nurses had been brought up on charges.

"Yup. Started here as a young nurse. Then when they shut us down, I went up to a hospital in New Hampshire. Worked there until last summer when we reopened." The wind rattles the windows, and the lights flicker.

Glenda nods, as if reading my thoughts, her eyes hidden behind her glasses. "It wasn't as bad as reported. I mean, it wasn't perfect, but psychiatric hospitals are scary places to outsiders, especially the other building." She tips her head toward where Nathan's facility is located. "Now that was a tough place. We had some dangerous patients over there."

"You worked over there?"

"Occasionally. When they were short staffed." She snorts. "Which they were half the time."

I shudder. The wind howls and batters the windows with shards of ice that clang like broken glass.

Glenda rips open her pastry. "At least you didn't have to deal with family too much over there. A lot of the patients weren't allowed visitors, not that too many people wanted to see them."

Even now, here, there aren't a lot of visitors. "Like with Frances," I say. "No one's come to see her since she's been here."

A shadow slips across Glenda's face. "Her family bugged out years ago. But she's a tough nut, Frances. Don't know that she'll ever get on her feet. She'll be back on the streets if you let her go."

"You worked with her before?" I'm astonished. I'm racking my brain, trying to remember what I read of Frances's background. I knew she'd been hospitalized many times, but I don't recall the details.

Glenda points at the floor. "Yup. Right here. Years ago."

"Before the hospital was shut down," I murmur half to myself.

"Frances was a regular." Glenda's brow furrows.

"What happened to her family?" I feel my heartbeat pick up. I really want to find someone who'll look out for Frances, so she *doesn't* end up back on the streets.

Glenda shrugs, but there's something akin to anger in her eyes. "Look. Doc, I know you mean well, want the best for your patients, but sometimes there's nothing you can do. You need to do what you can, then you let them go."

Glenda finishes her pastry, wads the wrapper, and tosses it into a garbage can like she's taking a basketball shot. "Well, I better get to work." The lights flicker again. She chuckles. "In case all hell breaks loose."

On my way back to my office, I see no one, even Brian and the receptionist are gone. Mr. Jacobson is still here. I see the light under his office door and there are a couple of people still manning the nurses' station. But I don't see Glenda there. I call a quick hello as I pass with my tea.

Back in my office I check my phone to see if I have any texts from Joanne. But there's nothing from home, so I get back to work.

My tea gone, I stand and stretch, go to my window. In the light of the streetlamps, I see ice accumulating on the parking lot and the wires overhead. I glance at my watch. Normally I would be heading home soon. I hope the roads won't be too bad by then and the night staff can all get here, so that I can leave. But, regardless, I do need to do evening rounds first.

Then, with another flicker of the lights, the power goes out. Everything is dark. I stand still, wait for the little beep that precedes the generator kicking in. But nothing happens.

I feel my way to the door, but it's pitch black in the hallway, and quiet except for the roar of the wind outside and the crackle of ice pelting the window behind me.

"Brian?" I call, my voice echoing down the dark, empty hall. There's no answer. I squint my eyes trying to make out the lobby, but I can't see a thing. The generator should've kicked in by now. We'd only needed it one other time when we first moved into the building last summer. There had been a terrible thunderstorm, and the power went out for about an hour. But the lights had come back on quickly. Dim, emergency lights, but it was only a minute or less when the generator took over.

I make my way back to my desk and pull out my cell phone. I text Joanne and she reports that we have power at home but that some of the roads have been closed. She and Rosewyn are fine, not to worry.

I lean back in my chair and take a deep breath. I tap my computer pad and it springs to life, but I only have ten percent battery. Great. Why didn't I charge it when I had the chance? But then, I expected the generator would be working. Hopefully, everything will get sorted out soon, so I go back to my paperwork. No sense stumbling around in patients' rooms until the lights come back on.

It's been at least a half hour that we've had no power, my computer is dead, and I'm getting worried. There are medications that have to be refrigerated, so that's definitely a concern. At least we don't have ICU patients on vents or other devices that need power like a regular hospital, but still, this isn't good. Then I wonder if Nathan's building has been affected. I decide to feel my way to the lobby and see if I can see over there and find out if anyone has a clue about what's going on.

There's no one in the lobby. I walk up to the glass doors. There are lights on across the parking lot. Nathan's building either didn't

lose power or their generator is working. That's good. I turn back
to the empty reception desk. Our building has an eerie other world
feel, and I can almost hear the past around me. The old building
seems somehow more alive in the dark. I can almost hear nurses
scurrying about in starched white dresses.

Then I hear mumbling, patients. Are they out of their rooms?
Wandering the halls? Where is everyone? I turn around, but I can't
see anything in the dark.

Someone grabs my arm and I shriek. Brian.

"Sorry," he says. "Didn't mean to scare you. Where've you been?"
He shines his phone flashlight in my eyes.

"In my office. What's going on?"

"Generator isn't working. They've got a maintenance guy look-
ing at it, but this isn't good. We're trying to round up the patients.
A few of them left their rooms." There's exasperation in his voice.
"We could use your help."

"Of course." I pull my own phone out of my back pocket, flip on
the flashlight and wonder why I didn't think to use it before. I follow Brian down the patient corridor. I hear them murmuring and
the voices of the nurses trying to lead them back to their rooms.

Then the lights come on. And we stand still blinking for a second before we hurriedly usher patients back where they belong.
Just as we get everyone secure, a scream erupts from one of the
rooms. Brian and I sprint down the hall where a young nurse is
standing in a patient doorway. We step inside the room. Frances
Martin is lying in her bed, on her side, a pair of scissors sticking out
of her back.

CHAPTER 58
Rita

WE HAD A TON OF CALLS WITH THE ICE STORM FULL BORE AT RUSH hour, but the call from the Graybridge West Psychiatric Hospital was different. We were dealing with a homicide in the midst of everything else.

Strobing police lights cut through the dark as Chase and I pull into the facility lot. Seems like I've been here too often, and I wonder if this new incident is somehow related to Doctor Thayer and her husband. They seem to be at the center of everything lately.

The air is frigid although the ice has let up some. Chase loses his balance in his dress shoes and grabs the side of our vehicle to keep himself upright. I'm grateful for my boots.

Uniformed officers have gathered the staff in the lobby, while the patients are in their rooms behind locked doors. Apparently, they'd had a power outage, and in the darkness, a patient had been killed.

This is going to take a while to untangle. Chase and I head to the vic's room where the ME, Susan Gaines, has just arrived and is examining the body. We watch for a moment while our tech guy snaps pictures.

Susan sees us and steps away.

"Hey," she says. Susan and I began working in law enforcement about the same time, years ago. She left for medical school and returned as an ME. Her salt and pepper hair is held back with a head-band, and light crow's feet trail her dark eyes.

"What've we got?" I ask.

"A patient. Frances Martin. Fifty-eight-year-old female. Deceased. Scissors used like a knife in her back. Appears that there are multiple stab wounds." Susan moves aside so that I can get a clear view. Blood has saturated the bed and pooled on the floor.

"Hit her heart?"

"Could have, or she bled out, but I can't say what the cause was until the postmortem."

"Definitely a homicide," I say, half to myself since there's no way she could've stabbed her own back.

Susan smirks. "I'll let you know manner after the postmortem. But you make your own assumptions based on the evidence at the scene."

That's Susan-speak for "of course it's a homicide, but the rules are, I don't make any definitive statements until I complete my work in the lab."

"Thanks, Susan. We'll try not to get in your way."

"No problem, Rita. Do what you have to."

Chase is hanging back behind us, as if to give two much older and more experienced professionals room to work. I motion him to my side, and he starts making notes on his phone while I search my satchel for my notebook.

I walk around to the other side of the bed. The vic is lying on her side, eyes half-closed. One mottled arm is stretched out as if she had tried to get off the bed, away from her assailant, but didn't have the strength to move. I wonder if she was sleeping when she was attacked. I do a quick sketch of her, and Chase and I leave the room. We walk the hall, looking for clues there, and I notice an outside door at the end of the hall next to Frances's room. There appears to be a blood smudge on it. I pull on gloves and try the door; it's locked. But it might not have been when the power was out. We'll have to see. I call over a crime scene tech and show him the smudge.

We herd the staff down to the cafeteria. We'll interview them first before turning our attention to the patients. Uniformed officers established that Frances was alive before the power went out and that was after some of the staff was let go, so we don't have as many people to question as we might have had.

I call the head administrator into a conference room, while Chase sits with the others.

He's a tall man, forties, wearing a dark suit.

"Mr. Jacobson, I've looked over the report our officers put together before we got here and want to check a few things with you."

"All right." His face twitches. He's understandably concerned. He's the boss. This is his show and one of his patients has been murdered. I had talked to him briefly when the Liddle baby was kidnapped, and he seemed much more confident then.

"The power went out about five-thirty, is that right?"

"Yes."

"And your generator wasn't working?" We've already learned that the generator was tampered with. Officers interviewed the maintenance man when they got here. We also know that the power was cut as well, so someone apparently planned this.

"No. Well, you know what happened to it."

I nod. "Is there any way that one of the patients could've done that?"

He shakes his head. "No. The power was cut from the outside of the building. The doors to the patient wing would've been locked."

"Okay. After the power went out, those locks would've stopped functioning? Cameras too?"

"Right." He blows out a breath. "Normally, the generator would've kicked in and the locks and cameras would've kept working."

"So, someone would have to know a good deal about this building. Where to find the power source and the generator."

"Yes."

That doesn't necessarily mean that the power being cut and the murder are connected. It is possible that whoever tampered with the power had something else in mind, and one of the patients could've walked freely and killed Frances. But I'm thinking it was all one plan, which means it was either a staff member or an outsider who then got into the building.

"What about your staff? Where were they when the power went out?"

"We were all trying to round up the patients who had left their rooms. It was dark. It was difficult to see who was who."

"Any of the patients violent?"

"Some can be."

"Any of them have a beef with Ms. Martin?"

"Not that I know of. And most of them had headed for the common area. We didn't find anyone down at Frances's end of the hall, not that they couldn't have been down there before we started looking. But I don't think so."

We already know that no obvious blood was found on any of the patients, so it's not likely it was one of them. But we can't rule them out at this point.

"Just two doctors here this evening?" He'd already made a list of the names of the staff present. Officer Connors gave it to me when I got here.

"Yes. We have three, but only Doctor Tanaka and Doctor Thayer were on duty."

"Uh huh." There are four nurses listed, one aide, and the maintenance man. "Did you see Ms. Martin while you were rounding up the patients?"

"No. Not me personally. Her room is the last one on the hall. I was near the front."

"Who was looking for the patients?"

"All of us. Everyone who was still here, I guess."

"You saw them all? All the staff who was here?"

He shakes his head. "I don't know. We were pretty much fumbling around in the dark. Using cell phones as light."

"So, you can't say that you knew where everyone was?"

"No, Detective. I can't say that."

"Is there any way someone from the outside could've gotten into the building?"

"It's certainly possible. Once the power was out, the doors could've been manually opened."

And there's that outside door with the blood smear at the end of the hall, just past Frances Martin's room. It would make for a convenient getaway for the perp.

"Would the lock on the outside door at the end of the patient hall have been working?"

"I don't know," he says, shaking his head. "Probably not."

"Any threats that you're aware of to Ms. Martin or the facility in general?"

"No. Nothing like that," he says, his gaze in his lap.

After Mr. Jacobson leaves, I call in the nurses and the aide, one at a time. None of them has any apparent blood on their scrubs or their hands. And none of them has anything to say that is in any way helpful.

The maintenance man is also unlikely. He was actually at the other building attending to a leaky faucet over there when the lights went out.

I look down at the report. I still need to talk to Doctor Tanaka and Doctor Thayer. Then we'll interview the patients. But my mind keeps going back to the blood on the outside door next to Frances's room. Why would someone want to kill her? And is the culprit long gone by now?

CHAPTER 59
Eve

I'M SHAKING WITH COLD AND EMOTION. HOW COULD THIS HAVE HAP-
pened? I'm sitting next to Brian on stiff cafeteria chairs, while Detective Fuller watches over us like a schoolteacher. We aren't
supposed to talk to one another, just wait our turn to speak to Detective Myers. I feel like I know her personally at this point and
can't help but think this is my fault. Could whoever is out to hurt
me and Nathan have killed poor Frances? Someone went to a lot of
trouble to get to her apparently, and I'm distraught to think that
someone might've killed her to hurt me. Or to avenge me maybe.
Don Barry? Could Don see this as a way to show me he cares? Kill
the woman who attacked me and left me bruised. He probably
heard about the tussle I had with her. He seems to know everything
that goes on around here. My thoughts race round and round. But
I keep coming back to I'm responsible, in some way. How did my
life go so off the rails?

"You okay?" Brian whispers. "I can feel you trembling."

"Just cold. Upset too, obviously."

He looks at me and there's something in his dark eyes that
makes me shiver. Does he think I could've possibly done this? Does
my closest colleague actually suspect me? Then I think about his
concern lately for my mental health. Will he tell the cops that?

"Doctor Thayer?" Detective Myers is standing at the front of the room, her expression unreadable. "Would you mind stepping into the conference room?"

My pulse is pounding in my ears as I sink down into a padded, rolling chair. It's cold in here too. The heat hasn't been back on that long.

"How are you holding up, Eve?" she asks, her face a blank.

"Okay," I manage.

"Tell me what happened."

I draw a deep breath. "I was working at my desk, doing paperwork. I was about to do evening rounds when the power went out. I figured the generator would kick in, but it didn't."

"So, what did you do?"

"I stayed at my desk. Waited. Then I went out into the hall and started looking for everyone to see if they knew what was going on."

"Did you find anyone?"

"I ran into Doctor Tanaka in the lobby. The patients were out of their rooms, and I started helping everyone round them up."

"Did you see Ms. Martin?"

I feel tears collecting in my eyes and I can't control my shaking. "No. I didn't see her. The lights came back on and one of the nurses was at the end of the patient hall. She started screaming and we ran to Frances's room. That's when I saw her." I cover my mouth with my hand to stifle a cry.

"What did you see?"

"She was in bed. On her side with . . . scissors sticking out of her back."

"Then what did you do?"

"I watched while Brian, Doctor Tanaka, went over and checked for a pulse, but he shook his head. And someone called 911."

"Where did you go then?"

I squeeze the sides of my thighs trying to control their shaking, but I can't. All I see is poor Frances, blood all over her bedding, spilling onto the floor. "Back to the lobby. We all gathered in the lobby, except Brian and Mr. Jacobson, the administrator. They stayed with Frances."

"When was the last time you saw Frances alive?"

"This morning, during rounds."

"She say anything? Anyone ever visit her? Threaten her? Was she afraid of anyone?"

I cringe back into my seat. "No. Nothing like that. No one's been to see her. We can't find her family." Detective Myers is writing in her notebook. Everything is silent except the scrape of her pencil. My lips are trembling. I clear my throat. "Detective, what if this is my fault? What if Don Barry did this? He was really angry when he saw the bruises that I got from when Frances attacked me. What if he thought he was protecting me?"

She looks up from her notebook, ice blue eyes locking on mine. "Was he at the facility today? Did you see him?"

"No. I didn't see him, but he could've been here."

"We'll question Mr. Barry. We'll bring him in. We're still gathering evidence, so I might need to talk to you again."

I nod. "Can I go home?"

"Yeah. That's fine."

I get up, and as I get to the door, Detective Myers calls after me. "Be safe, Eve. The roads are treacherous."

CHAPTER 60
Rita

W E'D BEEN AT THE PSYCHIATRIC FACILITY, THEN THE STATION, UNTIL late last night, but we're all back at work bright and early this morning. What had started out as a quiet winter in Graybridge has turned into a nightmare that is garnering national attention. Reporters from multiple media outlets have swarmed our little town. None of what's happened seems to make any sense. The only thing that ties it all together is Eve Thayer.

The station is humming with activity. The chief is running on caffeine and sugar, and I hope like hell this doesn't push him over the edge and he has a stroke or something. And I feel the weight of this case crushing my shoulders. If I'd only been able to solve the kidnapping weeks ago, I feel like we might not be sitting here with a homicide on our hands now. Nothing to substantiate that but a gut feeling.

In the conference room, Lauren, Chase, and I run through the interviews at the psychiatric hospital, but nothing is jumping out at us. No one—staff or patient—had any visible signs of blood on them. Forensics is testing the blood smear that was found on the exit door next to Frances's room, and they found more blood outside in the parking lot. We'll have to wait for the lab to tell us who it belongs to. But it looks, to me, like someone was there, killed Frances, then they were gone.

I glance over at Chase, whose dark eyes are surrounded by dark circles. "You find Donald Barry?"

"Nope." He looks at Lauren.

"The uniformed cops that went to his residence were unable to find him there last night, or this morning either when they went back out," she says.

"Well, he was home the other day when I went to talk to him. Don't tell me he's left town again. What about his employer?"

Chase rubs his hand over his face. "They said he hasn't been in the office in a week."

"He still doing his work remotely?"

"They said he was. But they don't know from where."

"You think he's our best bet, Rita?" Lauren asks.

I blow out a breath. "Who else would have a reason to kill Frances? Everyone at the hospital knew that she attacked Doctor Thayer. I just don't know what to make of it otherwise."

The chief walks in with Detective Schmitt on his heels. They sit at the table, and we run through everything we've got, as Bob nods along. Finally, he leans back in his chair.

"Okay. This is what we're going to do. We have nothing solid at this point to tie Frances Martin's homicide to the kidnapping, so I've decided to put Doug on that. Rita, you keep your focus on the Thayer/Liddle kidnapping."

My mouth falls open. "What if they *are* related?" My voice rises. "I think I'm in a better position to sort this out."

His tired eyes shift in my direction. Chase and Lauren have gone silent, their gazes on the table. But I can't keep my mouth shut. Bob's known me for years, and I hope that buys me something.

He takes a deep, tired breath. "Rita, this isn't a reflection on you. I just think it would be a good idea to have some fresh eyes on this. You've been dealing with Doctor Thayer for a while now. It might be prudent to have Doug look at the homicide from the outside."

I clamp my lips together and nod slightly.

He continues, "If we find a link in the cases, you two work together, obviously, but there're so many damn pieces to go through, I think it would be a good idea to keep these investigations separate until there's a solid reason to tie them together."

I can deal with that, for now. I slow my breathing and play the obedient detective. But we'll see where this all leads.

Bob stands, and he and the others sort through evidence while I look back through my notebook. I reread my notes on our original kidnapping suspects. Barbara Singleton, Donald Barry, and Nicole Clark, with Rachel Chapman as a possible outlier.

I wander down the hall to my office, shut the door, and sit at my desk. Just me and my notebook. What do I know about my main suspects? They all had motives for going after the Liddles. And all of them needed a place to keep the baby out of sight and an accomplice to watch her.

I can't sit still, so I decide to pay them all another visit if I can find them.

I slip out the back entrance. I hear reporters, snatches of conversations, laughter, the thrum of their work truck engines, out front. I start my van and exit the lot onto a back street and head for Don Barry's apartment complex.

I don't see his vehicle in the lot, but I stop and knock on his door anyway. No answer. I walk around the building and try to see through his windows, but the curtains are drawn. Everything's quiet.

I jump back in my van and call Chase.

"Where are you?"

"At Don Barry's apartment complex, but he's still not here."

"Why didn't you say anything? I'd have gone with you."

"Sorry. I wasn't thinking. Anyway, do me a favor?"

"Sure."

"See if you can figure out where the cousin is, Paula Barry. We need to talk to her."

"You think she's the one who's been helping him?"

"Time to find out. See if you can locate her while I head over to Barbara's."

"Will do."

With Barbara's money, she might have been able to hire someone to watch the Liddle baby. And I'm thinking back to the Singleton lake house. What if Barbara had an accomplice take the baby out there? It might be worth a look.

The FOR SALE sign is still in the yard, I notice, as Mr. Singleton comes to the door. He doesn't look as dapper and rested as he did before. His hair is a little mussed and his eyes are bloodshot. He peers at me through the slightly open door.

"Mr. Singleton, I'd like to speak with Barbara."

"She's lying down, resting."

"Well, this will only take a minute. I just have a couple questions for her." I'm digging my notebook out of my satchel.

"I'm afraid that won't be possible, Detective. My wife isn't well, and she's not up to speaking with you." He goes to shut the door, but I stick my hand out, bobble my notebook, and stop him.

"What's wrong with her?"

"This whole matter has taken its toll. I won't have her harassed by you or anyone else. If you want to speak with us in the future, you'll need to contact our lawyer."

With that he literally shuts the door in my face. *Huh.* I make a few notes. Then get back in my van. I'll ride out to the lake house later and look around the property. Then, if I can get it, maybe a warrant to search inside. See if there is anything there that would implicate Barbara in the kidnapping. It's a long shot, but what else do I have?

Right now, the next stop is Nicole Clark's place. She didn't necessarily need an accomplice. She might've been able to hoodwink Granny into believing she was at home when she wasn't, but she couldn't have kept the baby there. Even someone with dementia would probably recall a baby in the house, so where would Nicole have kept her?

The blue house sits quietly on its equally quiet street. I see Nicole's car in the driveway though, so maybe I'll luck out with at least one of the people on my list.

She greets me at the door, a smile on her face, her long blond hair pulled up in a ponytail. "How can I help you, Detective?"

"May I come in?"

She opens the door wide, and I notice a change in the little house. The knick-knacks that had covered every shelf and end table are gone, and boxes sit in the middle of the living room floor.

"Moving?" I ask.

"Yes. My grandmother is in an assisted living apartment now. I moved her in last week. That's what's really kept me here, in Graybridge." Nicole wipes her hands on her yoga pants as if they're dusty. "It took a few months to get her a spot." Nicole rolls her blue eyes. "So, now I'm moving on."

"Where to?" I ask, pencil poised.

"New York. I'm starting a new job."

"You have an address?"

She flutters her lashes. "Someplace. I haven't memorized it yet. It's written down somewhere."

"When are you leaving?"

"In a few days." She leans over and closes the flaps on a box that is bursting with what looks like towels.

"Where were you during the ice storm?" I can't help but ask.

She stands up, puts her hands on her hips. "Here. I wasn't about to drive around in that. Why?"

"Anyone see you here?"

"No. I don't think so. Everyone was pretty much staying inside. I think. Is there anything else, Detective? I've got a lot to do to wrap things up. And I've got work stuff too."

Strange. I thought she'd been fired. "All right. But don't leave town without giving us a forwarding address."

"I won't."

I sit in my van, drum my fingers against the steering wheel. The afternoon has gotten away from me and it's nearly dusk. Maybe I'll head to Graybridge Square, check in with Ms. Chapman and grab a coffee at André's. But first, I read back through some of my notes on Nicole. I decide to give her ex another call.

This time he sounds wide awake. "How can I help you, Detective?"

"Just following up on a few things, Mr. Clark. You said you live in Hopkinton?"

"Yes. When I'm home. I travel a lot for business."

"You lived there with your ex-wife?"

"That's right."

"Does Nicole have a key?"

He grunts. "She's not supposed to. She did leave some of her stuff there. She said at the time she'd come back for it all later, but she hasn't. I've been meaning to give her things to charity. Why?"

"Just wondering. Would I have your permission to take a look through your house?"

"What for? You think Nicole might've been up there?"

"It's possible. I'd just like to take a quick look if you wouldn't mind."

"So, they still haven't found the person who kidnapped that baby?"

"We have not," I say.

"Well." He draws a deep breath. "I don't think Nicole had anything to do with that. But I wouldn't put it past her to break into my house. Yeah. Go ahead. Let me know if she's set my clothes on fire or anything, would you?"

"I can do that."

"There's a spare key with my next-door neighbor, Mrs. Wilson. I'll give her a call and let her know that you'll be coming by."

"I would appreciate that, Mr. Clark. And I'll let you know if I find anything amiss."

"Great. Hopefully all's well," he says.

"Let's hope." I end the call and Google the directions to Mr. Clark's house, but before I can get on my way, I get a call from Lauren.

"We got something from the lab, Rita."

"What?"

"The scissors that killed Ms. Martin?"

"Yeah?"

"They found prints."

I head back to the station, the trip to Hopkinton postponed. I know I'm not technically investigating the murder, but my curiosity is piqued.

CHAPTER 61

Nathan

*E*VE CALLED TO LET ME KNOW ABOUT THE POLICE ACTIVITY OVER AT her building last night. The power went out, and in the dark, in the commotion, one of her patients was killed. It makes my blood turn cold to think something like that went on just across the parking lot. And I'm afraid for Eve.

But my anxiety over my health seems to have settled down in the last few days. My thinking is not as muddled. My brain feels clearer, and I hope that means I'm healing. After Eve's last visit, I've reasoned through the last few weeks, and I believe her. Someone else knocked me down the stairs, and we're targets of that person's wrath, but why?

I'm anxious to get out of here and get home. I need to protect my family. The doctors have been telling me that I'll be discharged soon. Now that my vision is returning, at least in my right eye, rehab has gone much smoother. I'm stronger than I was just a couple of weeks ago. My health seems to be trending in the right direction, both mentally and physically.

But where will I go? I want to go home. I want to live where my daughter lives. But what about Eve? Is there any way that she would take me back?

I picture myself in some small, crummy apartment, alone. That's not what I want for myself or Rosewyn. She needs me. I remember after my mother died how lonely life became. How cold the house seemed. I don't want that for my daughter. I want her surrounded by people who love her, and not on a part-time basis.

It's almost dark when Eve walks in.

"Hi, I just have a minute, but I wanted to see how you're doing." She walks to the window, her pale hair pulled back in an old barrette, her white coat rumpled. Eve gazes out toward her building. She seems so different. Subdued, quieter even than usual.

"I'm getting some strength back. I'm feeling more normal. So, what happened yesterday? Did they figure out who killed that woman?"

"Not yet." Eve sighs and perches on the edge of the visitor's chair. "This is all related, Nathan. I didn't want to get into it on the phone last night, but whoever is out to get us, I believe killed my patient."

"I was thinking the same thing."

"The cops aren't saying it's related, but I guess they can't yet. They've got to follow the evidence. But whoever did it, planned it carefully. The power was cut, the generator tampered with."

I wonder why they didn't kill Eve. I shudder. If someone is after us, why not go for her? They tried to get me. "Are you being careful?"

"Yes. They're still keeping an officer in a patrol car outside the house. And Mr. Jacobson is bringing in security guards at the hospital."

"That's good. You think it was your old patient?"

"Don Barry. That's my guess. I told Detective Myers that. But who knows?"

"Hopefully, they'll arrest him soon and this will all be over."

Eve looks at me, and despite the blurriness in my vision, I can see the worry on her face. The tightness of her mouth, the circles under her eyes. I decide to broach the subject of my going home. It can't hurt. Eve's at a low point and maybe I'm taking advantage of that, but I plow ahead anyway. I think we'd all be better off together, under one roof.

"My doctor said that they're looking at releasing me next week."

Her head bobs up. "Really? I'm sorry. I didn't know. I haven't spoken to them in a few days." She collapses back against the chair, rubs her face with her hands. "We can fix up the den since it's on the first floor. That would make it easier for you until you regain your strength."

And just like that, I'm in, at least as far as the first floor, and a flicker of hope blooms in my chest. Maybe we can reclaim our old lives eventually, somehow. I sniff, take a deep breath. I didn't know how much I wanted to go home until this moment.

"That would be great. I can help with Rosewyn, at least a little."

"Joanne can do most of the work. She's been amazing and she already said that she could help with you, too."

Even with all the craziness in our lives, I'm happy. "I quit smoking," I quip. "Nothing like getting your brains nearly bashed out to get you to kick the habit."

Her face breaks into a smile. Something I haven't seen in a very long time. "That's one good thing, Nathan. I'll take it." She stands and leans over, squeezes my shoulder. "I'll get things sorted out for you at home."

"Can't wait," I say. "In the meantime, Eve, be careful, okay?"

She says that she will and that she needs to get back to work. I watch out my window until I see her jog across the parking lot and disappear into her building.

CHAPTER 62
Eve

*M*ORNING STARTS COLD AND ICY. IT'S BEEN NEARLY TWO DAYS SINCE Frances was murdered and the cops still haven't arrested anyone, and they haven't questioned me again, so I hope I'm in the clear. I don't dare ask because I don't know if I can deal with the answer. I walk through my morning in a daze, taking care of patients, doing the nonstop paperwork that is so much a part of modern healthcare. The mood around the hospital is somber, everyone looking at each other with suspicion. Crime scene tape cordons off the end of the patient hallway where Frances's room lies. Cops are still in and out of the building.

My phone rings and a man identifies himself as Detective Doug Schmitt. I think I remember him from Rosewyn's case. He works with Detective Myers. He asks me to come into the police station ASAP. My heart is thumping as I agree and end the call.

I stop by the receptionist's desk and instruct her to cancel my afternoon appointments.

Reporters are gathered in bunches in front of the police station, and they rustle to attention as I get out of my car. They call to me and follow me up the walkway, their breath steaming in the cold.

Inside, I'm escorted to a small interview room. I look for Detective Myers, but I don't see her. A man is waiting for me. He's tall, well dressed in a dark suit.

"Have a seat, Doctor Thayer," he says. "I'm Detective Schmitt."

I'm shaking as I sit in the stiff, metal chair opposite him. He has me run through the night Frances was killed, and I tell him everything that I can remember, which isn't much.

He sighs, leans back in his chair. "You keep a pair of scissors in your work office?"

"Yes." Sweat is sprouting on my forehead.

"Where are those scissors right now, Doctor?"

"They should be on my desk in the cupholder."

"Well, we searched the hospital, top to bottom. We didn't find a pair of scissors in your office. But you do have some, right?"

"Yes. We probably all do, on our side of the building anyway, not on the inpatient side. Sharp objects aren't allowed there." I can barely speak. My throat feels like it's closing up.

"But somehow a pair of scissors made it over there." He leans back in his chair. "Here's the thing. We were able to pull prints, or one fingerprint actually, from the scissors that were used to kill Frances Martin." He clears his throat. "That print is yours, Doctor."

He keeps talking, but I can't hear what he's saying, his voice bounces around the room like the adult voices on a Peanuts cartoon. *Wah. Wah. Wah.*

I manage to speak up enough to deny any involvement in Frances's death. I ask for Detective Myers. She knows what's been going on, how someone is trying to destroy my life. I ask him to question Don Barry. I tell him that Don had been in my office a few days ago, alone. He could've taken my scissors then.

Detective Schmitt stands, puts his hand on his hip. "Funny thing is, Doctor Thayer, yours is the only print we found."

"Do I need a lawyer?" I manage to ask.

"That's up to you," he says.

I get to my feet. "I'd like to leave now." My heart is hammering. I can't believe this is happening.

He smirks. I think he's considering if he has enough to arrest me. And I wait for what seems like an eternity, my fate swinging back and forth.

"Okay," he says at last. "But don't leave town or anything."

I rush out of the room, stumble along the hall to the lobby. The reporters are waiting in the parking lot, standing in menacing little groups. I lean against the door trying to catch my breath. I can't believe this is happening, even with everything else that has gone on.

Officer Connors appears at my side. I remember her from the time she spent with us at the house when Rosewyn was missing.

"Doctor Thayer?"

I nod. I can't seem to find my voice.

"You want me to walk you to your car?"

I nod again and tears tumble down my cheeks unabated.

CHAPTER 63

Rita

When I learned about the fingerprint, I cornered Doug before he questioned Eve. I went over everything I had that would tend to exonerate Eve as the murderer. No blood on her, her clothes, or shoes. Blood on an outside door and in the parking lot, indicating that the perp probably left the facility after the attack. And, of course, the incidents involving the Liddles that point to someone targeting them. Still, he was ready to slap cuffs on her, but the chief joined us and made the point that the DA was going to want more than a single print, especially with all of the extenuating circumstances.

In any case, we needed to bring her in for questioning. Eve's not in the clear yet. I wanted to speak to her after Doug's interrogation, but she bolted from the station after the meeting. She's free for the moment.

I settle down at my desk, focus on the kidnapping case. That's the key to everything, I believe. I really need to speak to Don Barry. He's still my number one, and it's interesting that he seems to have fallen off the grid lately, just when things are heating up. I need to talk to Chase but take the lazy way out and call him instead of walking down the hall to the squad room.

"You find anything on the whereabouts of Paula Barry?"

I hear Chase swallow, probably the coffee he lives on. "Not yet, Rita. Let me dig a little more into that and I'll let you know."

"Good deal. Thanks." Ten minutes don't go by before my phone rings.

"I've got a location for Paula Barry," Chase says.

"That was fast."

He chuckles. "Sometimes things work like they're supposed to."

"Sometimes." I fumble with a Post-it note. "Where?"

"You won't believe this, Rita. She's staying at a motel just outside of Graybridge. She's been there for quite a while."

"How'd you find out?"

"I called his ex again. She finally answered her phone. She told me that Don told her just yesterday—he was afraid she was worried about him with all the news coverage of the murder." Chase huffs out a breath. "He told her that his cousin was in town, and he's been staying with her off and on. The ex-missus Barry gave me the name of the motel where she said the cousin sometimes stays. I gave the front desk a call and found out that she's there."

"Great work. I'll head over there. You game?"

"Meet you in the parking lot."

The Graybridge Inn has seen better days. It's the kind of place where you took the family back in the sixties or seventies. A strip of small quaint rooms with shutters on the windows and a couple of aluminum chairs on the small slab of a concrete porch in front of each unit. The parking lot would've been filled with wood-paneled station wagons, and the pool out front would've been full of happy kids. But that pool is now covered with a rotting tarp, surrounded by leggy weeds, and the families have been replaced by down-on-their-luck people who have nowhere else to go. It surprises me that Paula Barry, she of the big insurance-fraud win, would stay here. But you never know about people.

Her room is the last one in the complex. It takes her a minute to answer the door. She leaves the chain on, and we're greeted with a waft of cigarette smoke. "Yeah?"

"Ms. Barry?

"Who wants to know?"

Chase stifles a chuckle at the cliché. We identify ourselves, hold up our IDs.

"What do you want?"

"Can we come in a minute? We just want to ask you a few questions."

"Fine. Sure, but he's not here."

The door closes, the chain rattles, then she opens up. The two double beds are neatly made with lumpy, blue-patterned bedspreads. There's an impressive collection of liquor bottles on the dresser. The room looks lived in, but tidy for all that. Ms. Barry is tall, heavy eyeliner circles her dark eyes. There are crow's feet at the corners and lines around her mouth. Her hair is highlighted to a puffy straw-looking blond.

"We're looking for Donald Barry," I say.

"Like I said, he's not here." She walks back into the room and sits heavily on the edge of one of the beds, tamps out her cigarette in a full ashtray on the nightstand. "I know this place is a dump, but you can smoke here. And we used to stay here when I was a kid, so it has some good memories."

"Okay. Was he here, Ms. Barry?"

"Yeah. He's been staying with me. He didn't do anything, but he said he was getting harassed by the police, so I told him he could hang over here with me." She eyes a pack of cigarettes on the dresser.

"Where is he now?"

She shrugs, walks over to the dresser, and pours herself a whiskey, trying to be nonchalant about it. "He went out to get us something to eat, but I don't know where he went."

I pull out my notebook. I hear Chase typing on his phone, while he stands near the door. I run through the day the baby was kidnapped.

"You were here that day?"

"I'd just gotten to town, I think. I don't remember, Detective, the exact day I came up, but Don didn't have anything to do with taking a kid, okay? And neither did I."

I keep the questions going, anything I can think of, hoping that Don will return soon, but, after a while, that doesn't look like it's going to happen.

"Okay, Ms. Barry. We'll get out of your hair."

I'm thinking that Don might've come back and seen the unmarked car in the lot and recognized it. There's a coffee shop across the road, so Chase and I circle the block, then park on a side street, sit at a table near the window where we can see the motel.

But after two cups of coffee, I'm wired, and we haven't seen anything of Donald Barry, so we reluctantly return to the station.

I work on my other cases. Bug the guys at the lab. The afternoon wanes and I want to get out to the Clark residence in Hopkinton before it gets too late.

Chase has left for home. I pack up my satchel. We'd wasted a lot of time today with Paula Barry and hope we haven't scared off her cousin. I hope like hell he hasn't hit the road for points unknown.

CHAPTER 64
Eve

I'M FINISHING UP MY DAY, ANOTHER HEADACHE THROBBING AFTER spending my afternoon being grilled by Detective Schmitt. At least he didn't arrest me for Frances's murder. Not yet anyway. I finish a cold cup of coffee. Probably not the best thing for a headache, but I'm too tired to go get anything else. Besides, I've been avoiding my colleagues. While no one has said anything, I see it in their eyes. They don't trust me, and I'm expecting to get called into Mr. Jacobson's office anytime now and given my pink slip.

My phone vibrates. A text from Rachel. She wants me to meet her at the gallery. It's important. Can I come right away? I respond that I'm leaving work and can be there in ten minutes. I can't wait to get out of here.

I wonder what's up. I don't even dare speculate anymore. Snow is falling in fat heavy flakes as I get out of my car in front of the gallery. When I pull the door open, the bell tinkles, but I don't see Rachel inside. A woman stands by the register. She turns.

Marie Williams, my former patient.

"Doctor Thayer!" she exclaims.

"Hi, Marie. How are you?"

"Fine. I just walked in, but it doesn't appear that anyone's here." She bats her eyes. She looks great, as usual. Expensive coat draped over her arm. Makeup and blond hair perfect. "I stopped in to look for artwork for my new apartment."

"Maybe Rachel's in the back," I say, and drop my purse on the counter and head through the door. There's a restroom on the right and another door to the left. I prop open the restroom door with my hip. "Rach?" No answer, so I turn to the other door, which is a workroom. It's dark, so I flip a switch on the wall. There's a table with tools and artwork sitting on it. Framed pieces are stacked on shelves against one wall.

I catch my breath. Rachel is sprawled on the floor. She's covered in blood. Her top is soaked. I rush over, drop to my knees and check for a pulse. She's alive and moans as I call her name. I hear a noise behind me.

Marie.

"Call 911," I shout as I look frantically for the source of Rachel's blood. Then I see a knife on the floor nearby.

I hear the door shut. "Did you hear me? Someone stabbed Rachel!"

"I heard," Marie says.

I push up Rachel's blouse and apply pressure to a gaping wound in her chest near her shoulder. I'm immediately assessing. Too high for lungs or heart. Not a bad place if you've got to be stabbed. But she's lost a lot of blood.

"We need help. Call 911!"

"In time, Eve."

I turn toward Marie and notice a smear of blood on her sleeve. My heart hammers. Realization hits me. She did this. Marie stabbed Rachel. But why would she do that? I can't make sense of it, and I can't seem to catch my breath. What do I do now? My phone is in my purse in the other room.

Marie paces between me and the door. "You have no idea who I am, do you, Eve?"

I'm completely confused. "Of course, I do."

"When I came to see you weeks ago about my parents, I was hoping you'd remember me." She laughs. "But of course, you didn't."

I slide off my haunches, fall flat on my backside, my hand firmly clamped against Rachel's wound. Sweat is dripping down my back. "What are you talking about?"

"You and Rachel still BFFs after all this time. I should've known."

"Where do I know you from, Marie? What are you getting at?"

"We went to college together. I was a freshman and you and Rachel were sophomores. I lived right down the hall from you. Rachel used to refer to me as Weird Girl. Remember now?"

My mouth drops open. Yes. Memories start to come back to me. In fact, Rachel had just brought her up recently. I had no idea she knew that Rachel called her that. I always thought it was mean, but Rachel could be thoughtless back then. I can't believe Marie is the same person.

Marie waves her hand in the air as she paces. Then she comes to a stop and her gaze meets mine. "We had that one class together. The Drama I class."

She looks so different from the girl I barely remember all those years ago, whose name I can't recall. I can't believe she'd be so angry with Rachel that she'd try to kill her. She's obviously unhinged. How did I not see it in our sessions? How did I not recognize her? "I'm sorry, Marie."

"You should be sorry," she says angrily.

My mind whirls. How do I handle this? Handle her? Rachel needs immediate medical attention. She's barely conscious, and I feel her slipping away. "Hold on, Rachel," I whisper to my friend. Luckily the pressure I'm putting on her wound seems to have slowed the bleeding, but I can't move. I can't take my hand off her wound.

Marie huffs out a breath. "Don't you even remember the class we had together? *I* won't forget it. We had monologues to perform in front of the class one day and my roommate told me she heard you and Rachel whispering after I returned to my seat. Rachel said my performance was atrocious. She said she hoped I didn't plan on becoming an actress someday. And you both laughed."

"I don't recall that, Marie. I'm sorry. That was unkind." Surely, we didn't mean for anyone to overhear a remark like that. I'm racking my brain, trying to figure out how to calm her down and call for help, but I'm afraid if I move, Rachel will start bleeding again.

"Of course, you don't remember. But I had the last laugh. You suck as a psychiatrist, Eve. I was totally acting as Marie Williams. My parents didn't die in a car crash." She chuckles and my blood freezes. "When I moved back to town and heard you were a therapist, I couldn't resist. It was after I got my divorce, and I was so angry. So many people in my life hurt me. And I was determined to get even. So, I figured I'd start with you and Rachel, and my mom, of course. It really started there, at the beginning." She waves her hand in the air.

"I'm so sorry, Marie. I never meant to hurt you. College kids can be insensitive."

"Too late." She smiles. "Anyway, I had a plan, starting with running you off the road two years ago. I had just come home, and I saw an article about you online, how you were some big-deal doctor."

My mind is whirling, trying to make sense of this, of Marie. Some careless remarks a million years ago have her *this* angry? "*You* ran me off the road?"

"Yes. I've been following your career, your marriage, and then the baby, of course. Your promotion. Everything perfect for perfect Eve. And then, *then!* You show up in the center of my life again. I couldn't believe it when I made the connection. I just can't fucking get away from you." Her eyes are wild. There are angry tears on her cheeks.

"What are you talking about?"

Marie shakes her head, bats her eyelashes. "Later. First things first."

"You're the one trying to ruin my life," I murmur. Could she be responsible for everything? I shudder.

"Only because you ruined mine." She swings in my direction. "You just won't go away, Eve."

I sniff, clear my throat. "Please, Marie. Let's get Rachel some help then we'll figure this out." How can I get her to calm down? *Think, Eve.* Dealing with distraught people is what I do.

"I've already figured it out," she snaps, and starts to pace again. "Maybe I can't blame you for not recognizing me at first. Since college I lost thirty pounds, got rid of my glasses, and dyed my hair blond. But in those sessions when you had a chance to observe me closely, listen to me, you still didn't remember me because I didn't matter. Even after that blowup with Burke."

"Who's Burke?"

"Professor Daniels!" she spits.

The drama professor. The young handsome one who always called me out for special praise, who gave me creepy, unwanted attention. Not enough, or so I thought at the time, to report him.

Marie nods. "Starting to remember? I got kicked out of school for 'harassing him' and it was all your fault."

"How was that my fault?" I remember she didn't come back to school the next semester. There was a new girl in her dorm room and the rumor was that Marie had been kicked out of school because of something with the professor.

"He and I hooked up, once anyway. After that he went and told the administration that I was a fucking stalker. They believed him and I had to leave school. My whole college career was gone just like that. And I loved him, but he only wanted you, Eve. It figures you'd mess it up for me."

"I had no clue, Marie. I wasn't interested in him. I tried to stay away from him."

"Yeah. Right. Perfect Eve. My life went to shit after that. Oh, I rallied after a while. I got a job, lost weight, did a whole makeover. Then I met my husband, and I thought my life was finally on an upward trend. And I was making progress in another area of my life, and I was full of hope. My husband was quite a catch. All those designer clothes I wore to our sessions, all due to him. He has a lot of money. But then, he stabbed me in the back. Cheated." Her gaze meets mine. "You know how that feels, don't you? After my divorce, I ran you off the road, but that wasn't enough when I found out about the rest of it, our connection from *hell*."

I still don't know what she's alluding to. What could I have possibly done to make her this angry? Then again, I remember my training. Sometimes patients see things in ways healthy people don't. Sometimes something minor sets them off. And sometimes it takes years to build.

Her gaze shifts to Rachel, whose face is white as ivory from blood loss.

I'm praying that Marie is winding down, that her anger is dissipating, but then she starts pacing again.

"We weren't even yet," she says. "Not after I found out about the rest of it. So, I decided to make an appointment with you. See if you'd recognize me, but you didn't. That's when I started watching your husband. He's really hot, Eve, a bit wimpy for my taste, but a pretty good fuck."

I fall back against the wall, my hand slipping off Rachel's slick skin.

"Get it now, Eve? My name is Nicole Marie Williams Clark."

CHAPTER 65
Rita

I DRIVE OUT TO MR. CLARK'S RESIDENCE IN HOPKINTON. IF NICOLE took the baby, his house would be a good place to keep her. I quickly collect the spare key from the neighbor and head inside. The house has that chilly, abandoned feel when no one has been home for a while.

I flip on the lights. The living room is like a museum of rich furniture and antiques, and I have a hard time picturing Nicole Clark living here in her yoga pants and T-shirts. The kitchen is equally well appointed and pristine. No signs that anyone was here in the six weeks since Mr. Clark left for California.

Upstairs, the master is also immaculate, untouched, masculine. No sign that a woman ever lived here. But then the next bedroom is a totally different story. The comforter on the queen-sized bed is rumpled. Like someone made it quickly or sat on it and didn't straighten it afterward. The closet holds expensive women's clothes and a few pairs of shoes—and a red scarf. Just as Mr. Clark said, Nicole had left some of her things behind. In the adjoining bathroom, a bar of soap next to the sink is still wet, and a hand towel nearby is damp. Nicole has been here recently.

With gloves on, I search through the drawers and find makeup and lotions and nail polish, all high-end brands. Stuff I'd never buy. I head back into the bedroom, turn in a circle. But did Nicole bring the baby here? Could she have gaslighted her grandmother into thinking she never left the house when she was here with the baby?

I head back downstairs, survey the first floor again, then go into the garage. In the corner is a trash bin. I slowly open the lid and there's a white garbage bag in the bottom. I take out my phone and snap pictures before lifting the bag out and setting it on the cement floor. I loosen the blue drawstring and a sour odor wafts out. There's a small blanket on top covering what's beneath it. I lift it up and there is a can of infant formula and a plastic bottle. My heart hammers as I weed through the rest. Dirty diapers and a wadded-up towel.

I pull my hands back out of the trash, peel off my gloves, turn away, and take a fresh breath. Then I pull my phone from my back pocket and call the chief.

"Rita? What's up?"

"The kidnapper was Nicole Clark." I gulp for air. "I'm standing in her ex-husband's garage. I went through the trash. All stuff you'd need to take care of a baby."

Silence. "Shit. Great. Good work, Rita." I hear noise in the background like Bob is walking through the station, barking out orders. "I'll send the crime scene team out. Text me the address and sit tight."

"Will do." But I'm antsy. I need to find Nicole, especially since she's planning to head out of town.

"Where do you think Ms. Clark is?" Bob asks.

I glance at the time on my phone. "I hope she's home. After the tech team gets here, I'll head over there." I'm pacing the garage. "Can you light a fire under Hugo? I'm thinking we don't have time to lose."

"I'm already on it."

I'm edgy while I wait, going over the case in my head. I circle the garage and notice a small toolbox in the corner. Looks a lot like the one Ms. Parnell described, so I take a picture of that, too. I decide to call Eve and let her know, but there's no answer. Keeps going to voicemail. That's strange. She should be home from work by now. I call her home number and that picks up right away.

"Eve?"

"No. This is Joanne Fraser, the babysitter."

"Is Doctor Thayer there? This is Detective Myers."

"No, she's not. She called me and said she needed to stop in to see her friend on the way home, but I haven't heard from her since." I hear concern in her voice.

"Which friend?"

"The one with the long dark hair, Rachel. She said she was going to the gallery."

"Hmm. Okay. I'm headed back to Graybridge in a few. Tell her to call me when she gets home, would you?"

"Sure, Detective."

I end the call and peep out the garage windows. No one yet. I head outside. I'll sit in my van and wait there for the team.

My phone rings. Mr. Singleton. "Hi, what can I do for you?" I hope this won't take long. Now that Barbara is apparently in the clear, I don't have time for him.

"She's gone, Detective." His voice is desperate.

"What? What happened?"

"My wife. I left this morning to golf with my friends. I shouldn't have left her. She's not well. I'm really concerned!"

"Slow down, Mr. Singleton. Tell me what happened."

"She's not here! Her car's in the garage. She's not answering her phone. I have no idea what happened to her, but I'm worried!"

"Okay. Maybe she's just out for a walk. Go ahead and report it. And we'll look into it. But I bet she's back soon." But I'm not sure. This is very strange. I hope like hell nothing's happened to her.

"All right. I'm calling 911," he says, and hangs up.

I flip back through my notebook, stop on a sketch of Barbara I made early in the investigation. Then I flip through the other pages. Huh. Something strange is going on here.

I need to get going and luckily the crime scene van has just pulled up behind me. I throw my notebook on the passenger's seat, get out, and have a quick conversation with Hugo. Finally, I'm on my way back to town.

CHAPTER 66
Eve

I GASP FOR BREATH. "YOU'RE NICOLE CLARK?"

"I was Nicole Williams back in college, but I guess you don't remember that either. Didn't even remember my name. Even when I came to see you as Marie *Williams.* Still didn't ring a bell."

It is all starting to make sense, crazy sense. "You had an affair with my husband."

"Yes. I was tracking you two. Knew where he worked. I suggested to my friend that we stop for drinks at the bar across the street hoping I'd run into him sometime and eventually, I did. And it was easy after that. He's like a lost puppy, Eve, so needy. I'm super surprised you two got together. But then, you probably were looking for a man you could bully."

I get up on my knees, one hand pushed against Rachel's wound, the other feeling for her pulse, which is thready.

"Well, you got me, Marie—Nicole." She's pacing and I wonder if I can stretch my leg out far enough to trip her. If only I could let go of Rachel, but I don't dare. "I need to get Rachel some help. Please. Call 911."

She looks at her watch. "I need to get going."

"Call for help, please. Then you can take off."

"I'll take off all right. Got my flight to Paris booked for tonight.

At least my dumb fuck of a husband gave me enough money so I could still live the good life. But I can't leave any loose ends."

She pulls something out of her purse. Waves it in front of me. It's a little pink sock. Rosewyn's sock. "I saved this for right now. You see Eve, I'm going to place it here so it looks like Rachel was the kidnapper. You found out and you stabbed her, which has become a thing for you."

"I didn't stab my patient. Why would you think that? I help people!" I scream, hysteria in my voice.

Nicole snorts. "Right. Anyway, after you discovered that your best friend kidnapped your baby, ruined your marriage, you couldn't take it anymore and you shot yourself."

I tremble as I watch Nicole pull a handgun from her purse. "Then I'm out the back door. My car is parked at the curb and I'm off. I get on my flight tonight and the past is rectified. Debts are paid. We're even."

I try to tamp down my panic. I've got to get myself back under control. *Think, Eve.* "Why don't you just leave right now? Don't make things worse. If you kill me, the police won't rest until they find you. Your DNA has got to be all over this place. Your plan won't work."

"Says the terrible psychiatrist." She smiles. "Thought you were so smart. Smarter than the rest of us. Well, you didn't just fail to see that 'Marie' was lying the whole time. You couldn't even help poor Frances Martin."

"I didn't kill—"

"No, you didn't." She pauses. "I did."

I shudder. "And Nathan? You knocked him down the stairs?"

"Well, yeah. But he survived, didn't he?"

She's at the point of no return, completely off the rails, in a full psychotic break. But maybe I can keep her talking until someone finds us. "How? How did you get into the building? How did you manage the generator and all that?"

A strange pensive look passes over her face. "I know that building inside and out. Years ago, when it was the old psych hospital, my mother was a frequent guest. See, when I was little, everything was great. I was happy with my mom and dad. That New Year's Eve memory that Marie told you about? *That* was real. But then my mom started having 'episodes' my grandma used to call them. She'd go out of her head. Take off for days at a time, then come back, dirty, smelling of alcohol. So, after a couple years of that, my dad left. Took off. Just left me with her. Anyway, when she was in the hospital, my grandma would take me up to visit, but I couldn't stand looking at her like that, so I used to explore the hospital. Nana would give me quarters for the vending machine, so I'd go and buy a soda or a candy bar, then walk all over that place. They didn't have the cameras and all like today, and the place was pretty lax about security. I knew where everything was. That remodel didn't accomplish much. It's still the same old place. And then as a teenager, when those buildings were empty, I'd come by. Look around. I know that building like the back of my hand."

"Why kill Frances?"

Nicole snorts out a laugh. "Well, I was hoping they'd arrest you for it. I took the scissors from your desk during one of our sessions. Anyway, I want no loose ends. Everyone I can get to who made my life hell is going down."

"Frances?"

"Yes, Frances." She sighs. "My lovely *mother*."

My breath catches. Frances was telling the truth. She did have a family. A daughter, a mother. I glance up at Nicole.

Her hand wavers, but she keeps the gun pointed at me. She's going to kill me and let Rachel die. I glance around the room, looking for some way to stop her. Nicole inches closer to where I sit on the floor. To make it look like a suicide, she'll have to get close, so I let her.

She leans toward me, starts to bring the gun up to my temple. I let go of Rachel and spring up like a tiger, knocking her arm away, and throwing all of my weight into her stomach. We fly backward, and I pin her against the wall. Sweat drips down over my face and into my eyes. Nicole is heaving for breath, her face purple with rage.

"You bitch!" she screams.

I grab her arm and slam her hand against the wall. The gun drops and tumbles across the room. I've got to get to it first, and I do. I slip and fall on my backside, but I've got the gun. I wrap my sweaty hands around the cold metal, but before I can pull the trigger, Nicole is on top of me, scratching and pummeling me. Pain sears through my core. We're locked in a desperate wrestling match, and I can't get the gun where I need it to shoot her.

We roll over and the gun is trapped somewhere between our thrashing bodies. And then it goes off.

CHAPTER 67
Rita

As I drive toward town, I try Eve's phone again. She doesn't answer and something about that doesn't sit right. I've called her a half dozen times with no answer and that worries me. When I arrive in downtown Graybridge, I call Chase and have him head out to Nicole's house to see if he can catch Nicole there. I tell him I'll join him as soon as I talk to Eve.

There isn't a parking spot in front of the gallery, so I drive past and park farther down. When I get to the gallery door, all's dark inside, and the closed sign is facing out. I try the door. Locked, but Eve's car is parked out front. I step back and gaze up the street. There are a number of shops and restaurants Eve and Rachel might've stopped in, unless they drove away somewhere in Rachel's vehicle. I'm standing in the cold, wondering if I should just head out to Nicole's when I hear a single gunshot from inside the gallery.

I freeze, pull my phone from my pocket and call for backup, and then instinct takes over. I pull my sidearm from the holster and shoot out the glass in the door. I crouch and step through, inching my way along the dark showroom. My pulse is racing. I don't see anyone here as I creep forward, past the counter.

CHAPTER 68
Eve

NICOLE IS SCREAMING IN PAIN, DOUBLED OVER, GRASPING HER FOOT where dark red blood seeps.

"Fuck. Fuck. Fuck, Eve! You shot me!"

We sit still facing one another. Sweat pouring down my neck, saliva dripping from the corner of Nicole's mouth. But where is the gun now? I had it, and in our tussle, after the one shot, it got knocked across the room. I see it in the corner. A fraction of a second of numbness transpires before we're both scrambling on the floor on our hands and knees.

Nicole gets there first and grabs the gun, points it at me. My heart sinks. I can't catch my breath and tears slide down my face. This is it.

Then there's a gunshot and a crash of glass from the showroom. Someone's here. Someone has come to help. And I can breathe again. Maybe Rachel and I will make it out alive.

Nicole struggles to her feet, the gun trained on me.

"Let's go," she growls. "Hurry up!"

"What?"

"Get up, Eve." She glances at the back door. "Now! Or I'll shoot you *and* Rachel. I need to be someplace, and you're going to have to drive me there."

"Where?" I try to stall.

"A nice lake house. Let's go!"

Blood is dripping across the floor from her injured foot. I stand and glance at Rachel. Someone is here. They'll get her help, so I comply with Nicole's orders, and we head out the back door and into the cold night.

CHAPTER 69
Rita

I HEAR VOICES IN A BACK ROOM. THERE'S LIGHT UNDER THE DOOR. I nudge the door open with my hip, gun drawn.

"Police!" I enter the room, but there's no one there except Rachel Chapman, who is sprawled on the floor, covered in blood. A frigid breeze blows through the room. A back door to the outside stands open.

"Rachel? It's Detective Myers. What happened?" But she appears to be unconscious. I call dispatch again. "I need that backup ASAP and I need EMS as well." Despite the shot I heard, it doesn't look like there's a gunshot wound on Ms. Chapman. Then I see a knife lying on the floor not too far away.

I crouch and check her wound. The bleeding seems to have stopped. That's good, but help needs to get here quickly because whoever did this and whoever fired the shot is on the run, and I need to find them. Then I see a little pink sock.

Could Eve have done this? Did she somehow think that her best friend was behind the kidnapping? And she snapped? Why didn't she shoot her then? Something's not right here. That doesn't fit, and I'm all but certain now that Nicole Clark is behind everything that's happened.

Where is my fucking backup?

Then I hear the sirens. "What happened, Rachel?" I yell, hoping to get some answers. But she's totally out of it. Then she stirs slightly.

"Lake house," she murmurs. Then she's silent again, as if she'd used all of her remaining strength.

Anna Connors is the first cop through the door. I give her a quick rundown then I'm gone, wending my way back through the gallery as cops pour in through the door. In my van, I grab my notebook, turn on the dome light, and flip back and forth between sketches I'd made of my suspects. On a hunch, and Rachel's mumbled words, I throw the van's gearshift in reverse and head out.

CHAPTER 70
Eve

MY TEETH ARE CHATTERING AS I DRIVE THE UNFAMILIAR VEHICLE, A gun stuck in my side.

"Where did you say we were going?"

"Never mind. You'll see when we get there. Christ, my foot hurts." Nicole squirms in her seat but holds the gun steady.

"I'll look at it when we get there." Wherever that is. "I can bandage it and see if we can find some pain meds." Hopefully, I can buy some good will here.

"Yeah. We'll see. I can't head to Paris like this."

The traffic is light. Rush hour is over. I can't help but think about Rachel. Hope that EMS has been called and that she's going to be okay. Tears drip down my cheeks, blurring my vision, making it hard to see the road.

At least Nathan is getting better. He'll take care of Rosewyn if I'm . . . We're out of town now. The houses and stores have fallen away. We're in the country and the night is very dark.

"Turn left here," Nicole says.

This is it, I think to myself. We're in the middle of nowhere. She's going to shoot me out here. I should've let her do it back at the gallery. At least I had a chance with other people there. When we get out of the car, I'll run. She can't catch me with her injured foot. Maybe I can get away before she pulls the trigger.

We're headed down a winding macadam road. Then it dawns on me. I know where we are, sort of. We're at the lake. And Nicole's words come back to me. We're going to a lake house. But why? There are a couple of big, expensive homes here along the shore. But they're all dark. Weekend places probably, so no one is likely around. No one to hear me scream.

"Turn into the next driveway," Nicole says, her voice shaking with pain.

My heart is thumping so hard it feels like it will explode. What's she got in mind? Why are we here? There's a car in the driveway, and I wonder who it belongs to.

Nicole limps behind me as we head up the snow-covered walk to the front door. She hands me a key. "Let's go, Eve." I feel the muzzle of the gun in my back, and it takes me three tries to get the key in the lock.

The foyer is cold, and Nicole marches me to the back of the house. She flips on a kitchen light and I blink, my eyes adjusting.

"Do you want me to look at your foot?" I ask.

Nicole nods and pulls open drawers until she finds kitchen towels. Then she picks up a bottle of water off the countertop.

"I can clean it with dish soap," I say.

She grabs that from beneath the sink, and with the towels and water tucked under her arm, Nicole sits heavily in a kitchen chair, her face contorted with pain. But she holds fast to the gun and keeps it trained on me.

"So, why did we come here?" I ask as I remove what's left of her shoe and begin to clean her wound, rinsing off the blood with the water, dabbing with the soap. The bullet went straight through the metatarsal bones near her toes, a bad injury, but not fatal or anything.

"Jesus that hurts." She draws her foot back.

"Sorry."

"If you must know, this was part of my plan all along. Well, it took a turn when you fucking *shot* me, but it was supposed to play out with me setting up you and Rachel at the gallery. Then I was headed out the back door on my own. I was coming here to finish it all and wait until it was time to leave for the airport."

"Why here?" I blot the cleaned wound with a towel. I'm trying to regain my equilibrium. Maybe I can still think of a way out of this.

"Because, Eve, I believe that people should pay for their mistakes. Don't you? Especially when they destroy other people's lives."

"I'm sorry if I hurt you in college. I truly didn't realize that I had."

She huffs out a breath. "Of course, you didn't. Anyway, I would've been okay with just running you off the road. I felt that was enough. We were even until I made my biggest discovery."

I still have no clue what she's talking about. "What was that? What could I have possibly done to you?"

"I'll show you. But first let's stop in the bathroom. Maybe we can find something to bandage my foot with and some fucking pain medication." She gets slowly to her feet and nudges me with the gun down a hallway.

Sitting on the toilet lid, Nicole sticks her foot out for me to tend. I find a roll of gauze and tape in the medicine cabinet along with a bottle of ibuprofen. While I dress her wound, she swallows a handful of the pills.

Nicole takes a deep breath. "Let's go. Let's get this finished."

We head farther down the hall where I imagine the bedrooms lie. Nicole stops in front of a door and smirks. "I want you to meet someone." She opens the door, and there on the bed is a woman, who's tied, a scarf over her mouth.

I catch my breath, peer into the woman's frightened blue eyes. Barbara.

"I don't understand," I mumble. "Let me take that off her mouth. Her color doesn't look good."

"Sure. Fine. If she screams, no one will hear her."

I lean over the bed. "Barbara, are you okay?" She nods. My fingers clutch her wrist, feel her pulse. It's rapid; her skin is clammy.

"She's fine," Nicole says. "I didn't hurt her. I just needed to get her alone. Confront her. I need her to know how much she made me suffer." Nicole's voice has risen.

"I don't understand," I say again, and turn to face Nicole.

"Jesus, Eve. For somebody so fucking smart, you're just plain stupid!" She spits the word at me. "Barbara is my mother!"

Barbara closes her eyes. Tears stream from the corners.

"But I thought . . ." I'm still reeling from her last revelation.

"Frances? Oh, yeah. Frances adopted me. She'd had a little boy apparently and he died, so they wanted a replacement. But I thought she was my real mother for the longest time. Then when she started having her 'episodes' my nana told me not to worry. I wouldn't inherit anything like that because Frances wasn't my real mother! I was nine. I was fucking devastated. I decided I'd find my real mother if it was the last thing I did. So, when I got a computer for Christmas the next year, I started my quest. But you'd be surprised how tough it is to break into a closed adoption. Those Torrences made it damn hard. They didn't want me to ever be able to track them down. But I did." She smiles. "Took me years, but I finally found her.

"When I moved to Graybridge after my divorce, I still didn't know who my real mother was, but over the years, I'd become a top-notch hacker, so those skills were pretty useful. Anyway, life went on. Then I saw that you'd gotten married, had a baby. And that kind of reignited my interest in you. Why had perfect Eve gotten everything she always wanted, while I suffered?"

Nicole forgets the gun for a moment, and I inch toward her. But she remembers in time and swings it up and points it at my chest.

"It gets better," she says, swallows. "I have my breakthrough. *Finally*, after years of searching. I find my lovely mother. And guess what? She's perfect Eve's perfect babysitter! Barbara didn't want me, but she sure as hell wanted Eve's little girl!"

Barbara makes a sound somewhere between a moan and a gasp. She manages to push herself to sitting. I let go a ragged breath. Now it makes sense, *finally*. For someone like Nicole, who's battling demons, anger off the rails, her quest for vengeance makes sense to her. But how can I get us out of this in one piece?

Nicole's eyes cut in Barbara's direction for a split second, but then she's looking back at me. "I watched them together. In the park, at her lovely home. I even followed them out here." Nicole takes a deep, wistful breath. "She loves that baby, Eve. All that love poured into *your* child." She sighs, whispers, "I wanted you to suffer, Eve, and Barbara, too. It's only fair."

Nicole licks her lips, swivels, and points the gun at Barbara.

CHAPTER 71
Rita

I'M SPEEDING DOWN THE LAKE ROAD. IF MY HUNCH IS CORRECT, I'LL find Barbara along with the woman who must be the baby in the photo. Nicole Clark. The baby given up for adoption years ago and is now a grown woman bent on revenge. How did I not see it sooner? The resemblance between mother and daughter captured in my sketches.

I see the Singleton house up ahead and, bingo, Nicole's vehicle is in the driveway, but there's another car right beside it. I wasn't expecting that. I call dispatch, *again*, and request backup at the Singleton home.

I can't wait though, so I get out of my van and quietly close the door. My gun in hand, I walk slowly up the sidewalk. I try the knob and the front door opens. There's a dim light way back in the house's interior. I slowly make my way inside. The dark living room is empty, but there's light, brighter down the hall, and drops of blood. Shit.

CHAPTER 72
Eve

I HEAR SOMEONE COMING OUT OF THE ADJOINING BATHROOM. THEN I remember the other car.

Glenda.

My mouth drops open. I can't make sense of *this*. Why would she be out here helping Nicole?

Glenda is holding a syringe. Her gaze cuts sharply to me then to Nicole. "What's she doing here?"

"It didn't quite go as planned. She shot me." Nicole holds out her bandaged foot.

"Jesus Christ," Glenda says, and quickly crosses the room. "Are you okay?"

Nicole sniffles. "Yeah."

Glenda puts her hand on her hip. "You bandaged it?" She's looking at me.

"Yes."

"How bad is the injury?"

"She'll live."

Glenda nods, turns to Nicole. "Let's take care of Barbara first." She raises the syringe.

"Wait!" I call. "What are you doing, Glenda? Why?"

She takes a deep breath. "Because I've got a heart. Years ago, when I was a young nurse, Frances was my patient. I *told* you that.

And her mother would drag Nicole to the hospital to see her." Glenda's dark eyes lock on mine. "A psychiatric hospital is no place for a child, Doctor Thayer. You should know that. Anyway, I felt so bad for Nicole. She was just a little thing. I used to try to keep her mind off her mother while she was there. I'd show her around. Buy her candy bars in the cafeteria. I had no family. I was taken from my alcoholic mother by the state when I was ten. Never adopted. I never had a child of my own, and Nicole seemed to need me. We stayed in touch over the years and when she told me she was moving back to Graybridge, I came back. And since they were reopening the hospital, it all made sense. And then she found out who her real mother was, and I knew Nicole would never have any peace until she made things right. I knew how she felt, and I was going to help her."

Glenda had always given me an uneasy feeling. Nothing I could put my finger on, but now I understand why. She's as unhinged as Nicole is. And now I know they bonded years ago and probably fed off their mutual demons. "Now what?" I ask. I take a deep breath. I've got to keep it together. I have *two* deranged people to outwit.

"Off to Paris for Nicole. She's always wanted to live there. But I'm headed to Canada. Paris wouldn't suit me. I've got a little place way up north where no one will bother me." She glances at Nicole. "You've got your passport? Suitcase packed?"

Nicole nods.

Glenda's gaze cuts to Nicole's bandaged foot. "I'll drive you to the airport." Glenda glares at me. Then her eyes are back on Nicole. "We'll find you some comfortable shoes. There must be some in this place. And I've got some pain meds that should help. Okay. We better get the show on the road." She lifts the syringe, eyes the contents in the light, and heads toward the bed.

CHAPTER 73
Rita

I HEAR VOICES. NICOLE AND EVE, AND SOMEONE ELSE WHOSE VOICE sounds familiar, but I can't place.

My pulse is racing as I creep silently along the hardwood floor. I stop right outside what must be a bedroom, listen.

"Please!" It's Eve. "Don't!"

I slip inside the room. "Police! Stop right there!" A woman in blue scrubs lifts her hands, drops a needle on the floor. But a gun goes off and Barbara falls back on the bed. Eve grabs Nicole around the waist and knocks her to the floor. I run to them and bring my boot down on Nicole's wrist, lean over and wrench the gun away from her and tuck it in my waistband. Nicole is sputtering, screaming. With Eve's help, I roll her over on her stomach and get cuffs on her.

But the woman with the needle is gone. She managed to get out of the room while we wrestled with Nicole.

Eve goes over to Barbara, checks her, and unties her.

"How is she?" I ask.

"I can't find a wound," Eve says, her voice trembling. As her hands search, Barbara sits up, pushes her away.

"I'm okay."

I look up at the wall over the bed. There's a bullet hole. Nicole missed.

"Thank God." I let go a breath. Fumble my phone out of my pocket and let them know at the station what's transpired and to put out a BOLO on the vehicle I saw in the driveway, which Eve tells me belongs to one of her nurses, a Glenda Rowley.

I hear sirens in the distance coming closer. Eve is sitting on the bed next to Barbara.

Soon the room is full of cops, and they haul Nicole to her feet. Before they can take her away, Barbara gets up from the bed.

"Wait. Please," she says. She stumbles over to Nicole and gently wipes the tears from her cheeks. "I never wanted to give you up, and I thought about you every day."

I watch as misery covers Barbara's wan face. And then, through her tears, I see joy there as her eyes hungrily take in the daughter she has missed and mourned for over thirty years. Emotions flood Barbara's face, happiness and sorrow, one and then the other, distinct opposites that seem to sum up this bizarre situation.

But the look in Nicole Clark's eyes is unreadable. Empty.

CHAPTER 74
Rita

*I*T'S NEARLY TWO IN THE MORNING AND THE STATION IS STILL A HIVE OF activity. Nicole Clark and Glenda Rowley are in custody. Before Ms. Rowley could get off the lake road, squad cars were there and blocked her in.

Eve and Barbara were checked out at the hospital. They gave their statements and then Barbara's relieved husband took her home. Eve stayed on at the hospital with her friend, Ms. Chapman. Rachel's in ICU but it looks like she'll recover. It's a blessing that Nicole and her sidekick didn't do more damage. It looks like poor Frances Martin was the only one to lose her life to those two.

I walk down to my office and turn on my radio. It's on commercial, of course. I look out my small window and watch the snow fall through the streetlight on the corner. The reporters are gone now, but I expect they'll be back full force bright and early in the morning. I sit heavily in my chair. I need to go home and get some rest, but I can't seem to move. Finally, a song comes on, Eric Clapton's "Wonderful Tonight," which makes me chuckle to think how bad I must look about now, hair falling out of my bun, mascara smeared under my eyes. But it also makes me think of Joe and his invitation.

I lean forward and open my notebook. The resemblance between Nicole and Barbara was there all the time if only I'd seen it sooner. The big blue eyes, the slight cleft in the chin. But that's the way it goes sometimes. I sigh. At least it didn't end any worse. Poor Frances. She didn't stand a chance.

I pull myself out of my chair, gather my satchel and purse, and turn off the radio.

CHAPTER 75
Eve

*I*T'S ALREADY TOMORROW, AND I DIDN'T KNOW JUST A FEW HOURS AGO that I'd see today. I sat with Rachel until I was falling asleep as the sun rose. Detective Myers told me that Rachel had whispered "lake house" and that pointed her in the right direction, saving my life and Barbara's even as Rachel's own life nearly ebbed away. For that I will always be grateful to my best friend.

I drove home, quietly entering the house so as not to disturb Joanne and the baby, but Joanne was sitting at the kitchen table drinking coffee, waiting. She had wanted to meet me at the hospital last night, but I told her I'd rather she stay at the house with Rosewyn. My mother showed up, so I wasn't alone—although I almost wished I was.

Joanne gives me a hug and it's all I can do not to fall apart. I "suck it up" as my dad used to say. I've got too many people depending on me.

"Why don't you try to get some sleep," Joanne says.

"Did you sleep at all?" I ask.

She smiles. "A little. But I don't need much at my age." I notice the pillow sitting on the neatly folded blanket on the sofa.

"How's Rosewyn?"

"Fine. She had no idea what was going on, Eve."

I swallow, a lump in my throat, and nod. "Maybe I'll jump in the

shower. I want to go see Nathan." I'd called last night to reassure
him that I was okay. My ordeal was all over the news, so I had to let
him, Joanne, and my mother know that I was all right.

Despite my plans, I fall asleep on my bed wrapped in a towel
after my shower.

When I wake up it's nearly ten a.m. At first, I panic. Rosewyn must
be starved. But then I smell bacon, coffee and I know that Joanne
is in the kitchen making breakfast and that she's tended my baby. I
wipe the tears from my face. People are sometimes more than you
expect and just what you need.

At the rehab center, Nathan is sitting in his chair, dressed in his
regular clothes, jeans and a flannel shirt. He looks great, and
Rosewyn leaps in my arms when she sees him. I place her on his lap
and he cuddles her, but his gaze fastens on me.

"Are you sure you're all right, Eve?"

"I'm okay." I sit across the room from him, and we both fall silent
while Rosewyn babbles and squeals.

"I'm so sorry about . . ." He can't bring himself to say her name.

"I know. I'm sorry, too. I missed every sign, every red flag."
Which has me questioning my competence as a psychiatrist. I push
that thought away. I'm not perfect. No one is. This is my new
mantra.

"That wasn't your fault," he says. "Who would've thought she was
so twisted. She put on an incredible act, Eve."

"Yes. She did." I tell him the whole story, things I've just learned
from Detective Myers after she questioned Glenda. Glenda's role
in helping Nicole cut the power at the hospital, helping her escape
after the murder. Kidnapping Barbara and waiting for Nicole at the
lake house. Supplying sleeping pills so that Nicole could leave
home without her grandmother knowing she was gone when she
took Rosewyn. Even sneaking Nicole into the patients' wing at the
hospital at night, where Nicole taunted Frances a couple of times.
Poor Frances. She wasn't hallucinating after all.

"I guess we owe Detective Myers big time," Nathan says.

I nod. "We do. If she hadn't found us when she did, I don't know
that either Barbara or I would have survived. We don't know yet

what was in the syringe that Glenda was going to inject Barbara with. Detective Myers said it went to the lab, so we'll see."

"Shit," Nathan whispers, and shakes his head.

I sniff back tears. I was so close to losing everything.

Nathan lets go a big breath, and Rosewyn reaches up her tiny hand and slaps him on the mouth. He makes a face at her, and she giggles. I laugh, a bubbling up from somewhere deep in my chest.

CHAPTER 76
Rita

I'M OFF TODAY. I SHOULDN'T BE. THERE'S A TON OF WORK TO DO TO follow up the Liddle/Thayer case, but I've decided that Chase can handle it for now. And, luckily, the chief agreed. I'm just drained. Things could've gone sideways a half dozen times yesterday.

Still, I couldn't sleep, so I decide to get some exercise to reset myself. I eye my stationary bike in the corner as I drink my morning coffee, but it just doesn't appeal to me. I want to get outside, so I put on my sweats, stick my hair in a ponytail and hit the pavement. The air is freezing, yet still, and the sky is a bright blue. The snow lies neatly along the edges of the sidewalk, and I breathe deeply of the winter air.

I run for probably thirty minutes, taking in Graybridge Square where the shops are just starting to open, and people stream out of André's Café with steaming cups of coffee. Then I head home. My little town is peaceful this morning. Only the plywood nailed across The Gallery door shows that anything had been amiss. People will catch up on the news and they'll wonder how someone like Nicole Clark could've been hiding in their midst, but the incidents will soon fade except for in the minds of the participants, who'll be changed forever.

I near my building, breathing hard. Danny's car is parked at the curb. Huh. I told him last night that I was okay. Wonder what he's doing here. He gets out of his vehicle as I approach and grabs me in a hug.

"Hey, I told you I was okay." I pull away, squeeze his shoulder. Slow my breathing from my run.

"Just wanted to see for myself, I guess."

"Want a cup of coffee?"

He nods and follows me to the front door.

When we're sitting in my living room, Danny takes a long sip, then sets his mug on the end table.

"So, any other reason for the visit?" I ask.

"I wanted to apologize," he says, his elbows on his knees.

"For what?"

"Dragging you down to Maureen's."

"You didn't drag me anywhere. I'd've said no if I really didn't want to go." Which is actually a lie, but I don't tell him that. He laughs. He knows me too well.

"I know you went because I asked, Rita."

"Okay. You got me."

"Anyway, thank you, Sis."

"Did it help? Going through Ricky's things?"

"I think so. It cleared him up in my memory. Good memories of before he died. I needed that."

I nod, shift my gaze out the picture window. "Then the trip was worth it." We don't mention Jimmy. It's as if our "partner in crime" as Ma used to call him, were only in the next room. The brother who completed our three musketeers. It's still too tough to talk about him much. We aren't there yet. Maybe after we think about Ricky for a while, settle him in our brains.

"You'd think we'd have this figured out by now, Danny. We're freaking senior citizens," I can't help but say.

Danny grins. "Speak for yourself, Rita. Age is just a number. Isn't that what they say?"

"Nice cliché, Professor."

He leans back on the couch and laughs. "I don't feel my age, do you?"

I swallow. "Not usually."

"Well, I guess you're never too old to work through life's complexities. It isn't always a smooth ride."

"That's for sure." I think back over the last twenty-four hours.

"You want to talk about your case? You had us up all night watching the news. Charlotte came over to my house and Maureen even called me."

"Naw. I'm good. Maybe another time."

Danny drains his mug and stands. "Okay. I guess I'll go home then. I've got some work to do to. Semester just started."

I walk him to the door and the hug lasts a little longer than usual.

The apartment seems quiet, empty, as I walk into the kitchen, drying my hair with a towel. Now that I've had my run, a visit with my brother, and a shower, I'm contemplating going into work even though I don't have to.

I walk over to my stereo and drop to my haunches. The stack of 45s sits on the bottom shelf, and I hesitate. Do I really want to do this?

I take a breath and pull out the top record. I swallow and sniff. Before I can change my mind, I'm loading it on the turntable, the little plastic insert sliding over the spindle. I hit the power button and drop the needle. That familiar pop and scratch fills the room and then Frankie Valli's falsetto fills the apartment. I straighten and close my eyes. I hear Ricky singing. Whenever I would run to him after getting into a fight with Jimmy and Danny, he'd play this song, "Big Girls Don't Cry." And for the first time in a long time, this big girl does.

CHAPTER 77
Nathan

I CAN'T BELIEVE I'M HOME, AND I CAN SEE IT, A LITTLE BLURRY MAYBE, but enough that I'm grateful beyond measure. While I was blind, my other senses sharpened just like you hear that they do, and that makes my homecoming even more special. I can smell and hear everything. I'm sitting at the kitchen table while Joanne makes lunch and Eve feeds Rosewyn who's sitting in her highchair next to me. Oscar winds around my legs and I lean over and give him a pet.

In the distance, behind the house, I hear the whir of a circular saw. Ms. Parnell is back at work. It gives me a little uneasy feeling to know that Nicole had been over there, watching us.

"I think we need to put up blinds," Eve says, as if she and I were thinking the same thing.

"Yeah. Good idea. Maybe I can manage that." I'm still trying to figure out what my future holds, work wise. They don't know if I'll ever pass the vision test to be able to hold on to my driver's license. I don't think my company would be too thrilled to have a manager of a collision shop who can't drive. But we'll see.

And I don't know what lies ahead for me and Eve. I guess we'll need to see about that, too. I only know that I'm where I want to be, with my family, and that's more than enough.

CHAPTER 78
Rita

I GET IN MY VAN AND HEAD FOR 495 BEFORE I CAN CHANGE MY MIND. Light snow is falling, and I know the air will only get chillier as I head north and toward the coast. I can think of a hundred reasons not to go where I'm going, but Maureen's words haven't totally left me since that trip down to the house with Danny. I'm not miserable, but she did have a point.

After an hour and a half of fighting Boston metro traffic, I exit the highway and head to Newburyport. I always liked this little town. I've been here a couple of times and if I remember correctly, I've been to this pub before. It takes me a few tries driving up and down the main street and circling the block, but I find the place I'm looking for.

It's afternoon, so it isn't too busy. It's an old building, mellowed red brick and a nice friendly atmosphere. I sit in a booth, peruse the menu. They carry some nice wines and a full selection of local craft beers. It's Boston after all.

I wanted to get here first, for some reason. And it looks like I did. I check my phone. I'm about ten minutes early, but when I look up, I see him striding down the sidewalk and my stomach flutters. *What the hell are you doing, Rita?*

I stand when he approaches the booth and he grabs me in a

tight hug, and I let myself relax into him. He smells of cologne and flannel.

"I'm glad you're all right," Joe says.

"Told you I was. Backup got there pretty quick, considering."

He smiles and shakes his head as he slides into the booth. Our server comes over and Joe orders a craft beer and I forgo my usual wine and join him in the IPA. It just sounds good on a winter afternoon.

Joe reaches across the table and takes my hand. We'd been talking on the phone the last couple of days as my case got hot. He'd been back from Maine for a while and wanted to get together. I guess he wants an answer to his Clapton invitation.

Our beers arrive and that distracts us from conversation for a moment. Joe sips and clears his throat.

"I wanted to talk to you about something," he says, and I feel jittery. "I've made a career decision, Rita, and I wanted to tell you first."

"Huh? Really? What?" That wasn't what I was expecting.

"I'm retiring from the FBI."

I lean back against the booth. "You're kidding? I thought we both said we were nowhere near the end of our careers." This somehow shakes me as if I should be thinking of doing the same thing.

Joe smiles. "I'm not done, Rita. Not by a long shot."

"What then?"

"I've decided I'm through working for the government. I've decided to get my PI license and work for myself after all these years."

"Wow." I can't help but smile. "You going to rent a dusty old office, start wearing a trench coat and a fedora?"

Joe arches an eyebrow. "Maybe."

We laugh and sip our beers in silence for a moment. I need time to think about this. Joe and I have been in steady careers for so long, it seems crazy, impulsive for him to make such a change. But why not?

"You'll make a great PI," I say at last.

"Thanks. And if you ever decide you're ready for a change, I could use a partner."

Heat rushes to my face and I take a big swallow of my beer. "Yeah, well. Good to know."

Joe laughs and squeezes my hand. "I value your investigative skills, Rita. Anyway, you going in to work tomorrow?"

"Yeah. We've got a lot to clean up yet from the Liddle/Thayer case."

We settle in with a second beer and a basket of fried clam strips, talk about our work and our families.

I know I have to give Joe an answer.

"I think I'm free that weekend," I say. "The weekend of the Clapton concert."

"Great. It'll be fun, Rita. We could both use a little of that."

I nod, glance out the plate glass window at the snow blowing out toward the ocean. "Absolutely."

CHAPTER 79
Eve

I FEEL LIKE I CAN BREATHE AT LAST. ROSEWYN IS SAFE, MY HUSBAND IS home, and Nicole Clark and Glenda Rowley are in prison. I can't fully process what's happened to us these last few weeks. It's too much, too soon. But I know that healing takes time and I try not to worry.

Rachel, thank God, is recovering. If EMS hadn't gotten to her when they did, she might not have made it, and that thought makes me queasy. She left yesterday for Florida. Her older sister asked her to come for a long visit. The sister was widowed last year, no children, and lives in a quiet neighborhood two blocks from the beach. It will do Rachel good to get away and rest.

I'm making a change too. I don't want to go back to corporate healthcare. The stress is too much, the hours too long. I've decided to open my own practice, and I'm grateful I have the means to do so. My mother, who cried all over me when she saw me at the hospital the night I was rescued from Nicole, has made me an offer. She owns a condo in Aspen she hasn't used in twenty years. She told me she'd sell it and give me the profits to help with my business costs. I appreciate the gesture. My mother doesn't know how to express love other than with material things, but she is what she is, and I accept that.

I'm looking forward to being my own boss and to helping people. That's why I went into psychiatry in the first place.

I went to see Barbara and brought Rosewyn with me. She was thrilled to see the baby. Barbara told me that she's gone back to therapy. She's seeing a terrific doctor who I've known for years. She's been through a lot, but I feel like she's where she needs to be right now. Barbara was pleased when I told her about Joanne. She realizes that she needs to concentrate on her own healing right now. She needs to take care of herself.

And Frances Martin fills my mind. I'm saddened over what happened to her. And there are so many Frances Martins out there that society turns their back on. And like Frances, too many mentally ill people come to a bad end. I hope that in some small way I can help some of them.

I watch Nathan cuddle Rosewyn on his lap. Our baby smiles and my heart melts. This is what I want, for better or worse.